Rough Score

Kenna King

CONTENTS

Check out **www.kennakingbooks.com** for more books and information.

SCAN ME

CHAPTER ONE

Ryker

"Calm down?" I ask as anger and panic collide like a storm in my chest. "I'm about to get kicked out of the country because your administrative assistant forgot to send the check with my extension application, and you want me to calm down?"

"It was an accident, Ryker. She didn't mean to forget it," James Potter, my sports agent, says across his desk.

His gaze is sharp, and his dark hair is slicked back to the point that it would be immovable even in a Seattle windstorm.

An accident would be confusing wasabi for avocado at a sushi restaurant or hitting on a woman at an office Christmas party only to find out she's your boss's wife. This is way bigger than a mistake. It's a code-red emergency. I can't get sent back to Canada mid-season—sure, I'm old for an NFL player, but my career will only be done when I say it's done. I refuse to let down my Hawkeyes family over a damn administrative error. "And since you've come to expect the big payday that my NHL contract has paid you over the last eighteen years, I figured you'd be a little more empathetic to the fact that both of our livelihoods are at risk here."

"I get it, I do. But maybe this is the nudge you need," he says, his eyes not leaving mine.

I know that tone. He's got a wild plan brewing, and in my desperation, I'm all ears.

Anything's better than facing immigration's wrath.

"What nudge are you referring to?" I ask, my eyes darting across his fancy lacquered desk.

Behind him, the Seattle skyline stretches, a jagged silhouette of glass and steel against the evening sky, indifferent to the turmoil in this office.

He secured this office after my third contract, a milestone that now feels like a lifetime ago, considering our many years of success during my eighteen-year NHL career. Being my agent pays him well... just not well enough to ensure that his assistant knows how to slip the check I gave her into the application envelope right before I left with the guys to Seven's shack in Mexico for bye-week.

The visa extension should have been simple. I submit one every year around January and it's never been a problem before, but the immigration office is strict. The application and the check must be in the same envelope, or it's considered invalid. With their growing pile of applications, processing can take weeks, and I don't have that kind of time.

I shouldn't have left town. I should have handled this myself, but James's office has always gotten the envelope certified mail for me so I don't have to stand in line at the post office. We've been doing this for so many years— there's no way I thought she could fuck it up after all this time.

When I called the immigration office, after receiving their letter that my application was incomplete, I asked if I could send them a new application with the check. They told me that the new extension application would likely not get opened and processed in time before my visa status is revoked because their extension office is behind and understaffed after the Christmas break last month. Since everyone came back from the Christmas break last month, they're also seeing an influx of extension applications.

People told me to find a new agent once I hit the big time, but I didn't. Maybe I'm too stubborn to leave, or maybe I'm too loyal and don't believe in outgrowing people. And it's not like he hasn't negotiated some great deals for me in the past.

But whatever the reason for me keeping him on, it's turning out to be a poor business decision.

"That social media influencer you've been seeing for the past year..."

He snaps his fingers together as if trying to come up with her name.

"Six months..." I correct. "Amelia."

At just over a million followers online, being a social media influencer is how she makes her living.

"Right...right." He nods with a grin. "Six months is a long time for a professional athlete, isn't it?"

What does that have to do with anything?

"I guess that depends on the athlete."

He might have asked the question, but he ignores the answer and continues.

"I just spoke with a buddy down at immigration—"

"Wait, you have a buddy that works for immigration?" I ask.

"Well... more like an acquaintance at a men's club I play poker at once a week..." he admits.

I've always known James has a little bit of a gambling problem, though it hasn't seemed to affect his work, so it's none of my damn business.

"... and I told him about our missing check situation."

I nod to keep him talking. This is the part where he tells me he already came up with a solution to our problem and this guy is going to fast-track my application.

I knew James would redeem himself.

He continues, "I mentioned that you were planning to propose, and he said that he just had a couple cancel their appointment for three weeks from now. He could slide you into their spot."

What?... propose?

Who gave James that idea?

It sure as hell wasn't me.

"You want me to marry Amelia? That's your solution to this problem?" I ask, my hand pinching at my hips.

"You're going to marry her anyway, aren't you?" he argues quickly.

"I hadn't thought about it."

Because the truth is... I hadn't. Marriage hasn't been on my short list of priorities recently.

"These appointments don't become available every day. He's giving us a real opportunity here," James says, with a raised eyebrow.

"He's going to slide us into a spot... just like that?" I ask, my eyebrow raised in question at the convenience of it.

James's lips crinkle at the left corner of his mouth for a second. His 'tell' when he knows I won't like something he has to say.

"Well... he's a die-hard Hawkeyes fan with money on a hockey bracket where your team wins the Stanley Cup this season."

There it is...

"No more immigration paperwork... no more extensions. Permanent residency."

"I have a permanent residence... in Canada," I tell him, crossing my arms over my chest.

I love the United States, and I appreciate the opportunities I've had here, but Canada is still home. It's where I was born and raised, and it's where my entire family still lives. Even though I haven't thought much about settling down since my career has been my top priority, I always figured I'd do it in the same town I grew up in outside of Toronto.

I never expected I would outlive the four-and-a-half-year average lifespan of an NHL career. Even the top twenty-five percent of NHL players only see twelve years on average. At thirty-six, I'm still playing at the top of my game but I can't expect to stay here forever. My body has been beat down, and my mom hasn't let up for a second about me starting a family. She likes to remind me that my baby sister is going to have kids before me at this rate.

"We've discussed your plans for your life in Canada after the NHL. I know you want to follow in your father's footsteps and coach after retirement...but that day isn't today. Don't you want one more Stanley Cup win before you bow out?"

He knows I do, especially with the Hawkeyes.

I've got one championship win under my belt, but it was during my early years with a team I didn't stay with for long before getting traded. I haven't tasted victory in almost fifteen years. I want one more shot at it, and I want to do it with a team that's felt more like a family than any other team I've ever played for.

If I'm standing on the other side of the border watching my teammates hoist the Stanley Cup over their heads, that loss might haunt me for the rest of my life.

"Marry Amelia..." I mutter to myself.

I process the thought while staring down at my brown leather boots against the light oak floors of James's office.

I've always had a positive outlook on the idea of meeting someone and settling down but my focus has been to reach the peak of my career. Now, with this impending immigration issue, my career might end before I hold that coveted cup.

Amelia and I met only a couple of months before the season started and our weeks don't often match up. Some weeks, the only time I see her is when she's over at my house snapping photos in my jersey or off the balcony of my penthouse, all for social media.

She used to come to all of my home games, but since we started dating, she travels now as much as I do for product placement deals.

We're exclusive, but I never considered our relationship to be serious.

"Amelia is perfect. You've crossed the social continental divide with your relationship. It's boosted both of your careers to be connected and done wonders in your offerings for endorsements," he says, turning from me and pulling up a notepad he had on the corner of his desk. "We just had a meeting on the new deals coming through for you. A major cologne brand reached out just yesterday wanting you as their brand ambassador, and a huge fashion line wants you to do their Christmas campaign for next year. There's big money on this legal pad," he says, flopping the yellow pad of paper up and down as if to entice me.

I don't care about the fashion designer or the cologne brand, but maybe he's right.

Amelia is the quintessential WAG. She looks like she belongs in my season ticket seats, when she shows up, and she looks like she belongs on the passenger side of my Maserati. No matter how nice the charity event is, or how many Michelin stars the restaurant has, Amelia dresses like she belongs there. And I'll admit, she makes me look good whenever we walk into a room together.

But she's never met my family and I still haven't met hers, though she doesn't talk about them much.

The pressure from my mom for me to produce grandkids is getting a little heavier every time we talk. With my three other brothers already producing cherub-cheeked perfect offspring, and my kid sister just getting married last spring. I'm the odd man out and my mom won't let me forget it.

Maybe it's time. And marrying someone as career-focused as Amelia could be good for me.

Maybe I've been ignoring what's right in front of my face.

It's not as if she hasn't dropped the idea of engagement rings regularly. I've heard it.

I've just been too blind to see the obvious signs.

"I'm getting dinner with her tonight... I'll run the idea by her and see what she thinks about getting married."

"Great! I'll tell my buddy that you'll see him next week," James says, reaching for his phone and dialing the front desk.

"James, that's not what I—"

"Can you get Frank from immigration on the line for me? Great... and a turkey on rye for lunch. Fantastic, you're the best," he tells his assistant.

I groan internally at his praise.

Tell her to add a visa extension approval to that lunch order and then at least she wouldn't be the worst but she's been his assistant for years and he won't fire her.

He doesn't even look up at me as he waits for his call to get connected.

I guess this meeting is over.

I turn around and head out the door.

It doesn't matter what I say at this point—he's going to call and book the appointment.

I'm not expecting to get denied by Amelia anyway. She's been not-so-subtly sending me catalogs from the most expensive jewelry stores with a sticky note next to the ones she likes.

I got the message—loud and clear.

"Hey Frank... Frank, my man... It's James Potter. We're on for that meeting..." I hear him say before his heavy oak office door closes behind me.

I guess tonight... I'm getting engaged.

CHAPTER TWO

Ryker

"This place takes at least four months to get into, but I dropped your name, and they got us a reservation in one."

Amelia beams at me after the sommelier drops off the wine that he helped us pair with our meal.

They've seated us at the most private table they have, and I'm relieved considering the gravity of the topic I want to discuss with her.

"It's a nice place," I say.

I watch as Amelia picks up her cell phone and snaps yet another selfie with her wine glass. I'm not sure how many photos she's taken at this point, but at least a dozen.

"Did you know that this is the exact table where three A-list actors have proposed to their fiancées?" she practically squeals.

Her eyes glimmer back at mine and her excitement has me convinced that this whole idea James came up with actually makes sense—Amelia makes sense.

I reach out and grab her hand, pulling it into mine.

"Well then, I guess it's fitting," I say, smiling over at her.

"Oh my God!" She gasps. "You're proposing? Tiffany said she thought it would happen tonight. Thank God she talked me into those manicures today."

"Well... what I wanted to discuss was—"

Amelia doesn't hear a word I say and instead waves down the kid walking around refilling waters.

"Do you know how to work a phone?" she asks him in a serious tone.

"I'm seventeen... so yeah," the kid says, and then looks over at me. "No offense."

No offense?

What the hell does he mean 'No offense'? I'm thirty-six, not a hundred.

"Good, you'll have to do," she says, practically throwing her phone at him. "Now record this and make sure you get my right side —it's my best side."

The kid moves to her right side, and I do my best to ignore the few highbrow onlookers. They appear more concerned about Amelia having someone record in this upscale establishment than they are about our awkward proposal scenario.

I was hoping we could discuss it and come to a conclusion if this is something she wanted to do. But now I can see based on the mockup production Amelia is trying to toss together, she's expecting more than I planned.

"Perfect... right there should be good. And get an angle where you can see him in the shot but mostly me... and don't crop out my shoes. Keep rolling until I tell you. I'll just crop out whatever dialogue I don't want in post," she instructs.

In post?

And I guess the "him" she's referring to is me?

She turns back toward me, gives her hair a quick fluff, and then lays her hands gently down where mine sit on the highly starched white tablecloth. She gives me a demure smile that looks practiced to perfection.

"Ok, go ahead. I'm ready now," she tells me, batting her lashes.

"Uhhh... ok," I say, my eyes jetting up quickly to our 'cameraman'.

"Pretend he's not even there," she says, waving a hand in the kid's direction.

Right...

He's not here.

I'm no stranger to cameras and an audience. Every day I play a game that is televised at one level or another.

But this?

This is an unusual experience for me.

"So what I was going to say..." I continue, shaking off the weird start to this proposal and taking her hand in mine, wrapping my right hand around her left. "...is that we've been together for a while now."

She sits there nodding profusely with a pearly white smile. Her eyes glimmer back at me.

"...and with my visa about to expire, I think it makes sense that we get married," I say.

Her eyes go wide and her smile broadens. This was the reaction I was expecting, and I'm relieved to see it, even with the weird start.

"Oh my God, Ryker..." she says, putting her right hand against her chest as if she's surprised.

Then her eyes start to dart around the table for a second.

"What are you looking for?" I ask, searching the table as well trying to determine what she could possibly be looking for.

"Where's the jewelry box?"

Her face looks more and more confused by the second.

"What jewelry box?" I ask.

"The velvet one with the two-carat tear drop diamond I circled in that magazine that I left at your house."

Oh... she thought I already picked out the ring?

It's not as if I didn't consider that I'd need to buy her ring, I just wanted to make sure we were both on the same page before I dropped that kind of money on a clear piece of shiny carbon.

"I didn't get a ring," I admit.

Her eyes narrow as she stares back at me but her smile stays in place. Likely because the camera is still rolling.

"I wanted to bounce the idea off of you first, and if you agreed, then I thought we could go pick out the ring together," I say in an attempt to ease her concern.

Her face stalls with the same smile, but now that smile doesn't reach her eyes, and it's starting to look a little crazed.

I brace for the idea that the sixty-dollar-a-glass red wine she ordered is going in my face, but then her smile brightens back from the dead.

"Pick out the ring together?" she asks.

"Yeah. I didn't want to get the ring if you were going to say no," I admit.

She flashes a look at the cameraman. "Are you still rolling?"

He gives her a thumbs up and then she turns back to me.

"Oh. My. God!" she says, waving her right hand around her face as if to fan herself. "Picking out the ring together so that I get exactly what I want is the most romantic thing you could have ever done."

I reach behind and scratch the back of my neck. This exchange is getting weirder but I think this is what I was hoping the night would end with—a yes.

Tomorrow we'll pick her up a ring before my game next week, and then I'll ask the announcer to flash the kiss cam on her and announce our engagement. That will give this engagement the legitimacy that we'll need when we walk into the immigration office.

"Good, I'm glad you like the idea. Tomorrow we'll head down to whichever jeweler you want and you can pick out whatever they have in the case."

"Whatever they have in the case?" she asks, her smile falling a little.

"We'll need it before our meeting next week in the immigration office when we have our interview. You'll probably have to throw together a wedding quickly, too."

"Um, back up," she says, shaking out her right hand at me and then pulling her left hand out of mine. She turns to the kid and gives him the "throat cut" motion. "Cut it! Cut it."

He does... quickly, and then hands her back her phone and scurries off, back to doing his job.

"What do you mean immigration office and interview?"

"It's a K-1 visa—a fiancé visa. We have an interview next week to get approved and then we have to get married quickly after. I'd like you to come home with me for the annual charity hockey match. My family is going to want to meet you—"

"Wait... what happened to your extension?"

"I told you... they didn't get the check with the application, which means I have to re-send it, and since the office is inundated right now, my immigration paperwork will expire before they can approve it and I'll get deported. I'll have to start the process over from scratch back in Canada."

Her lips purse, but again, her forehead and eyebrows don't budge an inch.

"They're going to deport you?" she says.

"Yeah, that's why we have to get married within the K-1 visa time frame," I tell her.

"But I thought deportation was for like... normal people. You're famous. Don't you get... like... special treatment? A celebrity's phone line you could call to talk to someone more senior to push you through?"

I decide against telling her that the person pushing us through the fiancé visa could be giving us special treatment by giving us a cancelation, although I don't know how they run their schedules, maybe that's allowed. I just can't imagine that what James's "buddy" is doing would look good on his annual review if his superiors found out that he was giving favors out to a favored championship team due to a gambling bet he made.

"The immigration office is strict. If I don't get married, I'll get deported and have to wait out my new application. With the championship only a few months away, the Hawkeyes will have no choice but to drop me and fill my position," I tell her.

"You won't be a hockey player anymore?" she asks, her eyes narrowing on me again.

"No... I guess I won't."

"What happens if you get deported and we're married?"

"I thought you might come live with me for a while. Just until I get my visa straightened back out."

"Live in Canada! Are you crazy?" she asks, but it doesn't sound like a question.

"You can film anywhere, right?" I say, reaching for her hand again but she pulls it away for the second time.

That's not a good sign.

"Ryker, I was created for the spotlight. I need a place to shine. Who would I be if I'm just some old has-been ex-hockey player's wife, who lives in Canada?" she asks, a grimace in her voice as she says the name of my beloved country.

"You'd be with me. We'd be together. We could make a whole life in Canada. It's beautiful there—"

She bends down, grabs the overpriced handbag that I got her for Christmas, and then stands. The diamond earrings I bought her for her birthday catch and glitter in the mood lighting of the restaurant.

"It's nothing personal, Ryker," she says.

She steps forward, gently running her hand over my cleanly shaven jaw.

She never liked it when I grew out my facial hair. "It's just that being a professional player's girlfriend is part of my brand now. Don't you get it?"

She bends down and kisses me on the lips, and I'm stunned into silence, trying to figure out where this conversation derailed off the tracks that I let her plant a kiss on my lips.

Her lips used to taste like the signature Chanel lipstick she always wears, and her hair used to smell like the expensive hairspray she coats it with every day. But now, she tastes and smells like the jersey jumper she pretended not to be.

She turns to leave and I set my eyes on the lipstick smear she left on her wine glass instead of watching her walk out of the restaurant. The tealight candle set between our two chairs flickers as I listen to her high heels click-clack all the way to the exit, and then I listen for the sound of the doorman opening the door for her as she walks out into the windy Seattle January evening.

What the fuck just happened?

CHAPTER THREE

Three Weeks Later

Juliet

"I know what I want for Christmas next year," my assistant and best friend Shawnie says.

We both stand up out of our hockey stadium seats now that the game has ended, and the Hawkeyes hockey players are all exiting the arena.

The stadium is filled with excited energy as overjoyed fans, and really drunk ones, celebrate the Hawkeyes' win tonight. Fans from the out-of-town team that lost, sport permanent frowns.

"Oh yeah? What's that?" I ask, over the stadium music blaring through the speakers.

"A big hockey player wrapped up in a red bow, and sitting under my Christmas tree with mistletoe."

I laugh as we make our way out of our row. I follow behind her, watching her auburn hair cascade down her back in loose curls.

A non-stop stream of fans around us are doing the same thing.

Somehow Shawnie managed to get us these last-minute tickets this afternoon. I had zero notice about the impromptu hockey game and had to come straight from a meeting with a client at a wedding venue. Wearing a bodycon dress and sky-high heels isn't exactly freezing ice arena apparel, but I couldn't pass up the opportunity to see the space before my meeting with the Hawkeyes owner's wife tomorrow.

Marjorie Carlton.

The woman who will decide my fate.

A few days ago, I got the "congratulations" email from the Hawkeyes that my boutique party planning company, "Elite Event Planning," is being considered for a five-year contract as the premier party planner for the Hawkeyes franchise. Only five companies made it to this final round, and now all of us are expected to present our ideas in front of a small panel of decision-makers in the morning.

The problem is, I don't know the first thing about hockey or this brand, so when Shawnie got her hands on these seats, I couldn't turn them down. On my way in, I stopped off at the souvenir shop and found the warmest jacket I could purchase.

The jacket is three sizes too big for me and has the number 19 on it along with the name HAYNES on the back, but it kept me from hypothermia, so it was worth the outrageous price tag that I had to put on my credit card.

"If you win this contract, will it be enough to pay for the adult living care facility for Jerrin?" Shawnie asks.

Jerrin is my brother, and at 26, he's only a year and a half younger than me. He was diagnosed with autism when he was three.

"With our wedding season filled up and this lucrative Hawkeyes contract, it will be enough to make it all happen. But that's a big if." And it means I'll be eating ramen noodles for the rest of time, but I don't care... my brother's quality of life means more to me than anything.

He's been on the waitlist for three years. If I miss this opportunity, I'm not sure when we'll get another one.

"Can't your mom help cover part of Jerrin's housing?" Shawnie asks, dodging past a couple who decided to stop in the middle of a stampede of hockey fans headed for the exit.

Shawnie already knows the answer. My mom works as a CNA for the hospital, and even with extra shifts, it just isn't enough to cover her own expenses and the out-of-pocket medications that Jerrin needs.

"You know she can't. She's maxed out as it is, working every overtime shift she can get, and she's already at the top of her pay rate at the hospital."

"Did she apply for that Occupational Therapist Assistant program? That pays better, right?"

"Yes, but she doesn't have the time or money to do it. If I win this contract, I won't need her to pitch in for the new facility. The Hawkeyes contract will be enough to cover his room and board for the next five years."

A ding sounds on my phone. It's an urgent email from the supplier that they won't be able to send the cherry blossom flowers from Japan for a spring wedding that's only a couple of months away.

Damn it!

I find a bench to my right and plop down instantly to fire back. I can't fight the crowds of rowdy fans while my fingers are drafting an email back.

Shawnie looks over at me, but it's too late. The crowd is whisking her away. She'll have to flow with the current out to the exit.

"Don't worry. Just a few emails," I shout to her. "Talk tomorrow!"

She nods in understanding. She knows I take emails and phone calls from clients at any time, day or night. It's why we have such a high repeat clientele and constant referrals from happy customers. Our service and commitment are above the rest.

I watch as Shawnie doesn't fight the crowds and moves with the sea of hockey fans.

I desperately scour the internet for a new supplier who can supply me with the flowers that my bride demands. Without these cherry blossoms, the entire wedding theme will have to be redesigned, and my bride will be less than thrilled.

Before I know it, two hours have passed and I'm lucky that it's eight am overseas and a new supplier has confirmed that they can deliver on the order I need. And bonus, they're coming in under budget.

It's almost midnight when I look up from my phone and realize the only people left in the building are the cleaning crew.

"I don't mean to rush you, miss. It seems whatever business you needed to attend to was urgent, but we'll be locking up here soon," the older man in a medium grey janitorial jumpsuit says with a soft smile.

"Oh..." I look around and notice two other staff members cleaning behind the concession stand. "I'm sorry."

"No need to apologize. The name's Wilbur."

"Juliet," I say back.

"That's a beautiful name."

"Thank you," I say.

I gather up my things from the bench and stand to head for the exit. Wilbur looks toward the glass double doors that lead out to the parking lot.

"It's late, and there aren't many cars out there besides the cleaning crews. Do you want me to walk out to your car with you?" he asks.

"Oh no. I'm sure you have work to do. I don't want to trouble you." I wave off his offer.

"Ok, well, I'll at least walk out with you and take a look around the parking lot."

"Thank you, Wilbur. That's very considerate of you." I smile over at him as we walk side by side to the main entrance of the building.

"I have three daughters of my own and if my wife knew I didn't keep an eye out on a young lady out in a dark parking lot in the middle of the night, I'll be sleeping on the couch tonight. Make no mistake about that."

"Well, I wouldn't want you out on the couch." I wink.

He walks with me down to the curb of the parking lot and looks around to make sure there's nothing in the parking lot to cause him concern. Once he's satisfied, he turns to me.

"Good night, Juliet. Have a safe drive home."

I step off the curb and onto the blacktop of the parking lot, the glow of the parking lot lights reflects blue and orange off the wet asphalt.

"Good night," I say over my shoulder with a smile and a quick wave and then he turns and heads back inside.

Ryker

The chill of the night bites into my skin as I push through the side exit of the stadium. The asphalt, slick with a sheen of ice under the moonlit sky, threatens to dump anyone on their ass if they're not careful with each step.

Tonight's forecast: a plunge into the low 30s.

It's just about midnight but that won't stop the idiots driving like assholes in these road conditions.

Up ahead, a solitary figure caught in the glow of her cellphone screen navigates the icy terrain, oblivious to the lurking danger of the icy parking lot. She moves elegantly in a pair of heels and a tight fighting dress that wraps around her legs, stopping just above her toned calves. Her walking speed is at odds with the treacherous slick asphalt that she's moving across.

A familiar set of team colors catches my eye.

She's wearing a Hawkeyes jacket... and it has my number on it.

Number 19 with my name across her back. Her long thick, jet-black hair curled down to the middle of her back covers most of it, but I know it's there.

It's not unusual to see a woman in my jersey number coming out of the Hawkeyes stadium but something in the way she's dressed and the confidence in her walk, makes this pairing seem unlikely.

"Miss," I say to warn her, but she doesn't hear me over whoever she's talking to over the phone.

Those heels don't stand a chance against the slippery surface. And if she doesn't respect Mother Nature, she'll end up lying flat on her back before she even reaches her car.

I catch a glint of reflected light on an icy patch only a few feet out in front of her.

I pick up my pace to get to her first.

I hear her voice echo around us as she continues her conversation.

"I know it's a lot of money, Mom, but tomorrow I have a presentation with the Hawkeyes. If I win the Hawkeyes event planning contract then I can pay for Jerrin's care on my own."

The Hawkeyes event planning contract?

I heard Penelope, Autumn and Tessa discussing the position last week at Lake's birthday party. It didn't interest me until now.

"They're going to announce what company gets the contract in a few days. I'll know then," she tells her mom on the phone. "Yeah, dinner tomorrow sounds good. Ok, see you then."

Then she hangs up her cell phone.

I'm nearly to her when she begins to slip on the ice she didn't see.

Every instinct honed on the ice kicks in. I can't let her fall.

She lets out a small yelp as she slips. I reach her just in time and wrap an arm around her waist, pulling her tight against my body to assist me in my center of gravity to stabilize us both. We both narrowly avoid eating shit as I keep my feet from sliding out from under me.

Years of walking and skating on ice has me at an advantage over most.

Her left hand grips my jacket while her right hand, still clutching her cellphone, presses against my chest.

"Whoa, you ok?" I ask, my grip still tight around her waist.

"Yeah... I think so?" she says, her breathing a little labored from nearly taking a tumble and her eyes wide as if a little startled to see anyone else out here.

I release her once she seems stable enough but I stay close in case she slips again.

She smooths her hands over her tight, black dress.

From what I can see, she has an hourglass shape under that tent of a jacket she's wearing.

"Thank you," she says, looking up at me.

The parking lot is dark, but standing just under the overhead lights, her eyes almost look violet in color and catch my attention. I'm mesmerized by the deep blue/purple hue as they peer up at me through a thick frame of black lashes, complementing her warm olive skin. I've seen these eyes somewhere before. Maybe on someone famous, but I can't quite place it.

"What are you doing out here this late? The game ended nearly two hours ago. I figured I was the last one here, besides the clean-up crew," I say, searching her eyes.

Before she can answer, one of my assistant coaches walks past me.

"Great game, Haynes. Your defensemen played their asses off. That's what we need on the ice next week."

"Happy to give you the good D whenever you want it, coach," I say back, not breaking eye contact with the woman standing in front of me.

Though I play center-forward, I'm the captain of the team. This means I'm still responsible for every player on my team and the outcome of the game.

"Smart ass." He chuckles as he heads past us toward his car.

"You're a player?" she asks. Her eyes furrow as if she doesn't believe it.

Unlike Amelia's, this woman's eyebrows move.

That's oddly reassuring.

Another reassuring trait is that she isn't a jersey jumper.

She doesn't even know whose jersey she's wearing.

"Yeah, you were at the hockey game tonight, right?"

"I was, yes, but here for research. Sorry... I didn't pay all that much attention to the game."

Should I be insulted that I wasn't entertaining enough to catch her attention? The fans all seemed pleased so it couldn't have been that boring.

"Research for what?"

"The Hawkeyes party planning contract."

I heard her mention it to her mom over the phone but I wanted her to confirm it.

"Are you applying for it?"

What I'd like to know is why she needs the contract so badly. She mentioned something about paying for her brother.

"Yes, but I know there will be a lot of competition for this. I'm not so sure I have a shot," she says, her eyes casting down at her cell phone in her right hand.

She seems to think she already knows the outcome before she has even shown up for her presentation.

"You made your mom think it was a sure thing," I say.

Her eyes dart up to mine.

Judging from her confident posture and the way she carries herself, she seems like someone who doesn't readily offer her attention, as if she's inherently guarded... or maybe, someone made her that way.

I get the sense that she's a woman whose trust and attention must be earned. Admittedly, having to work for a woman's attention isn't something I'm used to in my line of work.

I don't use that to my advantage like other players do. Or at least, I don't anymore.

"You heard that?" she asks, watching me through her long dark lashes.

"Not intentionally but we're the only two out here so it was a little hard to ignore."

Her eyes leave mine again as she looks over toward one of the few vehicles left in the parking lot. The cleaning crew parks in the back and she was headed toward the SUV parked in the corner all by itself. It has to be hers.

"I just don't want her to worry about anything. My brother needs specialized care at a facility in the city and she can't afford it. I don't want her to worry about how I'm going to come up with the money," she says, blowing out a breath and wrapping her arms around her middle protectively.

The cold January night causes her warm breath to billow out from her painted red lips.

I have a feeling that was hard for her to admit to a stranger, but she said it like she needed to say it to someone else.

As crazy as it sounds, seeing her standing like that makes me feel protective of her. She shouldn't be staring off into an empty parking lot looking as defeated as she does.

"Anything I can do to help?" I ask.

"Not unless you can guarantee me the contract," she says, pulling her phone up and checking the time on it.

It's freezing and I should let her go home and warm up but then what she just said hits me.

What if I could guarantee her the spot?

Marjorie Carlton is the one who will be hiring for this position, and the Carlton's have a soft spot for their Hawkeyes families. If Marjorie knew that my soon-to-be wife wanted the contract, I'd bet the captain's position on the team that she'd give it to her.

"I can guarantee you the contract," I blurt out.

Her eyes flare up to mine in surprise. She wasn't expecting that answer.

"Is that right, Mr...?"

"Haynes. Ryker Haynes. And if you forget the name, you can just look at the name on your back."

"My back?" she asks, blinking up at me.

"You're wearing my name across your jacket," I tell her.

She attempts to look over her shoulder but can't see my name on her back from that angle.

"Number 19, Haynes," I say, to help jog her memory.

"Oh... I didn't know any of the names. I just bought the warmest-looking one."

I chuckle because that's the best answer she could have given.

She doesn't know who I am, and she doesn't care that I'm a professional hockey player.

"My number looks good on you. I'm glad you picked mine," I tell her with a genuine smile, because if she agrees... she might just be wearing that jersey for the next two years. "Now you know my name... what's yours?"

She bites down on her lip for a second and then looks back at the stadium.

"Juliet Di Costa," she says, and then looks back to me. "How exactly can a player guarantee me a position with the company? I find it hard to believe that you can promise something like that without being an owner."

"The Carlton's like me. If I ask Marjorie Carlton to give you the position, she will."

I leave out the part where Juliet has to be my wife for that to work.

"And what do you get out of all of this? I'm not going to sleep with you for a job." She scoffs, popping out a hip and raising an eyebrow at me.

I can't help but grin back at her.

The stern look on her face is cute as hell and after I tell her my terms, she'll probably wish I was only asking for sex.

What I need requires a much bigger commitment.

"No, that's not what I had in mind. I need a green card."

"A what?"

Her eyes go wide at what I just admitted to her, and she takes a half step back. Yeah... I'm pretty sure she wishes I only wanted sex now.

It's a lot to take in, I'll admit, but right now, she's my best shot. The meeting with the immigration officer is in three days and I need a fiancée. Preferably not one looking for WAGs status.

I have a feeling Juliet doesn't even know what that is.

This marriage needs a clean break at the end.

"I think you and I could help each other. You need a contract to help pay for your brother's care and I need to get married to stay in the country and take my team to the championship."

"Get married! Are you crazy?" she says, taking another half-step back from me.

"It serves two purposes. I need a green card and Marjorie Carlton likes to promote within the Hawkeyes family. If we're engaged, she'll give you the contract without a second thought. Especially if I introduce you as my soon-to-be wife."

She starts shaking her head. "This is insane."

She turns and starts heading for her car.

I follow behind her... at a safe distance.

I don't want her to feel uncomfortable with me following her to her car but this deal makes the most sense for both of us.

I need a temporary wife, and she needs something that I can guarantee her.

"Are you married?" I ask.

She shakes her head. "No."

We're getting closer to a small SUV and she hits the automatic start.

"What about a boyfriend?"

"No," she says again.

"Then you have nothing stopping you."

"Except that this is nuts. You don't just marry random people you met in the parking lot of a sports stadium in the middle of the night," she says into the cold parking lot.

"I know this is a little unorthodox but you and I both need something from this. I'll get you the five-year contract and all you have to do is stay married to me until the day we can divorce. We both walk away with something we want."

"What about your fan girls? What do you boys call them?" she asks with a sharp brow to provoke an answer.

I wasn't born yesterday. I might have taken several puck shots to the head in my long career but I'm at least I have enough brain cells to know enough not to walk into that.

I understand what she's aiming for and answering that question is the best way to get a "No thanks" from her.

"They're just fans," I tell her, sliding my hands into my pockets.

She smirks up at me like she knows I'm dodging the question strategically. She's smart, and she doesn't give a shit that I'm a hockey player. In fact, I think she might hold it against me... and I like her even more for it.

That makes her the exact woman I need for this.

Besides, it's been over a decade since I messed around with a puck bunny.

Most of the women I see now are people I meet organically outside of my Hawkeyes uniform. Most of those relationships fizzle out quickly too. My travel schedule and the fact that I live in Seattle during the season, and Canada during the off-season, creates a quick issue that ends the relationship before it even starts.

"Don't you have a DM list full of women who would love to be Mrs. Haynes?"

"I don't date women in my DM's. And a woman wanting to marry me because of what I do for a living is the exact person I'm trying to avoid. I need an arrangement with someone who understands this is temporary and is getting an equal benefit for our two-year marriage."

We finally reach her car and she stops. I reach for the door to open the driver's side for her.

She looks up at me, a little surprised by my act of chivalry. I was raised to open doors and pull out chairs for women but for some reason, the act takes her off guard.

What kind of relationships has she had if a man opening the door for her is unexpected? My curiosity about Juliet is growing. I want to get to know her and I might just get the chance if she'll agree to marry me.

"What's it worth to you to get your brother into that facility?" I ask, giving it my last shot to provide enough motive for her to take the leap with me.

My choice of wording could come off a little aggressive but the stakes here are high for both of us.

She stares up at me for a moment.

"I need to think about it."

I nod. "How about if you come to the home game in a couple of days and give me your answer then?"

"Isn't that Valentine's Day?" she asks.

"Yeah. Do you have other plans?"

She said she doesn't have a boyfriend but a woman this beautiful doesn't spend Valentine's Day alone.

"I guess not," she says, biting down on the inside of her cheek like she's trying to think of an excuse.

"Well, now you do... with me," I say, attempting to be charming while not creeping her out.

"And what if my answer is no to the arrangement?" she asks.

"Then I'll still take you out for a drink after the game. How about that?"

She rubs her red lips together as she debates her answer, her eyes glancing back at the stadium for a second.

"Ok." She nods but there's no smile in sight.

"Can I have your phone?" I ask, reaching out to her.

"Why?" Her eyebrows furrow immediately.

"I'm going to program my number in it."

She glances down at the phone in her hand and then reluctantly gives it to me.

I program my number quickly and then hand it back to her.

"Don't you want mine?" she asks.

"Nope," I tell her, shaking my head. "The ball is in your court, Juliet. If you have questions about how this arrangement will work, text me. I'll tell you anything you want to know. And if you don't reach out, then I understand."

There's an instant shift in Juliet's demeanor to what I said, a softening in her eyes and a more relaxed posture as if she's no longer on alert.

Do I want her number?

Hell yeah, I do. So I can check in every five minutes to see if she has an answer for me. I'm all too aware of how little time I have left to figure something out. But my gut tells me that I need to build trust with her, and this is my first attempt at doing that.

Not to mention, she's agreed to come to the date in two days. If I can read this woman at all, I'd say she's the type that sticks to her commitments.

She told me she would come to the game, and I have to believe she will.

I still do not know which direction she's leaning and I don't like the feeling that this proposal is a long shot.

If she doesn't agree to this arrangement, I'll get deported. Heading back to my family in Canada doesn't bother me. I've been gone too long as it is and I missed moments I'll never get back with my father.

I have an entire house and a whole life there. What bothers me isn't the leaving, it's letting down my teammates and the Hawkeyes family right before a championship. If I fail to stay in the country, I'll have to live with the disappointment of letting them down, forever.

And I have enough regrets as it is.

"I'll leave a ticket at will-call for you," I tell her.

She turns back toward the car and steps up on the running boards, taking a step in her heels on the icy black plastic. I grip onto her arm the second I see her slip a little and help guide her safely into her seat.

"Thank you for saving me... twice," she says reluctantly.

"I've heard that makes for great husband material," I say, hoping not to leave on the wrong note with her.

She lets out a chuckle and covers it with her hand quickly.

I can see her tough exterior starting to crack the more I show her who I am.

If I want to win her over, I have to make her laugh and show her I'm a good guy she can trust.

I can do that.

I wait until she buckles herself in and then I close the driver's side door gently next to her.

"See you soon, Juliet," I say to the glass window between us and then take a step back to show her I'm easing off now and giving her space.

She gives me a look that almost suggests she's considering saying something but then puts the SUV in drive and eases onto the gas, leaving me alone in the parking lot.

This is it.

This is my last shot.

I marry Juliet, or I get deported.

CHAPTER FOUR

Juliet

"You're going to be great. You've prepared and your presentation looks incredible," Shawnie says.

I wish she were here in person, but we have a large fiftieth wedding anniversary party that requires one of us to be there to ensure everything goes perfectly for our clients.

I'm lucky that Shawnie is so amazing and can handle all the hoops I throw at her. Someday I hope to make her partner. She's certainly earned it since she started with me four years ago.

"I hope you're right. This means so much to me, and I need to impress them with my presentation," I say, pressing the elevator button to ascend to the corporate offices, following the instructions in their email.

Being back at the Stadium the day after Ryker's offer to secure this contract in exchange for marrying him, has my nerves on edge.

He asked me if I had plans for Valentine's Day and then invited me to the game to hear my answer. My stomach has been in jumbled knots all day, wondering if I just agreed to a date with Ryker and whether or not I would run into him this morning at the stadium.

Do I want to see him?

I can't make up my mind but since I don't have an answer for him, it's probably better I don't see him.

I went to visit Jerrin this morning on my way to the Hawkeyes stadium at the center he has an apartment at, and told him about my trip to the hockey game. He didn't say much, but his eyes lighting up told me everything I needed to know.

I don't like labeling my brother's autism, but his specialists say his ASD level ranges between a one and two. He's very capable of doing most things on his own, which is why he can live in an assisted facility, and in an apartment he shares with another resident, but his desire to communicate verbally is minimal. I believe that's a product of the trauma from our father leaving him at such a young age. However, he and I communicate just fine, whether he chooses to use words or not. Maybe it's that brother/sister bond or the fact that he knows I'll do anything for him.

His favorite nurse called me right after I stopped at the cafe for my coffee on my way to the Hawkeyes stadium to tell me that Jerrin is wearing the Hawkeyes jacket that I brought him. And asked her to find him old replays of Hawkeyes games.

In an hour, he already has a favorite player: center forward Ryker Haynes, captain of the team, and Hawkeyes number nineteen.

I suppose I brought that upon myself.

Riding up to the third floor, I fidget with the strap of my laptop bag and stare back at the reflection of myself on the metallic surface.

I look the part in a designer pant suit with cropped blazer and heels. My raven hair slicked back into a low bun at the base of my skull.

I'm wearing my signature red lipstick, meant to signify power, but right now, it isn't giving me the confidence boost it usually does.

Impostor syndrome sets in, and I take a deep breath to calm my nerves.

The thing is, I know I can do this.

I might not have as many years of experience as some of the other planning companies coming in today, but I know I'm the best. I know I can do this job. I just need a chance to prove it.

But what if they can't see past the small boutique wedding planner who's never held a contract this size before? What are they aren't willing to take the chance on me?

"Everyone has to start somewhere," my mother always reminds me, and she's right. I guess that's why growing pains are just that—painful.

"I can almost hear your panicked thoughts from here," Shawnie says, her voice clear through the receiver.

I'm surprised to still have such good reception in the elevator.

"I'm not panicking."

"Yes, you are. Take a deep inhale because you're about to ace this thing."

Before I can say anything back, the elevator doors ding on level three and the doors start to open.

The third floor opens into a modern space with tall ceilings, dark espresso wood-stained floors, and grey and turquoise painted walls.

A tall reception desk sits across from the elevator doors in the lobby. An older woman with a bob haircut is perched on the other side of it. Her inviting smile beckons me forward.

"I just got here. I have to go. I'll call you later," I tell her.

"Break a leg!" she says before hanging up.

I cut through the distance between me and the receptionist and head for the front desk to check in for my appointment.

"Hello, Juliet Di Costa. I have a nine am with Marjorie Carlton," I tell her.

She glances down at a clipboard on her desk.

I don't mean to but my eyes follow her line of site and I see the other four companies that made it to the shortlist, right below mine, in order of appointment time.

I swallow hard at the gravity of knowing that all of my competitors are companies that have been around many more years than me and have far bigger budgets than I do.

The bit of confidence from Shawnie's pep talk has all but dissolved into thin air.

"Welcome," she smiles. "I have you down, Ms. Di Costa. There's coffee and sparkling water in the lobby. Help yourself.

Penelope Roberts will be out to get you when they're ready," she offers.

I walk over to the well-stocked table that has a single-serve coffee machine and every creamer flavor imaginable available for consumption.

A small fridge with a glass door sits under the machine with three rows full of sparkling water flavors and bottled water.

Although coffee sounds amazing right now, I've already had three cups today, and one more might make me too jittery for my presentation.

I bend down to open the fridge, pulling out a single bottle of water and then I close the fridge door.

"Juliet Di Costa, Elite Event Planning?" A woman a little younger than me with long blonde beach waved hair says, smiling from the opening of the hallway.

"That's me," I say, raising my hand quickly.

I head for the woman in the hallway.

"Good morning. I'm Penelope Roberts and I will be sitting in on your presentation today," she informs with her pearly white smile and bright blue eyes.

"It's nice to meet you," I say. "Thank you for having me."

"The pleasure is ours. Follow me down the hall and we'll get started," she says, turning and giving her back to me as she starts walking.

I do as she says, following closely behind as I take it all the large memorabilia boxes attached to the walls. Each displays pictures and old equipment, showcasing the Hawkeyes' history over the many years.

"I'm the Administrative Assistant for the GM and I will be acting as one-third of the panel in today's interview," she says over her shoulder as we continue down the hallway. "Autumn Daughtry, our PR guru who handles a lot of our charity functions and team appearance, will be our second on the panel, and of course, Marjorie Carlton, the owner's wife will be the third and largest deciding factor on our panel today."

She stops and then offers out her hand to signal us to enter the conference room, where a table is already set out and two women are already seated.

They both stand as we enter. The youngest of the two, with medium-length light brown hair and a friendly smile greets us first.

I walk up to the conference table and reach out to shake her hand that she's extended to me across the narrow table.

"I'm Autumn Daughtry. It's very nice to meet you," she says, as we shake.

Then the older woman stands and does the same, offering her hand across the table. Her smile is warm but her handshake says she means business.

I like her already.

"I'm Marjorie Carlton. Thank you for agreeing to meet with us on short notice."

"Absolutely! I wouldn't have missed it. I can't tell you how much I appreciate you giving me an opportunity."

"Well then, let's jump right into it," she says, leaning back over the conference table and taking a seat.

I see a sheet in front of me with the whole first-year's calendar laid out with the events and dates of everything the winning company will be expected to take care of. Seeing the much larger list than I was expecting has my heart racing. A lot of them are small team signing or media days that won't require "the works" like bouncy houses and cotton candy machines, but having this much work might even mean bringing on a second assistant.

The potential is so exciting that I have to keep my mind on the task ahead. I haven't won them over yet.

"As you can see on the list," Marjorie says, pulling out a pair of glasses and adjusting them as she peers down at the list. "This contract will encompass many different projects over the years. Although I have done most of this myself with the assistance of Penelope Roberts, the sports world is changing, and with it, higher demand for public displays, flash and pizazz." She says.

"And that is exactly what we plan to do," I say, nodding in agreement and glancing up from the calendar in my hand. "May I plug into the projector for the presentation that I prepared?"

"Yes, please do," Marjorie says. "We love a tech savvy planner."

I watch as Penelope and Autumn make a note.

Penelope gets up from her chair to make sure I don't need any help, and within a few minutes, we are up and rolling.

Twenty-five minutes later, the allotment of time I was told I had in the email, we are through my presentation of what I can bring to the Hawkeyes and some examples of work I've done in the past.

My presentation was flawless but whether or not that will be enough to win them over with the steep competition waiting out in the lobby... I don't know.

I shake hands again with all three women before I exit the conference room and head for the elevator.

Hitting the elevator button, the first thing I want to do is call Shawnie and tell her about the stiff competition we have up against us but my phone rings in my hand.

The bank.

Elevators are notorious for bad reception, but I can't let this go to voicemail in case this is an approval phone call. And I can't have a call with the bank about winning this contract while standing in the lobby.

"This is Juliet," I say at the same time as the elevator doors open.

"Hello, Juliet. This is Stewart from the bank regarding your loan. Do you have a moment?"

"Yes. I do," I tell him.

I step into the elevator, willing it not to drop my call.

"Great. I just wanted to verify that this loan is contingent on you winning a five-year planning contract with the Hawkeyes hockey team. Is that correct?" he asks.

"That's correct."

"And have you been awarded the contract?" he asks.

"No, not yet. I just met with them this morning."

"When will they be awarding the contract?"

I don't like the hesitation in his voice after hearing my answer.

"In four days. But I need those funds now for the down payment in order to secure the spot for my brother."

"I understand Ms. Di Costa but without the contract, we can't approve the loan—"

"If I don't have the down payment and sign the contract by the end of the week, they'll give his spot to someone else. I don't have that much liquid cash available right now," I explain.

Not to mention that signing that contract holds me to paying the monthly payment for my brother's care for the next twelve months... whether or not I win the Hawkeyes contract.

"I'm sorry Ms. Di Costa. If we can't verify income, we can't distribute the funds. Let me know as soon as you are in contract with the Hawkeyes, and we will reopen your request for a loan."

"Reopen my request?" I blurt out in frustration.

Without this loan, there isn't any way I can pay the first and last, plus the deposit required to lock in Jerrin's spot.

I open my mouth to ask for some kind of exception, but he hangs up, or the call drops, I'm not sure which one.

"Damn it," I mutter to myself, staring down at my phone that shows "Call Ended".

Then the memory of last night and what Ryker offered comes flooding back.

He said he can guarantee the contract for me if I agree to marry him. This man is a complete stranger to me, but he has more to lose if he doesn't hold up his bargain.

It isn't the ideal solution to my problem, but I'm on a time crunch here and my plan A just fell through.

The deadline for the facility is the day before the Hawkeyes said they would make their decision, February sixteenth, and the facility has already been kind enough to extend the deadline a couple of weeks while I waited to hear from the bank. There's no way they'll extend again.

The way things are looking now, I don't have another choice. But there's one more condition I'll need in order to make this deal work for me and my hands shake as I pull up my phone to text Ryker. I hate seeming so desperate, but I have to swallow my pride and do this for Jerrin.

It's for my brother.

The elevator doors open and I exit as I type up the text before I chicken out.

> Juliet: I have another condition. I need a down payment for Jerrin's apartment, and I need to know that if the Hawkeyes contract option falls through that you'll guarantee to cover my brother's facility expenses.

Now this really feels like I'm taking money for services rendered. Even though he said this isn't for sex, it still feels like a grey area.

The bubbles signaling his incoming text have me gripping my phone tighter.

> Ryker: Your terms seem fair considering you're bailing me out and I said I would guarantee you the contract. How much do you need for the down payment?

> Juliet: $35,000 is the deposit and I have to make it in three days.

The second I send it off, I hold my breath. I'm not sure whether I want him to agree or tell me the deal is off.

> **Ryker:** That's not a problem. I can get you the money today if you need it. Cash or certified check?

Really?

That easy?

I internet stalked him last night. I couldn't help it.

Ryker was recruited right out of high school. He's been playing for the NHL for almost two decades. His contract salary is public knowledge and was listed on a website ranking the highest paid hockey players in the league. With all those zeros for so many years I suppose it's not shocking that thirty-five thousand dollars is easy to come by for him.

I hold my phone in my hand and get cold feet at the last second. I can't pull the trigger just yet. I need one more day to wrap my head around what I'm about to do.

Two years married to a man I don't know.

> **Juliet:** Can I have one more day to think about it?

> **Ryker:** Of course. Do you think you'll have an answer for me tomorrow at the game?

Tomorrow's game... the idea of having to give him an answer tomorrow has my heart racing.

Even if I wanted to take more time to overthink this... I can't. Both Ryker and I have impending deadlines. His meeting with the immigration officer and my brother's lease contract are all due in a few days' time.

> **Juliet:** Yes. I'll have an answer for you tomorrow.

Thank you for understanding that I need more time.

> **Ryker:** See you then. Don't forget... I'm the guy on the ice. And take good notes because I'm going to quiz you later. Let's see how much you pay attention this time.

I smile at the text. He's teasing me because I didn't pay attention to the game the last time I was in the stadium.

> **Juliet:** I'll be watching. I swear.

> **Ryker:** Do you need me to remind you of my jersey number again in case you forgot already?

I catch myself grinning again as I text back.

> **Juliet:** I won't forget. Haynes #19.

> **Ryker:** That's my girl.

My stomach flips unexpectedly.

I read the text over and over again, half expecting that the text is a mirage, or I read it wrong, but it doesn't change.

My thumb hovers over my screen's keyboard, debating if I should respond back... and how. Conflicting emotions flow through me as the reality of what Ryker, and I are about to do soaks in. A marriage of convenience... a decision from both of us because of our desperation.

And yet...

There's a thrill in the uncharted territory of doing something spontaneous. Letting down my guard a little for a new adventure.

But any bit of excitement I feel is overshadowed by the uncertainty of how Ryker and I will pull this off.

And survive each other for the next two years.

With time dwindling quickly for both of us, I have to make a decision.

And I already know what it has to be.

Ryker

I smile down at my phone as I hibernate it and stick it in my front pocket after agreeing to Juliet's condition.

Juliet's coming tomorrow.

I don't care about the thirty-five thousand dollars; it's a drop in the bucket for me, and if she had just asked for the money for her brother's care instead of the contract, I would have agreed to that just as quickly.

I make more than enough to afford it and staying with this team to finish the season is worth every penny.

"Haynes! Stop sending dick pics and spot me," Seven, one of our goalies and most veteran players on the team, says by the bench press.

I chuckle at my teammates' crass comment.

"Jesus Wrenley. You're clingier than plastic wrap in a hurricane. Keep your jock strap on, I'm coming," I tell him.

I walk around the back of the weights while he lays flat on the cushioned black bench and positions his hands on the barbell.

"Did you get your visa approval back yet? You sent it off before we left for bye-week, right?"

He does a set of reps, and then I outstretch my hands to help

Of course. My luck... the player who talks the least on the team is the only one asking the hard-hitting questions.

"Uh... actually, Potters's assistant forgot to mail the check in with it," I tell him.

He knows James Potter well enough since he also used to be Seven's agent. But Seven made the move to a bigger agent years ago. I don't know the details of why he moved agencies, but there's so much bad blood there. Wrenley doesn't talk about it, and I don't ask.

"She fucked up the application?" he asks.

He reaches for the barbell again and wraps his hands around the cold metal.

"That's the gist of it, yeah."

He shakes his head.

"I told you to move agencies before some shit like this happened."

Then pulls the barbell off the rack again, doing another set of reps.

He warned me... once when I moved to the Hawkeyes team years ago.

He finishes his reps and then I repeat helping him place the barbell back in place.

Then he spins his legs back over to one side of the bench and leans up to sit, and looks at me sideways.

"What are you going to do then? You're our captain and we're weeks away from playing in the finals for the championship."

"I'm working it out," I say, hoping that's enough for him to let it go.

"Did you send in a replacement application with the check?"

"No. They wouldn't be able to process it in time."

I rub the back of my neck at the information that I should be keeping my mouth shut about.

He turns towards me, still sitting on the bench.

"Ryker... what are you going to do?" he asks, his eyebrows furrowing. "Did you tell Sam about this?"

Did I tell our General Manager that I might get deported and to start looking for my replacement? Hell no.

I have a plan and I need to hope that Juliet decides to bail me out.

"And have him start warming up my replacement? No... I've got a plan."

"A plan to stay in the country without a visa? Do I even want to hear more of this? Will this make me an accessory to whatever laws you're about to break," he scoffs.

"I'm not going to hide out illegally. I'm a public figure anyway... I'd last a day if that."

"So what's the plan?"

I debate whether I should tell him but if anyone can keep a secret, it's Seven. He wouldn't tell a soul.

That's why he has a shack on the ocean in a tiny village in Mexico. During his off-season he hides out in seclusion for months on end... just fishing and whittling on the beach by himself.

It's not my idea of a good time, however, everyone deserves their peace. Our job is stressful and hard on your body. If he wants to zone out for a while to get his head right again before another crazy season, then let him be.

"I'm getting married," I tell him, though I'm not sure if I have a bride yet.

"To Amelia?" he asks with a grimace.

Good to know he's a fan. I'm not surprised he hasn't seen the social media evidence that she's not dating me anymore.

"No, not Amelia. Someone else that needs my help just as much as I need hers."

"You sure that's smart."

"Nope. But if I want to play hockey for the Hawkeyes, I have to come up with a way to stay in the country. I don't have a choice at this point."

"Did you tell Sam what's going on?" he asks.

Telling Sam so that he starts looking for my replacement is not on the top list of things I want to do.

"No. I'm going to fix this myself. I might need a witness to stand up with me."

"You're asking me?" he asks with a lifted eyebrow.

"Would you?"

He nods. Seven is the guy you count on to hide a body. He'll show up, not ask too many questions, and never tell a soul.

"Yeah man, I'll be there. I just hope you know what you're doing."

Yeah... me too.

CHAPTER FIVE

Juliet

"Mom…" I call out as I push through her apartment door on the third floor. "I'm here."

The minute I walk through the door, the smell of freshly baked ziti and garlic bread wafts past my nose.

After all the stress of my presentation this morning at the Hawkeyes stadium, it's nice to be back in my mom's apartment.

It smells like her cooking and my favorite childhood dish, offering some much-needed comfort. "In the kitchen, Juju bean!" she responds.

It's her only day off this week from her job as a nursing assistant at the hospital. I wish she would take it easy but my brother is going through a phase where he'll only eat my mom's baked ziti and peanut butter and jelly sandwiches without the crust.

Every week she takes the package to his group home and gives it to the nursing staff for his meals during her frequent visits.

I walk into the kitchen to find four foil baking pans full of the delicious pasta dish.

"You made four pans? Can he eat all of that in a week?" I ask.

Though my brother is younger than me, he towers over my mom and me. He got our dad's six foot one height. He could probably eat it all if the nursing staff let him.

"No, of course not," she says with a grin. "I like making a couple extra for the staff; they enjoy my cooking too.

"Of course they do," I smile back, taking the last few steps towards the small four-person table at the end of her small galley kitchen.

It's not like the huge kitchen I grew up in when my father was a pro baseball player for Seattle. But when he got injured, he lost his contract and sunk into a deep depression. Then, slowly, we lost everything else. The house... the cars... everything, including him.

Last I heard, he lives in an RV trailer park on the ocean in California. He retells his glory days at some local bar to anyone who will listen.

He doesn't reach out and neither do I.

He doesn't even call to check in on Jerrin or offer to help my mom pay for anything. That's what gets me the most.

"Here," she says, setting down a plate of piping-hot noodles, melted cheese, and sauce, along with a glass of milk for me. "I made enough for us, too. I'd never forget my best girl."

She leans down and kisses the top of my head.

Her best girl...

How do I tell her I'm about to disappoint her in a way I never thought I would?

"Well, I hope you still feel that way when I tell you some good news."

"No matter what news you have, you will always be my best girl... you know that."

My mom heads back down the narrow kitchen and starts to dish herself up a plate as well.

Now is the time to break the news so I don't have to tell her while she's staring back at me face to face.

"So the bank won't be coming through for me in time to secure Jerrin's spot, but I have a better option," I say quickly.

My mom pauses mid-spatula scoop. "No bank?"

"No, not the bank. But I've found a better solution where I won't have to repay the money. I'll earn it."

If you can call marrying a man for two years "earning it".

"You're going to earn thirty-five thousand dollars in three days? What exactly will you be doing?" she asks, her brow lifting in concern.

She doesn't like the sound of it already and if I were in her shoes, I wouldn't like it either.

She still hasn't scooped her portion of dinner out of the small glass casserole dish she made just for us.

I wish she would do something besides stare at me.

Why do I feel like a call girl when I'm trying to explain it to my mother?

I shouldn't feel that way. Ryker even assured me that sex wasn't what he's looking for in exchange. But we will be married and living under the same roof. I guess those details will still need to be ironed out if I agree.

So I do what any daughter of a mother who's half Italian, but full temper will do... I lie.

"I have a friend who needs some help staying in the country."

"Juliet..." she starts, that tone of disappointment in her voice already.

"He has connections to the Hawkeyes and will secure me the event planning contract and will give me Jerrin's down payment. I just have to help him get his green card and that's it."

"His green card? You have to marry this person? Juliet, this is absurd," she says, lifting the spatula and pointing it at me.

"He'll pay me the money for Jerrin's down payment, and I'll get a five-year deal with the Hawkeyes that will be sure to pay for Jerrin's monthly lease."

"I told you already, Jerrin is fine where he is. And if it's between you marrying some strange man and Jerrin getting better care, then I'll just bring him home."

"You can't mom, you know you can't," I argue.

I love that she wants to take care of him, but we've tried this. She works too much and Jerrin needs more hands-on help.

"I can take care of him just fine. He's my son."

"Mom, he's twenty-six years old. He needs some independence and someone who will work with him every day. You work six days a week and mostly the night shift or swing shift. You're asleep while he's awake."

"The state-paid facility he's in is fine then. We don't need to move him."

"It's practically a daycare, mom. They do their best, I'm sure, but this other facility has its own home economics classes where he can learn to cook and do his own laundry. They help him to become more independent. And he'd get his own apartment instead of sharing a bunk bed with other residents. Plus he gets assigned an Occupational Therapist that works with him daily."

She lets out a sigh, dishes herself a plate of baked ziti, and starts walking towards me. We've been through all of this already, but the price tag is hard to swallow.

She sets her plate down and pulls out the chair across from me.

"A good mother would never agree to let you go through with this. Your brother's care should fall on his parent's shoulders... not his sisters."

I hold my tongue, wanting to curse my father for not being here and lending a hand with everything. But it only hurts my mother more when I bring him up.

"I found a way to make this work. I don't need you to agree, I just need your blessing... please," I say, reaching out and covering her right hand lying on the oak table with my own.

"How does someone who's struggling to stay in the country have that kind of money and influence with an NHL team to give you that? And if you say he's a mob boss—"

"No! God no," I chuckle, although sadly, she would like that answer better than the one I'm about to give her.

That's how much she hates pro players. She'd rather I married an Italian mobster than marry a rich jock.

This is the question I've been dreading most all evening.

I pull my hand back off of hers in an effort of self-preservation. She might bite my hand off when I give the last damning piece of information.

"He's a... well, he's a hockey player that I met the night I went to the game with Shawnie."

"A hockey player!" my mother practically screams. "Oh no—absolutely not. You know how I feel about professional athletes."

"This isn't an actual marriage. I'll be in and out, two years max."

"Two years? Juliet... that man is going to ruin your life."

"You don't even know him."

"I don't have to know him. They're all the same. It's all rainbows and puppies now but wait until the career he spent his life dreaming of burns down with a line drive to the kneecap. Just wait until the man you fell in love with turns into a shell of the man he once was and tries to grasp at his old glory days by spending his nights with women half your age."

"Mom, I know... I'm sorry that happened to you, but this isn't real. I just have to pretend until he can get permanent status and then we'll divorce."

"I won't give you my blessing to destroy your best years, Juju Bean... I won't. We'll find another way to get Jerrin more help but not like this. I'll take more shifts at the hospital."

"You're already overworked as it is."

"This discussion is over," she says, standing out of her chair instantly and picks up her plate.

She stomps out of the kitchen and into the small living room just past the kitchen.

I don't have to look to know that she's sitting on the couch in front of the TV with her wooden tray table out in front of her.

This is how she eats when she's home alone for dinner.

She and I eat in separate rooms with only the sound of Jeopardy reruns filling the void between us.

I finish my plate of food, rinse off the dirty dishes and load them in the dishwasher. Then I walk out to the living room to say goodnight.

She doesn't look up at me.

I know she isn't mad at me. I made her relive a painful part of her history that she tries to forget.

I walk over to the couch and lean down, setting my lips against the top of her head and kiss her.

"I love you, mom. I'll call you tomorrow," I say softly, leaning back up.

I head for the door, not far from the living room and as I turn the handle on her apartment door, I hear her voice.

"Text me when you get home safe, Juliet."

Then I walk out the door and close it behind me.

I wish she would have given me her blessing. The weight of a decision this big would have become a little lighter if my mother could have assured me that this was the right thing to do for my brother. Now, being at odds with her makes this decision harder, but not impossible.

Her past with my father is clouding her ability to see this clearly for what it is. A chance to give my brother a fuller life with more opportunities for independence, however small it might be.

I prepare myself for the decision that has to be made for Jerrin's sake. Tomorrow at the hockey game, I'll give Ryker my answer.

CHAPTER SIX

Juliet

> **Juliet: I need a new outfit for tonight. Going to a hockey game.**

> **Shawnie: Yes girl!!!**

Why is this reaction not shocking? I know well enough at this point not to engage with her when she's on an emoji bender. I'd better save my energy for the questions I'll get while we shop.

> **Juliet: Meet in an hour?**

Shawnie: Wouldn't miss this!

Freaking emojis. Shawnie has a bet with herself for how far she can carry on a conversation in all emojis. It wouldn't hurt my feelings if emojis were deleted from the keyboards across all operating systems.

I meet Shawnie at our usual spot—the coffee shop near the mall's entrance. While we wait, I spill the entire parking lot story on her, not missing a single detail... because she needs all the facts if she's going to answer the question I've been struggling with.

Even though Shawnie and I differ in many ways, when it comes to advice, no one gives it as straightforwardly as she does. And no one knows me better than she does, either—not even my own mother.

"So that's his offer — a marriage of convenience with a two-year commitment with no strings at the end. Do you think I'm crazy for considering it?" I ask, even though I don't know what I'd do if she says yes since I've come to terms with the fact that this is my best bet.

"Uh... do I think you're crazy for considering marrying a drop-dead gorgeous hockey player and living in his penthouse for the next two years while you secure the biggest account Elite Events has ever had? Let me think about it," she says, dramatically putting her index finger to her chin. "No! I think you're crazy for not agreeing the second he pitched you the idea."

Of course, she would be on board with this— it's right up her alley. And if she hadn't just started dating her perfect match, she would probably offer to take my place.

"Marriage is kind of a big deal, and did you miss the part where I could get in trouble if this whole thing goes wrong?"

"No. But I did miss the part where you have to pay back the thirty-five thousand in sexual favors. I would love to know that part of the agreement... in greater detail," she says, wiggling her eyebrows at me.

I shake my head at her and take a sip of my iced coffee.

It could be negative ten degrees and I will still always order iced coffee over hot.

"I already told you, he said he wasn't looking for sex. This isn't that kind of agreement."

"Not looking for sex and not wanting sex are different. And did you see the size of that man's glutes? I bet he has a nice power play he could show you."

The memory of how effortless it felt when Ryker caught me around the waist right before I fell on my ass in the parking lot, comes back to me. There's no denying that the man is in good shape.

"We're not going to be sleeping together. This is transactional only. We get married, he gets me the contract, we jump through all the hoops for his green card, and then a quick, painless divorce."

Shawnie pulls out her phone from her back pocket as we continue walking through the mall.

We already picked out the warmest knee-length camel peacoat jacket I could find and a cute beanie and matching gloves from one of the designer department stores.

I'll pair it with a pair of straight-legged dark wash jeans and my high-heeled booties that I already have at home.

If I'm going to be meeting Marjorie Carlton again, I want to look as professional as possible, and not freeze my ass off in the process, like I did last time.

"Give me your phone," she tells me.

"Why?" I ask, but when Shawnie wants something, it's better to give in.

It's not as if I don't trust her.

She knows every password to every account I have, including the code to my cell.

"Just give it here," she insists.

"Fine," I say, handing it over with a huff.

We pass by one of the boutique wedding shops in the mall.

Seeing the dress has me thinking about the fact that in less than ninety days, I might be walking down the aisle to Ryker. It's an odd vision — not how I pictured my first wedding.

Ick... first wedding.

I promised myself that when I got married I'd do it right so I never go through a divorce like my parents, and here I am, already planning to have a second wedding before I even have the first.

" Look," she says, holding my phone up to my face. "You're going to be living under the same roof as this."

I stop at the abrupt swinging of my phone in my face and when I finally focus in on the picture, I come face to face with a half-naked photo of Ryker in only a pair of boxer briefs.

I've internet-stalked him a little—I'll admit, but I've never seen this picture. It's an underwear ad for a large men's brand and Ryker has all the right assets to belong in it.

His muscular arms fletching with his hands behind his head...

His rippling abs draw your eyes down to the deep V of his pelvis...

That bulge in his boxers and those thick glutes.

Ok, the man has a drool-worthy body, but that is for someone else to fan themselves over. I can't let myself think of him like that.

Our marriage has an expiration date shorter than an over-ripened banana.

"What's your point?" I ask.

"This man is going to be your husband. The one man on earth you absolutely should be screwing on the regular, and you're asking me what my point is?" she asks, her eyebrows stitching together.

I roll my eyes at her—screwing Ryker is not on my list of things to do. I have too much on my plate already. I click the side button to hibernate my phone and this slide it into my pocket.

I hear her huff to the right side of me. "Fine, be like that, but just so you know, I think you just wasted your money on a peacoat when you should have blown your entire budget on lingerie," she says. "The assless kind."

I can't help it as a chuckle bubbles out of me.

"I'm going to take that to mean that you think I should go through with it."

"Hell yes, you should, and if he has any friends needing a green card, you're welcome to send them my way."

"You're in love with the accountant. Don't play tough with me," I tell her.

"Yeah yeah... I think I'm going to marry the Poindexter. Will you plan my wedding?"

I shake my head. Shawnie is just as talented of a wedding planner as anyone I've ever met. She could go out on her own if she wanted, but she'd rather work with me.

"Plan it yourself," I tease, though I would love to help her.

"Fine..." she says, linking her arm with mine and pulling me close so there's no gap between us as we walk. "Will you be my maid of honor?" she asks.

"Yes," I'm almost too scared to say it out loud but I need to come to terms with the fact that saying yes to Ryker is my only option. I'm out of time, and so is he. "...will you be mine?"

She squeals with excitement and squeezes my arm with hers until I swear it cuts off the circulation.

"Yes! Come on, let's look at wedding dresses for you before I have to set up for the gender reveal party for the Carter family," she says, tugging me against my will to the other end of the mall.

There's no point in struggling... resistance with Shawnie is futile.

Ryker

She agreed to Valentine's Day and coming to the game. I know she needs the money and the contract to secure her brother's lease.

She asked for more time, but she and I both know that we're each other's last hope. She's supposed to have the down payment to the center in a matter of days, or she'll lose Jerrin's spot.

As the team captain, I'm always here early, but today, I needed to make sure to get here even earlier in order to set everything in motion.

I know our cameraman and announcer usually get here before the team to make sure mics are cued up and everything is ready to roll.

"Doug," I say, walking up to the sound podium where our announcer sits for the game.

"Haynes, how's it going? You ready for the game tonight?"

"Feels like a winning night. The team's ready," I assure him. "Hey listen, I need a little favor tonight."

"Sure, whatcha got?" he asks, spinning his rolling chair to face me with his list of roster players that he was memorizing before I walked up.

"It's Valentine's Day. I need a little help."

I set out a piece of paper with Juliet's name and some information he'll need not to get taken off guard.

He looks down at the sheet of paper and his eyebrow lifts for a second. "No problem. I'll take care of it."

"Thanks. See you later," I say and turn out of his bird's-eye view of the rink below.

I head back downstairs in search of one more missing component.

"Kenny!" I call out down the hall at our mascot that just got into the stadium for today's game. "You got a minute?"

CHAPTER SEVEN

Juliet

Ryker: You still coming tonight?

Juliet: Of course. I'm just about ready to get a rideshare and head to the stadium.

Ryker: Did you make a decision?

Juliet: Yes I did.

> **Ryker:** Make sure not to leave your answer at home when you head over here. I have a surprise for you tonight.

Oh great. I'm terrible with surprises.

> **Juliet:** What kind of surprise?

Then nothing... no more bubbles.

> **Juliet:** Ryker... what surprise?

More time passes as I stare at my phone every few seconds as brush through my eyelashes with mascara and line my lips with lip pencil.

Finally, the bubbles return and my heart leaps.

> **Ryker:** Don't forget, you agreed to be my Valentine today.

I didn't actually agree to be his valentine. I agreed to drinks after the game.

Nervous energy starts to rise at the thought of being his valentine and an unknown surprise.

I've been called a control freak before but it doesn't bother me. In my line of work, being detailed and wanting everything to be perfect is why people hire me and why my business is growing so rapidly.

After that last text, Ryker doesn't text again.

My notification dings that my rideshare has arrived and I head out the door.

Whatever it is, I'll know soon enough.

"Hi, I have a ticket waiting for me on will-call. Juliet Di Costa," I tell the man at the ticket window in front of the stadium.

"I'll just need to see some ID," he says, turning back into the building and going through a file folder.

He pulls a ticket from the folder and then lays it on the counter, taking my ID that I already have out for him.

Once he verifies it's me, he slides the card back in my direction.

"Have fun tonight," he says.

I nod with a smile and then turn from the long line behind me and make my way through security at the front entrance.

Walking into the stadium tonight, the atmosphere is electric. I navigate through the sizeable crowds as I head for the section that Ryker got me a seat for.

Walking into the arena, it's just as cold as I remember and I'm glad I opted for jeans instead of a dress tonight.

Once I find where I'm supposed to be, I notice that my seat is only six rows up from the home player's box and not far from the player's tunnel. I'll be able to watch Ryker from behind the player's box.

Excitement bubbles in my belly, anticipating the first moment that Ryker and I will lock eyes and he'll see that I came like I said I would.

I settle into my seat as the surrounding seats all fill up with excited, boisterous fans. The smell of popcorn and beer... but also the clean smell of ice, fills the surrounding space.

After the opening music and monologue plays on the two large jumbotrons, the players start coming down the tunnel.

"Seattle.... here are your Hawkeyes!" the announcer says as strobe lights go wild and the stadium is illuminated with multi-color lights.

Sitting with the tunnel to my left and facing the ice, I can't see the players until their height peaks past the tunnel walls.

I watch as player after player races out through the tunnel and onto the ice.

My eyes meet the jerseys of every player as they pass by, but I still haven't seen the number I'm waiting for.

Number 19.

My heart rate increases with anticipation, wondering if he'll spot me in the crowd when he's out on the ice, or if it's too hard for a player to see into the stands from out there. I have no idea. This is only my second game and I have so much to learn.

So many players have passed the tunnel and are out circling the rink. For a moment, I think I might have missed him, and I quickly look out to the players skating rounds, checking for that elusive #19, but I don't see it.

I hear the crowd around me start to cheer toward the tunnel, and when I look over, Ryker is standing near the end of it, his gaze fixed on me with his helmet in his hands.

He flashes a disarmingly beautiful smile towards me and my belly flutters with excitement. Between all the fans he could be looking at, he's staring straight at me.

He gives a little wave and then pulls on his helmet and skates out onto the ice.

A warm blush spreads across my cheeks, physical evidence of the emotions going on inside me. Ryker's focused attention, in front of hundreds of adoring fans, sends a thrilling yet unnerving shiver down my spine.

Though I don't enjoy being in the spotlight, opting for being behind the scenes, like the elaborate weddings I plan, Ryker's attention sparks a feeling of being singled out and special. Something no one's ever made me feel before. Or, at least not at this level.

"Well, someone has a new fan," the woman sitting to my right says, leaving over and giving me a playful elbow.

"Huh?" I ask. "I wouldn't really consider myself a fan—"

"Oh, no, honey. He's the fan," she says, looking over and smiling at me. She looks a few years younger than my mom with a daughter in her early teens, both of them in jerseys that say AISA on the back. The goalie if I remember right from the game Shawnie and I attended. "I'd say he is totally smitten with you."

"Totally smitten," her daughter agrees with a nod, cramming a handful of popcorn in her mouth while keeping her eyes fixed on the players skating rounds on the ice.

The freshly smooth ice is now chewed up by their expertly applied metal skates.

"I don't think I've ever seen him do that in a game," she says, squinting as if she's trying to recall another instance but coming up empty. I think the captain has a crush on our girl here," the woman says, smiling over at me.

She and her daughter giggle together at the thought of it and I can't help but chuckle at their contagious enjoyment.

"We're still getting to know each other," I blurt out honestly and then instantly wish I hadn't.

If we get engaged tonight, I'm sure she'll find my comment odd.

"New or not darlin', I love seeing big hockey players falling hard. Good for you honey," she says and then reaches over to her daughter and takes a handful of popcorn.

She switches her attention back to the players on the ice.

Ryker? Falling hard?

I don't think so.

I join them in turning my attention back on the ice... my eyes locking on him and only him as he skates. His movement so technical but fluid at the same time.

"Hawkeyes fans," the announcer's booming voice comes over the loudspeakers. "... here is your Hawkeyes starting lineup."

The jumbotron sparks to life with bright color graphics and the crowd around the entire stadium starts cheering.

A few players are called out and their team picture flashes onto the jumbotrons. I don't know any of these players yet, but after tonight, I'll probably have to become familiar with it all.

I might be the captain's fake wife but I need to play my role and know just as much as any real wife of a player would. What if the immigration officer asks me about questions that, clearly, Ryker's wife would have the answer to?

"Number 19," the announcer calls out in his deep voice. My heart thumps wildly against my chest at hearing Ryker's number. I'm taken by surprise at how I'm affected by it. "...Center Forward and your captain, Ryker Haynes!"

Chills run down my arms at hearing his name over the loudspeaker.

The fans go wild and I don't know why but a puff of pride sweeps over me at the thought that in a few short days, real or fake... that man might be my husband.

The gravity weighs heavy, but then Ryker skates by pointing his hockey stick toward me, and suddenly, the nervous energy turns into excitement.

This isn't a real relationship and we're both here to get what we need out of this arrangement, but the small things he's already doing to let me know he's watching me and knows where I am at all times is an unexpected sweet gesture.

The woman next to me chuckles and elbows me lightly again.

As the game starts, my eyes don't leave Ryker for even a second. I know exactly where he is on and off the ice at all times.

Finally, it's the first period and I watch as the team exits the ice as music starts to blare through the sound system. Everyone around me seems to know what this sound represent but me.

"The kiss cam," I hear a woman behind me tell her friend.

Oh, that's right. Now I remember from the game Shawnie and I came to.

I look up at the jumbotron to see that the woman behind me is right. The cameraman is already looking for suspecting couples.

With the seat to my right still open and the woman who was sitting next to me having already left for the bathroom, there's no chance the camera will fall on me.

I watch for a few moments while the camera men find unsuspecting victims. Some couples practically blush when the camera falls on them, while other couples really get into it.

I feel my phone buzz in my pocket and pull it out to find Shawnie's name on my phone... and the half-naked picture of Ryker on my phone with that tan build body and that sexy smirk.

I need to remember to change this but now isn't the time. I'll do it when I get home tonight.

"Hey," I yell over the loud music.

"How's it going? Have you told lover boy that you'll marry him yet?"

"Not yet. It's the first period right now. I'll have to wait for the game to get over before I get to see him."

"Yeah, I know... I'm watching the game at home," she says.

What... really?

"You are?" I ask.

"Of course. My best friend is marrying a hot hockey player, and we're about to get a huge contract with the team. I should know the players a little."

"Right... I guess that's a good idea."

I watch as the Hawkeyes mascot skates on the ice with the Hawkeyes dancers. After a minute, he skates off the ice and disappears.

"How did your mom take the news when you told her?" Shawnie asks.

My mother is the last thing I want to think about right now.

"Not well, and I haven't exactly told her that I'm going to do it yet."

"You haven't? I don't see why she's even that mad about it. It's short term and your brother is going to get more specialized care."

"I know but—"

"Oh my God! You're on the screen," she yells.

"What?" I ask, looking up to find myself with my phone to my ear, staring back at myself. "How the hell…"

The picture changes from me to the top of the stairs of the stadium where the massive Hawkeyes bird mascot with his double 0 jersey comes running out and down the stairs.

Where is he coming from?

I don't spot him across the rink from me. I look to my right and then to my left but I still don't see him until all of a sudden I hear Shawnie shriek.

"He's behind you!" she yells with glee.

I turn in my chair to my left to find him taking the last couple of steps into my row.

The golden brown fury-looking bird, covered in a turquoise, black and white Hawkeyes jersey, takes a step into my row, taking up the full width of the area due to his wide costume.

He looks down at me and makes a motion with both of his hands to stand up, though I don't hear any words coming from the suit.

For a moment I do not know what to do.

Am I in his way?

Does he want me to move?

I try to push my knees in one direction to let him past me but he shakes his big bird head to signal that's not what he wants.

His hands signal and up motion again.

"He wants you to go with him," someone yells up at me from a couple of rows below.

"Go girl!" someone behind me cheers.

A few people smile at me while giving me the shoeing motion with their hands to go with the oversized bird.

"He wants you to move your ass, Juliet. Go!" I hear Shawnie on the line say.

Finally, Shawnie's voice jostles me into movement.

I forgot we are still on the phone with all the confusion about what's happening.

Something on the ice catches my eye.

Ryker.

With the biggest bouquet of roses I've ever seen in his hand.

My jaw drops and my eyes widen.

What is happening... and are those for me?

"OH. MY. GOD!" Shawnie screams over the phone.

"I'm going to have to call you back," I say.

"Yeah, I think so," she says and then she hangs up and I push the phone into my peacoat.

He's staring back at me as the crowd goes wild.

Even from here I can see that panty-dropping smile as he watches me walk to the end of the row towards the tunnel and take the Hawkeyes' hand.

I walk hand in hand with the man in the Hawkeye suite as he leads me over to the metal side panels of the tunnel where the players come out.

Two security guards are on the other side waiting for me.

People jump over the seats to get out of the row we're walking through to make room for us.

What the hell is happening?

I look back at the ice to see that Ryker's eyes haven't left me for a second. He watches patiently as we make our way to the tunnel.

The mascot turns to me behind him and points to the security guards.

"He's going to lift you up and we're going to help you down," one of the security guards says to me.

Since I guess the mascot is mute?

Are they not allowed to talk while in costume?

I nod to the security guard even though this whole thing is insane and I wish someone would tell me what's going on.

The nerves hit me as thousands of people watch the mascot pull me in front of him and then grip around my waist, hoisting me up and over the railing. If I was ever self-conscious about my weight, it would be in this very moment. But if the mascot is struggling to hold me up, he's hiding it well.

Both security guards on the other side take my hand and help me down while the mascot tosses himself over the railing as comically as possible.

The crowd is cheering and laughing as he gets back to his feet.

"You ready?" the security guard asks.

"For what?"

Please just tell me what's going on.

I look up to see that Ryker is front and center on the jumbotron standing out on the ice with a smile across his face still.

The stadium is a packed house tonight, and being in the spotlight has never been my things. In fact, I'd probably rather swim with a shark than do any public speaking.

"To walk out on the ice. He's going to take you out there."

"He's going to do what?" I say, my voice cracking with nerves.

The mascot doesn't give me much choice as he takes my hand and pulls me the few feet to the opening of the ice rink from the tunnel.

"I'm going out on the ice?"

He doesn't answer as he steps out onto the ice and watches me take my first step as he gently pulls me out with him.

I've never been ice skating a day in my life, and I wouldn't have selected these chunky three-inch heeled boots if I knew Ryker was going to do this to me.

My thoughts are now debating the options of how I'm going to get back at him for this. If he thinks this is funny, he has a sick sense of humor.

Should I be marrying a man this deviant?

I take one more step, staring down at the glassy ice under my feet with the blade marks from the hockey players earlier.

I hear the sound of metal against ice and then a familiar voice.

"I've got her from here. Thanks man."

I look up to find Ryker standing in front of the mascot.

I shouldn't feel relief that Ryker is standing close, but with how we snatch me up in the parking lot before I slip, I feel safer with him near. I know Ryker won't drop me and the realization takes me off guard.

I don't even know this man but I already trust him not to drop me.

The mascot nods and then carefully hands me over to Ryker.

The Hawkeye leaves the rink quickly, closing the door to the rink behind him.

"What am I doing out here?" I ask but before he answers, he wraps one arm around my waist and pulls me off the ice and against his chest, while his other hand holds the three to four dozen red roses wrapped in tissue paper and cellophane.

A yip squeaks out of me, to my surprise, and he chuckles. Yet again, bringing attention to my weight and whether or not he can hold me up.

"I won't drop you, I promise," he says... and I believe him.

He skates us to the middle of the rink and then sets me down softly on the ice.

"Are you going to tell me why I'm out here now?" I ask.

He hands me the roses, "It's Valentine's Day. Perfect day for a grand gesture," he says, his green eyes pop against the bright white of the ice below us.

"Is it now?" I ask, pulling the roses up to my nose to take an inhale.

I've always loved the smell of fresh roses.

"Have you made a decision on my proposal?" he asks, his eyes searching mine.

"Is that why you brought me out here? To apply the pressure of thousands of fans to my answer?"

His lips uptick at the left corner of his mouth. He thinks this is funny.

"Couldn't hurt."

I take another smell of the roses to distract myself from the crowd all watching us. Whistles and cheers ring out and echoing off the ice below our feet. It's loud out here with the rink acting as a sound board.

"Yes... I have."

"So you have an answer to my question?" he clarifies.

"What question?" I ask.

Ryker drops gently to one knee and the crowd in the stadium erupts with cheers. I've never heard something so loud but the only thing I can think of is him.

Down on one knee.

Those honest eyes of his staring up at me.

He reaches for something tucked under her jersey or pants... I'm not sure but the second my eyes catch on the small box, I feel my heart thump wildly against my rib cage.

I've never been proposed to before, and I never expected Ryker would do it. This is a business arrangement if anything. But he went as far as to buy me a ring before he even knew my answer?

I didn't expect this.

He holds up the ring but he stops before opening it.

"Juliet Di Costa, will you do me the honor of marrying me?"

The moment his long fingers open the box, a diamond far bigger than he should have bought for me glimmers in the florescent blue stadium lighting. The facets are so brilliant they're almost blinding.

My free hand flashes up to cover my mouth and dropped jaw as I stare down at the ring and then at him.

"Be careful what you say... they can read lips," he warns just loud enough for only me to hear.

I glance from him to the crowd, and my eyes catch on the cameraman, who has a portable camera on his shoulder and is out on the ice with us, only a few feet away. I never noticed him until now.

This was planned... in great detail.

That's why he wanted to make sure I was coming tonight.

The world is watching and I can't turn him down now. Not after I already decided to go through with this.

My brother deserves better care and Ryker can ensure I have the funds to make that happen.

If I say no, I'll be booed out of this arena and I'll lose my brother his chance at a better life.

I nod, "Yes, I'll marry you."

Ryker smiles up at me and then pulls the ring out of its box and slides the cold platinum band with the small planet sized diamond onto my left hand.

If I didn't think the stadium could get any louder, it does. The entire stadium erupts, my ears ringing from the applause. All I can do is stare down at how the ring feels on my finger.

This is temporary... so why does this ring feel so permanent?

Either way, there's no going back.

This ring seals my decision.

I'm marrying Ryker Haynes.

Ryker stands and pulls me into him. I wrap my arms around his neck with the bouquet still in my hand.

I take the chance to bury my face into his shoulder, seeking just a moment to hide and get some privacy from the crowds of people watching on.

Ryker's mouth presses against the left side of my head as he holds me even tighter like he knows I need the reassurance that he has me, more than just physically.

That we're in this together.

"You won't regret this. I'll make it worth it. Your brother will get the care he needs, I'll make sure of it."

"Thank you," I say against his shoulder.

A second passes and then he speaks again.

"They're going to expect us to kiss."

My stomach flips instantly at the idea.

I hadn't considered it but I know he's right.

"And the games about to start back up so I need to put you back," he says.

I nod in agreement.

There's no way out of it.

Getting engaged and not kissing would be odd, even with so many people watching.

"We'll keep in PG. Little kids are watching and all."

I pull back, and our eyes lock onto one another.

His eyes dart between mine for a moment, and then they drop to my mouth.

His head dips down and his lips lock onto mine.

The kiss is soft and sweet.

It's more than a peck as his lips engulf mine but the kiss is fit for family consumption.

The kiss only lasts a few seconds but the way the butterflies break loose low in my belly tells me that kissing my future husband for the cameras over the next twenty-four months won't be such a difficult task.

He pulls back from our kiss but his eyes stay glued to mine for a moment. Those sage green eyes glimmer against the reflection of the icy blue rink surrounding us.

Whatever you do, don't fall in love with him.

I remind myself.

This isn't permanent.

None of this is real.

We're both doing this out of desperation, and I'll remind myself of that for the next two years.

"The game is about to start up. I have to take you back," he says.

"That's a good idea."

Just like he did to get me out to the middle of the ice, he lifts me up again and skates me back to the opening that leads down the tunnel.

One of the security guards opens the door for us and we exit the ice.

"Can you take her back to her seat?" he asks one of the security guards.

"Not a chance," I hear the voice of Autumn Daughtry, from the meeting yesterday, walking up to us. "She is practically a Hawkeyes wife now. She's coming with me," she tells Ryker.

She links an arm around mine and Ryker releases me.

"Break her in softly. I don't want her changing her mind before she says I do," Ryker teases.

Autumn gives him a playful eye-roll and then pulls me down the tunnel, towards the underbelly of the stadium.

"She safer with me than with you," Autumn hollers back.

"Probably," Ryker agrees.

Then Autumn hangs a right at the bottom of the tunnel and I look over my shoulder right before we turn and we leave Ryker standing where we left him.

I hear the announcer start back up and then I hear the players marking out of the locker rooms behind us and headed down the tunnel towards Ryker and the rink.

"You didn't mention that you were dating Ryker Haynes in your interview," Autumn says.

Damn it!

Why didn't Ryker and I work out what we were going to say ahead of time? He left me completely defenseless to come up with my own explanation. Hopefully, he hasn't said anything to anyone I'm about to meet that I might contradict.

Just stay vague.

"I didn't want special treatment," although I didn't mind marrying for it, I guess. I hate that I'm lying to her already. "We were keeping it quiet."

"If quiet is proposing in from of a stadium full of people... then you two suck at it," she says, looking over at me with a grin.

"I wasn't expecting that," I admit, grateful to be able to tell the truth for once.

"Yeah... I could tell."

She could tell?

I look up at her for a second but she just keeps walking, smiling and waving at people she knows as we make our way out to the main area of the stadium where people are still in line at the concessions and lines for the bathrooms are backed up out of the door.

If she knows something, she's not letting on.

She leads me to the elevator I took yesterday up to the third floor for my interview.

"Where are we going?" I ask.

"To the owner's box. There are a lot of people eager to meet you," she says, pressing the button on the elevator.

Once the elevator opens, she releases her hooked arm around mine and we walk inside.

A quick ride up to the third floor and then we head for a dark mahogany door.

A tall security guard, intimidating enough to be a bouncer at a night club stands by the door. He reaches over and opens the door as Autumn and I walk up.

"Thanks, Gerald. This is Juliet Di Costa. She doesn't have an Owner Box pass yet but I'll ask Penelope to get her one tomorrow."

"Awe, Mr. Haynes' fiancée. I heard about the proposal. Congratulations, Ms. Di Costa."

I can feel my cheek warm at the title of fiancée.

It feels too new for it to sink in but I guess I'd better get used to it, and fast.

"Thank you," I tell him as Autumn and I walk through the door he's holding open for us.

The first thing I notice when walking through into the owner's box is the large room with floor to ceiling glass windows directly across from us.

The room is designed the same as the offices with dark stained wood floors and grey-painted walls with jerseys from what I assume to be retired players.

To the left is a bar with a bartender mixing up drinks and to the right is a huge buffet of food that would feed the whole stadium, never mind the thirty or so people in this room.

Maybe the players come up after the game and eat?

I have no idea. There's so much I don't know about this team and about hockey, but I guess I'd better learn. I'm now the company's party planner and a player's fiancée.

For better or worse, Ryker and I are about to be stuck together for the next two years. I have a part to play, and I intend on holding up my bargain.

CHAPTER EIGHT

Ryker

She said yes.

If I'm being honest, I wasn't confident she would.

I went into tonight with my best foot forward, but I knew there was a chance she was going to turn me down.

Sliding that ring on her finger felt better than I thought it would. I have a good feeling that she and I are going to pull this off.

"Did Haynes just get fucking engaged on national television?" Brent yells out as I walk through the locker room after Autumn stole Juliet at the bottom of the tunnel.

I'm glad she did, though, because Juliet becoming friends with the girls will make the next two years a little easier for her.

Now, she'll have people to sit with during home games and friends in the same building when I'm at away games.

"I thought you were dating that social media chic. Where the hell have I been?" Briggs asks.

"Pussy whipped on the sixth floor," Lake blurts out.

A few of the guys laugh as we all move around getting ready to head back out for the second period.

"You should know since Tessa keeps your balls in her purse," Briggs fires back. "When's the last time you've seen them?"

"Yeah Powers, does Tessa let you have visitation from time to time?" Brent jumps in.

Oh shit... here they go.

I can feel the nervous energy of wanting to get through this game. Winning tonight will get us just that much further to the championship.

We need to pull off a victory tonight, and with all of us playing the way we did in the first period, I think we have a good shot at it.

But another reason I want to get through the game is talk to Juliet. We haven't said more than a couple of words since we got engaged, and I want to feel her out. There was an obvious panic in her eyes when I pulled her onto the ice with me. All I can hope for is that she doesn't bail on tonight and change her mind.

She agreed to go out to the bar with me tonight so we can talk about the logistics of everything, I just hope that after post-game media, she's still around.

"Who gives a fuck? That chic was a user... I never liked her," Kaenan says, walking past me and slapping my shoulder.

That might be the most words I've heard Kaenan speak on a situation like this in the locker room. Kaenan's always had my back, and I now appreciate it more than ever.

Although, it would have been nice if Kaenan had warned me. It might have saved me some time. However, Altman isn't one to chit-chat.

"Ladies ladies... save your useless gossip for The Commons where you all live. You have a Stanley Cup to win me this season, remember?" Coach Bex says, coming out of his office. "Now get your asses out there and bring me back a win."

I grab my hockey stick and helmet like everyone else and we all head back out for the tunnel.

In about twenty minutes, we'll be skating back off the ice with a win, and then the only thing standing between me and a much-needed conversation with my fiancée is a room full of nosy media vultures looking to pry into my life. They're worse than my own mom who's probably blowing up my phone as we speak.

Things with my mom are going to go one of two ways. She's either going to kill me for not telling her I was getting engaged tonight, or she's going to be elated.

Either way, I'm going to find out next week when I take Juliet home for the charity hockey match.

Juliet

"Come on. Marjorie Carlton is here tonight. Let's go say hi and then I'll introduce you to Isla and Tessa. They're also dating players on the team," Autumn informs me. "And you're the newest member."

She grins over at me.

My stomach drops at the idea of lying to these women whom I barely know and will have to work with for the next five years. And what happens when Ryker and I divorce? How awkward is that going to be at work if no one knows this was our plan all along?

I knew Ryker and I would have to lie to the immigration officer and in some ways, lie to the Hawkeyes...but this? Lying to these women who are bringing me into their circle of friendship as another player's wife?

This feels wrong on a whole different level.

I try to hide the look of dread on my face and force a smile as I nod following Autumn further into the room. I follow behind looking around for Penelope, the other woman I met who was in our meeting yesterday.

It only takes a second until my eyes catch on a vigorously waving blonde in the back corner of the room with a huge smile across her face.

Penelope Roberts.

She's sitting with two other women at a bar-height round table by the glass windows. I can only assume that the other two women are the ones that Autumn was referring to. Tessa and Isla.

I follow Autumn further into the large room and spot Marjorie sitting in the right corner of the room.

"Juliet! What a surprise, dear," she says as we draw closer. "I did not know that you are dating one of our star players. Ryker is like family to us, isn't he, Phil?"

I look around her to find Marjorie Carlton beaming up at me from her spot on a couch near the opposite side of the room as the girls. Tucked in the corner with a great view of the rink below.

Marjorie looks over to the man sitting to the left of her.

I recognized him immediately as Phil Carlton for the research I did on him when I found out about the Hawkeyes contract.

He's talking with another man who I also recognize from the digging I did on the team's website before my interview.

Sam Roberts.

The current GM of the team and an alumni player who was the team captain the last time the Hawkeyes won a Stanley Cup twenty years ago.

Phil is a husky man with a short build and greying hair. From the internet search I did on him, he's around his seventies and Sam is tall from what I can tell, even though he's sitting. His dark hair is hidden under a Hawkeyes hat with light peppering around the ears.

Phil turns his attention to me and smiles, "Yes, he is, and he made quite a splash with that proposal tonight," Phil beams. He looks over at Autumn quickly. "We should capitalize on the media attention as soon as possible."

"I already have the videographer processing a few still shots for me to upload to social media. I already have news outlets blowing up my phone asking for an exclusive interview with Ryker," she tells him.

Social media?

Exclusive interviews?

Yeah... this is all getting out of hand.

Did Ryker know this would all happen because of his proposal? He must have.

"I wish you would have told us sooner. We wouldn't have wasted anyone else's time," Marjorie says with a kind smile.

"I'm sorry... what?" I ask.

"You're our captain's fiancée, soon-to-be wife. We take care of our own around here," I look over to Autumn who grins over at me as well. "It's a formality at this point to wait a couple of days before turning down the other candidates, but it goes without saying that the position is yours."

Just like that? It was that easy?

"Whoa, umm... thank you," I tell her, stepping forward to shake her hand.

She reaches out for mine as well and I can barely believe that I'm shaking on a deal I didn't think I had any chance of winning.

This is why I'm doing this. To get this contract and make the money, I need to get my brother into better care. Tomorrow, when I head to my brother's to have our weekly dinner together, I'll get to tell him he's going to get to move after all.

Change can be tough for Jerrin, but once he sees the therapy pool and all the other amenities, I think he'll warm up to it quickly.

Ryker said he could guarantee that if I was his fiancée that I would get the contract and he wasn't lying. It was practically instant. Now more than ever, it's important that I hold up my part of our deal and help get Ryker his green card.

"I will ask legal to draft everything up and we'll get the contract sent over to you to review in a day or two," she tells me, taking a sip on her blueberry mimosas.

"I can't even tell you what this means to me and my family. I won't let you down," I tell her and then look to Autumn to make sure they know that I'm telling them both.

"We have every faith in you," Marjorie says. "Now go have fun tonight. I'm sure you'd rather watch Ryker out on the ice than chat about work tonight."

"Congratulations on your engagement," Sam says, looking up at me from the couch. "Ryker is a stand-up guy and you couldn't have selected a better man to spend your life with."

I can feel my hands clam up as Sam stares back at me.

His sentiment seems sincere but there's also a twinkle almost in his eye. Does he know this is all fake? Ryker never told me who on the team knows about his visa issues but it would make sense that he would possibly confide in his GM. Though I wish I knew who is in the loop and who isn't.

I'll have to ask tonight if we get alone time together.

"Thank you. I feel very lucky that he picked me," I say, which isn't a lie.

Ryker did pick me.

Maybe out of desperation and because I needed something in return. But nonetheless, he's a good-looking hockey player with an eight-figure income. Finding someone to play his wife couldn't really be that hard for him.

"We'll be in touch soon," Marjorie says, releasing me from any further conversation.

It's a relief since all of these people have known Ryker for a long time and if they quiz me on Ryker Haynes trivia, the jig will be up and it will be obvious that Ryker and I don't know each other at all.

I nod and smile at her, and then give Sam and Phil a smile as well before Autumn turns us around, leading us towards the four-person bar top by the window. Three women and a toddler are waiting for our approach.

I glance out the window to see that the game has started and the players are all out of the ice.

"Juliet, you know Penelope," Autumn says as we walk up to the girls at the table.

"Hi Juliet! I had no idea you were dating Ryker," she says, jumping up from her seat and coming around. "I need to see this ring. You could practically see it sparkle from here."

Penelope walks over and takes my hand to look at the ring. The other girls "ow" and "ah" too. They all look genuinely happy that I'm engaged to Ryker.

"This is Isla and Berkeley," Autumn introduces, pointing to the blonde at the table that I haven't met yet.

"It's nice to meet you, Juliet. I'm Kaenan Altman's girlfriend. We're so excited to have a new girl to add to our group."

Her sincere smiles and softer voice give her a sweetness about her.

She seems just as genuine to have a new member as Autumn did when she snagged me downstairs and brought me up.

"And this is Berkeley." Isla introduces the little girl with wild deep chocolate curls.

Isla bounces the cutest toddler on her lap.

"Berk is the rowdiest one of the bunch," Penelope teases.

"Hi Berkeley," I say back.

"And this is Tessa," Autumn introduces the last of the four women sitting at the table.

Tessa's dark brown hair frames her face as she smiles back at me and reaches her hand out to shake mine.

"I heard you impressed everyone at the meeting yesterday," Tessa says.

"I did?" I ask, a little surprised that I was anything worth discussing.

"Your presentation was fantastic. Marjorie loved it," Penelope chimes in, handing Berkeley a cupcake that she must have gotten from the buffet table.

"Really?" I ask, feeling a little more confident about my presentation than I did before.

"You're going to make a great addition to the team. Tessa and I have a media event we'll need help with so we should make plans to meet next week before you leave," Autumn says.

"Before I leave for what?" I ask.

"We figured you're going to Vancouver with Ryker for the annual charity hockey tournament he does every year," Penelope says.

A charity event? In Vancouver?

"Oh... right, sure," I say, though not convincing.

"We'll make plans to meet up before you go," Tessa nods.

"Ryker just scored!" someone yells nearby.

We all turn just in time to see Ryker, skate around the goal.

I walk up to the window and he looks up at the same second. He sends up a little wave and my heart jumps.

"Ryker's such a great guy. I'm glad he's finally settling down," Autumn says.

"Yeah and not with Amelia... she was a bitch—" Tessa starts.

"Tessa!" Autumn says.

"Oh right. Sorry, Juliet," Tessa says.

Amelia?

Who's Amelia?

CHAPTER NINE

Ryker

The minute I got off the ice and changed into my suit for media, I checked my phone... which was my first mistake.

I open my mom's text because a little guilt seeps in that I didn't give her a heads up and she watches all of my broadcasted games.

> Mom: You're in so much trouble for not telling me!

> Mom: When do I get to meet her? Please tell me she's coming for the charity event.

> Mom: She's gorgeous. Why do I know nothing about her?

I shoot a text quickly.

> Ryker: Going into media. Can't talk right now. She's coming with me to Vancouver. Love you.

Then, because I know my sister has some comments to make, I check.

> Harper: Amelia's old news, huh? You move quick.

> Harper: You knocked her up, didn't you?

> Harper: NASA just announced… they can see her ring from space.

I decide my sister can wait for a response.

By the time I check my phone tomorrow, she'll have thought of a few more backhanded, witty comments. I might as well let her tire herself out first.

The number of missed calls and texts is ridiculous and there's no way I have time to get back to any of them until after I get home.

Going into media, no one could have prepared me for the assault of questions about Juliet, our wedding plans, and when we foresee starting a family. Eventually, Sam pulled me out as the media started fighting over getting their questions in. Tessa had to come in and put them back in their place before sending in the next player.

The second my eyes fall on Juliet wearing a number 19 jersey with her peacoat hanging on one arm and her bouquet in the other hand. She's standing with Autumn in the hallway and I let out a breath of relief. She didn't leave, she stayed.

I walk up to Autumn and she gives Juliet a wink and then leaves to give us a minute.

"Congrats Haynes. This one's a keeper," Autumn says, retreating from us.

"Yeah... she is," I say, my eyes locked on Juliet's.

Who else would bail out a total stranger?

"My jersey?" I ask. "When did you get this?"

I walk around to see my name printed on her back. I should be used to seeing my jersey around the stadium, but this time is different.

"Penelope asked if I had one and I told her I didn't. She ran down and got me one as an engagement present," Juliet says, watching me as I take her new look in. "This one actually fits."

I grin. "Yeah, it's better than the XXL jacket you bought last time." Though she looked cute as hell wearing it over that bodycon dress and heels. "How did you do upstairs?" I ask with no one close enough around to hear us.

"I got the contract," she says.

I'm relieved but not surprised to hear that Marjorie offered her the job after seeing me propose on the ice.

"I told you. The Carltons like to hire within."

"You weren't kidding," she smiles. "They all seem down to earth. I kind of feel bad though because everyone seems happy that you're settling down. I didn't know what to say."

Lying to the team and my Seattle family doesn't feel good, but I'm doing this to keep the team together so that we can bring the Hawkeyes a Stanley Cup win at the end of this season. This isn't my first choice, but I think the means justify the ends in this case.

"Sounds like you handled it like a pro. Let's head for the bar, we have a lot to work out," I say and then I lead her with my hand on her back out towards the exit.

Before we walk out the exit, I take her coat and help her into it. It's not supposed to be as cold tonight as it was the first time we met in the parking lot, but with The Commons so close, and Oakley's only a few blocks away, I don't drive to the stadium usually.

Walking into Oakley's, Juliet and I are immediately congratulated by every single person inside.

I want to celebrate the win with my teammates, but Juliet and I need to talk.

"Do you like beer?" I ask over the loud bar music as we venture toward the back of the building towards the bar.

"Yeah, whatever is fine."

I squeeze in against the thick-cut lacquered wooden top and order two beers.

Oakley slides two draft beers in glasses to me and I give him a nod up toward the ceiling.

Oakley has a rooftop terrace at the top of the bar that no one knows about except for a few people, me included. He lets me go up there on occasion, though I don't often take anyone with me.

It's the quietest spot in the bar and no one will interrupt or overhear us up there.

"All yours, and congratulations. I saw the proposal on TV," he says.

"Thanks... I got lucky," I tell him because Juliet showing up tonight feels as unlikely as hitting the winning numbers in a six-digit lottery.

I grab the two beers off the bar top and then turn to Juliet.

Someone catches her eye, and she gives them a smile and a wave.

I follow her eyeline to find Tessa, Autumn, and Penelope at a bar top waving back.

Even though I'm happy that Juliet is making friends with the girls, I know well enough that if anyone is going to sniff out our secret, it's those three.

"Come on, follow me," I say, turning back to her with both beers.

We walk up the steep stairs, Juliet in front of me in case she trips. Just like the parking lot, I watch her carefully in case she makes a wrong step.

"What's up here?" she asks, her voice tinged with a blend of curiosity and anticipation.

"Privacy and a good view."

She makes it to the last step and then pushes through the rooftop door, the night sky illuminating the space.

It's a warmer night than usual and the full moon casts a glow on Juliet's face. The small amount of tanned skin peeking through in the few places not layered in clothing looks like velvet.

The wind picks up and her cinnamon vanilla scent fills my nostrils.

She smiles back at me when she sees the view of the Seattle skyline she wasn't expecting, and her violet-blue eyes sparkle back at me.

"I would have never guessed this was up here," she says, still making her way towards the ledge of the building that comes up just past her hips.

"It's a hidden spot that Oakley lets me use from time to time."

Juliet lays her bouquet on the ledge and then I hand her the other beer in my hand.

"To bring a woman up to? Is this 'your spot'," she asks, gazing over at me with a glint in her eye as if she caught me.

"I don't bring women up here," I tell her honestly. "I haven't brought a single person up to the terrace beside you."

"Really?" she asks as if surprised by my answer.

"I usually only come here if I want to be alone. Bringing someone with me would defeat the purpose."

"Oh," she says, looking down at her glass and smiling to herself. "Should I feel special?"

I look at the woman who agreed to marry a stranger to help him stay in the country so that she could spend every dollar she can to give her brother a better life.

"You are special, Juliet," I tell her, holding my beer in one hand and tucking my other hand into the front pocket of my jeans.

Her eyes break away from her glass as she stares up at me. Her eyes search mine for sincerity.

I caught her off guard.

She wasn't expecting that answer, and neither was I. But it's true. Who else would offer so much of herself for someone else?

When the silence grows, I realize now is the time to break the ice and start learning about each other by way of rapid fire.

"Tomorrow, we have a meeting with the immigration officer. I thought maybe we could play a game to learn as much as we can in a short amount of time," I suggest.

"Like truth or dare?" she asks, her nose scrunching up like she doesn't like the idea.

At least occasionally, she makes her thoughts easy to read.

"No. I was thinking more like twenty-one questions but instead of the original rules, we take turns asking a question that we both have to answer."

She thinks about it for a second and then agrees.

"Ok, you go first," she says.

"Tell me what concerns you the most about our arrangement."

I want to do everything I can to mediate her concerns so things can go as smoothly between us as possible. I don't want her getting cold feet at the immigration meeting or at the courthouse when we get married.

"The fact that if the U.S. government finds out that this marriage is a fake, I'm looking at criminal charges," she says, pulling out her phone and opening up a screenshot of something she took online. "Criminal charges, fine, and up to five years incarceration."

Ok... maybe that wasn't the best first question to ask. That turned pretty dim, and I'll admit, in comparison to the penalties, hers are more severe than mine.

But they would have to prove it's fake, and if she and I go into this a little differently, maybe this doesn't have to be a fraudulent marriage.

"Who said this marriage has to be fake? It's only fraudulent if we believe it is, right?"

"Isn't it, though? We're not in love."

I look out at the illuminated skyline for a second to think through her question.

"Does love have to exist for a marriage to be real? My mom once told me that a successful marriage is when you're equally matched with your partner. When you both want more for the other person than you want for yourself. When you lift one up to reach their dreams and they do the same for you. Isn't that what we're doing?" I say.

I glance over to find her watching me.

She sets her phone down on the ledge and pulls her glass up to her perfectly painted lips and takes a sip of the amber liquid.

"Is that what a successful marriage looks like? I wouldn't know. I have no point of reference for a marriage that lasts," she says, a little sadness in her eyes.

From the look on her face, edging into discussing her parent's marriage might not bode well for me. I want to know everything I can about her but this might not be the best timing.

"My parents were happy for thirty-plus years. I think they did something right," I tell her.

Thinking about my parents and how we lost my dad a few years ago, I can only imagine how hard it has been on my mom.

My contract with the Hawkeyes will be over in four years and then I'll be a free agent. Maybe it will be time to head home.

"Ok, it's your turn to answer. What is your biggest concern about this arrangement?" she asks.

"That tomorrow they'll deny us and my visa will expire. Then somehow I'll have to tell my team that I fucked them over and that they're on their own to find a replacement for me before the championship. Or if we do make it through this, and immigration finds out about us later, I'm looking at deportation and ineligibility for getting a visa in the future."

"Do you think something will go wrong?"

"No. I think as long as we agree that this marriage is real, there's nothing they can prove."

It completely changes the dynamic of this agreement, but it's the only way to remove the fraud from the equation and give her reassurance.

"Alright, you're up. Ask away," I say.

"You're from Canada? I think I should know your background in case they ask."

"What do you want to know?"

I pull the glass to my lips and take a drink, watching her over the rim.

"How about, where did you grow up? How many siblings do you have? Did you have a pet parakeet that I can whip out as Ryker trivia in case it seems like the immigration officer might be on to us? That sort of thing."

Her question has me entertained and I like this side of her... making a joke about a very serious thing we have to deal with tomorrow.

"You're cheating. That was more than one question," I say, setting my beer down on the ledge of the building.

"I'll answer the same question after you. Only, I didn't have a parakeet. But we did have a Boston Terrier when I was a kid named Bruno."

"A dog person? That tells me a lot about you," I say, though I'm full of shit.

I couldn't tell you the difference between a dog person, a cat person, or those people who buy miniature ponies and let them live in their houses. The way I see it, people are just people.

She takes a sip of her beer and stares at me, letting me know that she's waiting for my answer.

"Let's see... I grew up in a town outside of Vancouver. I have two older brothers, Camden and Everett, and then a younger brother and sister... Austin and Harper—"

"That's a big family. Your parents must have been busy with five of you," she says.

"They were, but they loved it. I come from a long line of hockey players. My grandfather is a three-time Stanley Cup champion and my father coached one of the most prestigious college hockey teams in Canada for most of my life. Then he coached for the Vancouver Vikings NHL team at the end of his career. With five of us and my dad, we had a full team so we'd play in city leagues and wipe the ice with them."

"Your little sister played too?"

Juliet hasn't met my sister yet, but when she does, she won't be surprised.

"Harper's five foot two and her leg is probably no bigger than the circumference of my biceps, but she can be as mean as a rattlesnake if you underestimate her."

Juliet laughs. "Well, no wonder if your brothers are all as big as you. It's survival of the fittest out there in the wild."

I think about my sister and what it was probably like for her growing up with four older brothers.

"I guess you're right about that."

She has a point. That's probably what happens to a girl when she's raised by a household of boys.

"My mom is sweeter than maple syrup and never could get control over us... she had a hard enough time just containing us. And my father was the ringleader of our crazy circus."

"Sounds like you had a great childhood," she says.

"I did."

"And your parents are still married? You mentioned they've had a thirty-year run."

I didn't want to bring this up now, but she's right. She should know it all.

I reach back and rub the back of my neck. This conversation never seems to get easier to talk about. "My dad passed away a few years ago."

"Oh my God," Juliet steps forward and puts her left hand on my other bicep and I like the feeling of her touch. It's oddly familiar, though it has no reason to be. "I did not know. I'm so sorry."

"Thanks," I say back because what else do you say in a conversation like this? "It came out of nowhere. He had a heart attack in the Vikings weight room while with the team."

My hand releases the back of my neck and falls to my side. Juliet puts her left hand on my other bicep and steps closer. She doesn't say anything, she just listens.

I don't like talking about my dad passing and how I hadn't seen him in over a year since it seemed our schedules never matched up, besides the one game the Hawkeyes and the Vikings played against each other.

Guilt from not seeing him more, even all the years before, always sets in when I talk about my dad. I missed so much and now I don't get those years back.

It's the reason I spend my off-season in Vancouver now. I don't want to miss time with my sister or watching my brother's kids grow up.

"Anyway, I grew up in a loving family, came from a hockey dynasty, got drafted out of high school and moved to the US to play for the NHL. And no animals to speak of. I think we were enough to try to keep alive as it was with all the crazy stunts we'd get into." I chuckle.

We also traveled too much on the hockey teams we played for to properly care for an animal.

"That sounds like you had a good childhood," she says.

"I did. Now it's your turn. Let's hear it."

I lean against the ledge facing her.

She lets out a sigh, but she's not going to get away without telling me something. This woman intrigues me and I need to know more about her family dynamic and her brother.

"As you already know, I have one brother, Jerrin. My parents married young and had kids young. They seemed happy, but then my father got hurt on the job and he was never the same after that."

"Got hurt on the job? What did he do?"

She pauses for a second and reaches for her cup running her thumb over her red lipstick on the rim of the glass.

"Uh... he played for the Portland Pirates."

Hold the fuck on.

Her dad was a professional baseball player?

Then her name finally clicks and those violet eyes... I knew they looked familiar. Her dad has them too.

"Philipe Di Costa is your dad? The shortstop for Portland?" I ask.

He's a legend. Or at least for the time he played. It's a shame what happened to him out on the field. No great player should go out that early in their career.

"That's the one," she says, casting her eyes down to her heels.

"He was my brother Camden's idol growing up. He wanted to play professional baseball but hockey runs in our family and my dad pushed him towards the ice. I'm sorry about his accident," I tell her, remembering the moment on live TV when Di Costa took a line drive to the knee-cap that ultimately ended his career before his time.

"I'm glad he was your brother's idol... but he's not mine," she says, her eyes back on the skyline.

Now I remember her saying that her dad wasn't around to help with her brother's expenses. I didn't realize that she meant that Philipe Di Costa abandoned his family.

"When was the last time you saw him?" I ask.

It doesn't feel like the right time to dig into something this deep but I'm not sure when she'll open up like this again.

"The night my mom kicked him out. I was six and Jerrin was four and a half. My dad moved us to Seattle because there was a sports physical therapist who thought he could help my dad, but his knee just never worked right again. Over time, my dad kept coming home smelling like alcohol and perfume and my mom had enough. She told him to leave, and I never saw him again," she says, crossing her arms over her chest. "The first couple of years he'd call on our birthdays and Christmas, promising he was on his way up to see us from California with presents... but then he'd never show."

"Shit, I'm sorry Juliet. I wouldn't have brought it up if I had known your history."

Though my history is painful, the memories of my father are good ones. I hate that Juliet has a father that doesn't even call.

My father was sports-obsessed and a workaholic who expected a lot from us kids, but he was always present whenever we needed him. I can't imagine what it would be like to not have had a relationship with my father.

"It's ok, and I know I'm the one who asked. It's why my mom doesn't like this idea. She doesn't want me dating a professional athlete."

The information she just dropped takes me off guard. I would think most mothers would be ecstatic to know their daughter is dating a man with a decent-sized bank account to take care of her.

"Hold on... your mom doesn't want you dating a professional athlete? What does she have against pro players?"

"She was married to one, and it didn't end well. But I shouldn't have said anything. This arrangement is between you and me, and this conversation about my mother's preferences is getting off-topic. Can we talk about what we need to prepare for tomorrow?"

Even though I want to press her more on this issue about her mom, she's right.

"Yeah, sure. What should we discuss next?" I ask.

"You said we need to live together? When do you want me to move my things over?"

"I thought you could bring over whatever you want tomorrow after the meeting with Immigration. You can keep your apartment if you want, or get rid of it and save the money. Either way is fine but for the next two years, you'll need to live in the penthouse. If we don't live together, it'll give them a reason to ask questions."

She nods. "I'll pack a few bags before the meeting and I can move in after."

"What else should we cover?"

Her lips purse for a second and then she speaks.

"Am I right to assume this is an open marriage?" she asks, no hesitation in her voice.

I clear my throat and pick up my beer off the ledge and take a swig.

This was something I knew would have to come up, and this is the best opening I'm going to get for it.

"I've been meaning to talk to you about this. I know this is a lot to ask, but since I'm a public figure, I have to," I set my beer down on the ledge. "With the tabloids always trying to get a story, and with us trying to make immigration believe this is real, it would look bad on our relationship if you were caught having dinner with another man, or if I was caught with a woman at the bar. It could be grounds for immigration to dismiss our claim."

"What are we supposed to do then? Sneak around?" she asks.

Sneaking around might work for her, but I'll be done for when a story about an NHL player having an open marriage with the woman he married to get his green card rolls out in the tabloids.

"No. I was thinking more that we agree not to date anyone until my green card is approved and we sign divorce papers."

Her eyes widen as she stares back at me like I've lost my mind.

"You want us both to refrain from dating other people?"

"Yes," I say simply.

I know what I'm asking for is a lot.

I'm asking her to put her life on hold for two years for me, but neither of us can risk this marriage looking like a contract agreement.

"No sex for two years?" she asks, a single eyebrow lifting. "You're going to refrain from puck bunnies at your away games?"

I guess she found out what the boys call them. A quick internet search probably gave her a laundry list of things I wish she didn't know about hockey players.

But she says it like she can't believe I'd survive without meaningless hookups at the bar.

Those rookie years where one-night stands seemed like a good idea are years behind me.

I take a step closer and reach for her left hand that hangs at her side. I pull her hand into mine and run my thumb over the edges of her three-carat cushion-cut diamond.

"I didn't say you couldn't have sex," I tell her, taking my eyes off the ring and locking them on hers. "I'd be happy to take care of my wife's needs whenever she wants it."

It's dark out on the rooftop but I swear I see her eyelids hood and those violet eyes dilate at my offer.

Sex might complicate things, I get it, but I'm asking her to give up her life for two years. The least I can do is make sure there's one less thing she has to give up.

Not that servicing my wife would be a hardship. Nothing could be further from the truth.

Juliet is gorgeous, there's no disputing it, but I won't make the first move. I kicked the ball in her court. It's up to her if she wants to return it. Otherwise, we'll live as roommates. And that's probably the smartest choice we could make since we have an expiration date.

"How generous of you," she says, taking a sip of beer.

Juliet's phone rings on the ledge.

MOM, reads on the screen. But then I notice something unexpected.

My underwear shoot from three years ago as Juliet's background.

She reaches over and silences her phone, letting out a frustrated sigh before taking another sip of her beer. She stares back out towards the city center.

Does she not know that I can see the screen?

Or does she not care?

"That doesn't seem fair. I don't have one of you," I say.

"What are you talking about," she asks, turning back to me.

I nod down to her phone that's still lit up from her mom's ignored call.

The second her eyes drop to her phone and connect with the same image, her jaw drops, and a look of pure panic covers her face.

"Oh my God! I didn't do that — I meant to change it — my best friend... she's the one, "

Juliet dives for her phone, her fingers tangling together to hibernate the screen as quickly as she can.

"That photo wasn't taken from my good side. I have a better one if you'd like," I tease.

She holds her phone in one hand and covers her eyes with the other.

She's embarrassed, but she shouldn't be.

She said her friend did it, and maybe that's true, but I still like that it's on her phone.

"I'm mortified and half tempted to just toss myself over the ledge of this building," she says, her hand still covering her eyes.

I reach for her hand and pull it from her face.

"Please don't do that. We came up here alone and without a witness, someone might think I pushed you for the life insurance policy," I tell her, trying to lighten the mood.

She lets out a little snicker and looks up at me.

"And besides, you shouldn't be mortified— I'm your fiancé. You can look... and you can touch," I say.

I guide her hand to lay on my abs, hoping to get a laugh or a chuckle out of her.

She pulls her hand away instantly and rolls her eyes but can't stop the grin from forming across her lips, though I know she's trying to resist.

"Fake fiancé, remember?"

I shrug my shoulders and reach for my beer, finishing off what's left of it.

Below us, I hear a few people exit the bar. It's getting close to closing time and the temperatures are starting to drop.

"I should take you home. It's late and tomorrow we have our interview with immigration."

Juliet looks down at her phone in her hand and checks the time.

"Oh... I didn't realize it was after one in the morning. Yeah, I'd better get home and get some rest before tomorrow."

I nod, I'd like to spend more time getting to know her a little better before our meeting, but we'll just have to wing it.

"Come on. I'll drive you."

"Are you sure? I can take a rideshare," she offers looking down at the beer in my hand.

It's the only one I've had tonight. I'm not buzzed, not even close.

"I've only had one beer. Oakley's isn't far from the apartment building. We can walk over and get my car."

"Really Ryker. I'll just take a rideshare. You don't need to go through the trouble."

If she had already moved in, we could just walk back to The Commons a few blocks away.

"Looks like there's a lift only two minutes down the road. You won't have to wait long," she says.

"I don't mind waiting," I assure her.

And I don't.

She grabs her flowers and I grab our empty glasses.

We walk down the flight of stairs to get to the bottom level of the bar. Half the guys have already left and there are only a few people still in the bar.

I drop the empty glasses at the end of the bar.

"Night. We're out of here." I call out to Oakley, who's wiping down the bar top as we walk through the space and toward the exit.

A few goodbyes call out from who's ever left in the bar right before Juliet pushes through the door in front of me.

The February night air hits against my face the second we exit the bar.

"Are you sure you don't want me to take you home?" I ask.

I don't like the idea of her in a rideshare at one in the morning.

"It says he's a block away. I'll be fine. I only live twenty minutes from here."

I push my hand into the back of my pocket. I have one last thing to give her.

"Here," I say, handing her an envelope with a check made out to her. "Your down payment for your brother's lease contract."

She stares down at the envelope in my hand for a second before reaching out for it.

"You're giving it to me now? I don't need it for another couple of days, and we haven't even had the interview to make sure this is going to work."

"I know but you're anxious about the contract deadline and I wrote up the check the day that you texted me with your conditions. I know you're going to be more relaxed at our meeting tomorrow if your brother's contract is signed and paid for."

"Ryker... I don't know what to say."

She stares down at the white envelope now in her hands, creased in the middle from where I folded it to fit in my pocket.

"Say you'll see me tomorrow."

The rideshare pulls up, but she doesn't acknowledge him; she's still smoothing her thumb over the white envelope I handed her.

"Thank you," she says and reaches her arms around my neck, like she did at the game after she said yes, and I slipped my ring on her finger.

She pulls back and looks up at me, her hands still around the back of my neck.

Déjà vu from my proposal hits me, and I contemplate dipping down and trying that kiss again- this time without thousands of witnesses applauding. But this situation is delicate, and if I make a move that she isn't comfortable with, it could cost me a fiancée.

It's better not to chance it.

I kicked the ball in her court by telling her I'm available to meet her needs for the next two years. If she wants something to happen, she'll have to make the first move.

If she doesn't make a move, a clean-and-cut marriage and divorce will probably suit everyone better anyway.

She gets into the rideshare and I shut the door for her.

She waves goodbye and I wave back as the car pulls off the curb.

I walk back to The Commons while replaying what she told me about her dad, and how her mom wouldn't be happy if Juliet dated an athlete.

I wonder what her mom thinks about her marrying one.

Chapter Ten

Juliet

The loud thumping of knuckles on my apartment door wakes me from a deep sleep.

Oh God... if my mother walks in here yelling at me, she's going to wake the whole floor.

I quickly get up at the second set of loud knocks against my apartment door.

"I'm coming!" I yell as I grab the fuzzy pink robe that Shawnie bought me a few Christmases ago.

I think it was meant as a joke since I look like a bubblegum version of the cookie monster when wrapped up in it, but jokes on her. It's so comfy.

I stomp up to the door and look through the peephole... It's Shawnie.

Thank God... and with coffee.

I let out a thankful breath that it's not my mom and begin to unlock the two deadbolts on my apartment door. I yank the door open to let Shawnie in.

"You're my savior! Gimme that," I say, reaching for the clear plastic coffee cup filled with iced liquid heaven.

"Hold on a minute there missy. You owe me a story," she says.

"Are you kidding? I'd give you a kidney right now if you asked for it in exchange for that coffee."

"Here," she says, taking a step into my apartment and handing me the iced drink. "You're too pitiful looking when you beg like that. But I refuse to feel sorry for you now. You just got the hottest fiancé on planet earth."

I grin just before I wrap my lips around my straw and take a long pull off the vanilla cream coffee.

Ryker is attractive, I'll agree with that. And the minute he pulled my hand against his abs, I can't deny that my body reacted. But it's that smile he has and the fact that everyone I met last night loves him. You can see it in the way the crowds cheer for him in the stands and in the way that everyone talks about him in the owner's suite when he isn't even around to hear it.

He's too easy to like, which has me worried. As long as I keep a little distance between us and remember that this is a business arrangement, then it will be fine.

"I need to know everything. Did you know he was going to propose?" she asks.

I close the door behind her and then walk to my small living room to sit on the couch. She's going to be here until she gets everything she wants out of this.

"No. I told you, we hadn't even talked. He didn't know what my answer was going to be. I could have said no for all he knew."

"I have to tell you. From a viewer's perspective... his proposal didn't look fake at all."

Don't say stuff like that.

"Shawnie... it's all fake, no matter what it looked like from your television screen at home. This isn't real," tell her.

And then I remember what he said last night. About how if this is real, even if it's temporary, then who can argue our claim?

"Oh my God! Well, that diamond sure as hell looks real!" she screeches and reaches for my left hand. "This is the diamond you get for getting the man a green card? Does he have any Canadian friends?" she teases, her eyes as wide as saucers staring down at the ring on my hand.

I almost took it off last night, but I was sort of worried that if I took it off, I'd lose it.

"I know... it's too big, isn't it?"

"Uh, no ma'am. It's freaking perfect. Honestly, this whole thing is perfect."

"Don't start that again—"

"Juliet... I'm serious. The man looked like he was proposing for real."

"Don't get ahead of yourself. He mentioned divorce plenty last night, so he doesn't have 'til death' on his mind," I tell her, bringing the straw up to my lips again.

"What else did you talk about? Did you tell him you're worried about getting caught?" she asks.

I wish she hadn't asked that question. When I tell her what he said, it only encourages her more. But I'm a horrible liar, and she knows my lies.

"He said that a marriage based on encouraging one another and mutual respect is a real marriage. And he doesn't want either of us to see other people during our two-year marriage due to the tabloids."

Shawnie's face almost looks like I pushed pause. She's staring back at me with a wide grin and she hasn't blinked.

"I freaking knew it," she cackles, slapping her hand on her knee.

"You don't know anything," I say, taking another sip and glancing off at my tv across the room.

"So when are you two getting hitched," she asks.

"We have an interview tomorrow morning with the immigration officer. Once he signs off, we'll go down to the courthouse."

"The courthouse? You're a wedding planner. There's no way I'm letting you get away with a courthouse wedding. What kind of terrible friend would I be?"

"We don't have much of a choice. We have to do this soon and honestly..."

"And honestly, what?" she asks.

"I know I hate my dad and it's not like I'd ask him to walk me down the aisle. And my mom is about ready to kill me and dump my body in Puget Sound for marrying a professional athlete. She's refusing to come."

"She said that? She actually said that she won't come. Even though you're doing this all for Jerrin?"

Shawnie's appalled reaction to my mother's response gives me a little vindication that my mom is overreacting about this.

"She thinks he's going to ruin my life, but he's only getting two years of it. How much damage could he do?"

She studies me for a moment, and I don't like that look. That's a look from a best friend who knows your deepest darkest demons.

"Are *you* worried he's going to hurt you?" she asks.

"No... why would I. We have to stay together for two years for him to get his green card. Then, I'm out as fast as the ink dries on our divorce papers—clear-cut rules." I say, barely registering what I unconsciously admitted to her.

I try to distract by bending towards the coffee table and setting my half-drunk coffee cup on the white-washed wooden furniture in front of us.

"Bingo," she says, raising a finger into the air. "Out before the ink dries. Why does that sound like exactly how you'd react?"

"Oh shut it, you know nothing," I say, shaking my head at her.

I hate when she tries to connect my "daddy issues" with the reason why I'm still single at twenty-eight years old.

I have enough going on in my life. Between trying to build a successful event-planning business and making sure that my brother and mom are cared for, I don't have time for the men of my generation.

"Really? We've been friends since freshman year of college. I am well versed in Juliet's quick escape the second the wind changes direction."

"What does that even mean?" I ask, with a grimace.

It's less than a question and more of me attempting to convince her that her comment is completely off-base.

"Oliver, your boyfriend from college..."

I shake my head and turn to look to my left out the window over my shoulder. "You always make him out as an example."

"Juliet... you two were serious. That kid loved you and the second he got into law school two hours down the road, you practically changed your number and ghosted him."

I turn back to her and roll my eyes. "I didn't ghost him. We broke up. Long distance never works."

"He sent you flowers to our dorm room every day for a week, begging you to reconsider. He told you he wouldn't go to law school until after you graduated if you'd agree not to break it off."

"I wasn't that into him," I lie.

"Bullshit. You two already had your first two kids' names picked out. His family adored you and you spent more time with them than with your own. You two were happy."

"We were still just babies Shawnie."

"No... you were just scared."

I hate when she does this.

Her dad's a shrink so she thinks she is by proxy and tries to psychoanalyze my childhood trauma and make it out to be the reason I do everything.

Though I think she's just a psycho.

"I'm not talking about this anymore. Oliver and I have nothing to do with my fake relationship with Ryker," I say, standing up and heading for my kitchen.

Yes, I'm basically running away from this conversation... but that proves nothing.

My kitchen is small and L shaped but clean and updated with white cabinets and white countertops. It's hard to get an apartment in the city for a decent price but the space was renovated recently and the one-bedroom apartment is plenty of room for me.

Shawnie gets up and follows me.

I head straight for my freezer and open it, pulling out a box of frozen ham, egg and cheese croissant breakfast sandwiches.

"Want one?" I ask, walking over to the microwave.

"Sure, I could eat."

I pull two out, rip off their plastic containers, and wrap them in paper towels. I set the microwave to a minute and a half and then I pull out a gallon of orange juice.

"The only reason you're agreeing to this is because it has an expiration date," she says.

I pull out two glasses above the counter and start pouring juice in each cup for us.

"Shawnie," I say, turning to her with her glass of OJ and setting it on the countertop overhang where two short bar stools are tucked underneath. "Of course, I only agreed to it because it has an expiration date. We're strangers."

She walks over to the counter, pulls out one of the stools and takes a seat.

"What if, in two years, things change between you two and he tells you he doesn't want to divorce at the end of your arrangement?"

I hate what-if questions.

What's the point of considering things that may or may not happen? Making decisions at any given moment is hard enough without having to factor in multiple other scenarios.

Life isn't a "choose your own adventure" book. You're lucky even to get one choice because most of the time, it feels like you have no choice at all.

I didn't get a choice in my father leaving.

I didn't get a choice in him not wanting to see us.

I didn't get a choice that my brother has daily struggles that I wish so badly I could make all go away for him.

I can't live in what-ifs.

They only lead to disappointment and misplaced hope.

"He won't want to stay together in two years so there's no point in considering it," I tell her.

I walk over and set her plate down in front of her with the piping hot breakfast sandwich.

"You can't know that," she says, lifting the glass of orange juice and takes a sip.

"He'll be ready to move on by then. The divorce rate for professional athletes ranges between sixty to eighty percent. He won't stick around," I tell her, even though I know that I just gave her more ammo to use against me.

She thinks I'm a flight risk when it comes to relationships because of my experience with my father.

Maybe in previous relationships, I jumped a little prematurely, but Ryker doesn't count as a relationship. This is no more than a business deal.

"I just don't want you closed off to the possibility of what could happen just because of what happened between your parents," she says, lifting her sandwich from the plate. "Ryker's proposal didn't look like a man trying to find his way out."

"He wanted to make a splash to make it seem real for the immigration appointment we have today."

"Your appointment is today? And then what?"

"If we get approved... we get married," I say, the words wanting to clog my throat.

The weight of the fact that I might be getting married in a matter of days is feeling as real as the ring he put on my finger.

I don't know what has me more nervous. The idea of marrying a total stranger or the possibility that we'll be outed and I'll be playing Texas Hold'em with my brother over a video screen from jail.

"Have you thought about where you want to have the wedding? I can call around and see what venues we can book—"

"No, we won't need any of that. We'll go down to city hall," I tell her, turning around back to the counter for my sandwich.

Being an event planner and not planning my dream wedding is weird. But with the turnaround of a few days, the courthouse is our best option.

And anyway... my dream wedding should be reserved for when I say "I do" and mean it forever.

"Really? City hall? Are you ok with this?" she asks.

"Of course. The marriage certificate is just part of the arrangement... it means nothing."

I look over at the time of the stove.

This morning got away from me with Shawnie's impromptu visit.

I still have to get across town to drop off the check and sign the lease for Jerrin before meeting Ryker at the immigration office.

"I really have to get ready and get out of here. See yourself out?" I ask, already making my way out of the small kitchen, headed for my bedroom on the other side of the apartment with my breakfast sandwich in my hand.

"Yep, call after your appointment. I want to know how it goes."

"I will," I call out to her, speed walking down the short hall to the one bedroom I have.

"Like right after," she yells after me.

"I know. I got it," I say and then close the door to my bedroom to start trying on outfits.

I have all of twenty minutes to toss something on, pull my hair up into a bun and get down to the new center for Jerrin if I want to get the deposit and contract signed and still make in time for our ten am appointment.

I can't be late for our interview. He just gave me the check I need and I'm about to spend it. I have to make sure I hold up my end of the bargain.

"Ms. Di Costa," the woman at the front desk of the new center says as I walk through the double automatic glass doors.

She was the one who also gave me a tour of the facilities the first time I came in to look at the place.

"I wasn't expecting you for another couple of days. Were you able to get everything squared away?" her warm smile and the warmth of the front office remind me of why I decided that spending the money for Jerrin to be here is worth it.

"Yes, I did, thank you. I have the deposit and I'd like to lock in his spot here."

"Fantastic," she says, almost leaning out of her seat to reach a file cabinet under her desk. "I already have the paperwork drafted up for you. I had a good feeling that this was all going to work out. Jerrin is going to love it here. I think he'll be a perfect fit," she says, her head ducked behind the tall desk where I can't see her.

I look around the lobby. There are several small living room-like setups for families to come to visit or for residents to come down and grab a puzzle or deck of cards for a change of scenery from their studio apartments.

Fresh flowers in vases adorn several tables around the space. One large vase of spring flowers sits on the reception desk. This is going to give him that home feel that the other center lacks. Not that they can help it. The center he's in now runs on government funds, whereas this place has private money running through it.

"I think he's going to fit in here really well too. I told him about swim therapy and the painting and gardening classes. I think he's most excited about the chess club you have here, though," I tell her, remembering my brother's eyes lighting up when I mentioned the many different clubs he can participate in... if he chooses to.

"Well, then, I have a surprise. I spoke with our resident coordinator and told her that Jerrin loves Poker. Turns out one of our occupational therapists has poker night at his house once a month so she's setting him up as Jerrin's therapist. That should give them something to bond over."

I can't stop the stupid grin forming across my lips.

I'm grateful that my brother has had a safe place to be during the time he's been at the other facility, but it's time for his personal growth to expand as much as possible.

Change can be hard for him but this center understands that and is working to find ways to help Jerrin assimilate as quickly as possible.

Jerrin might not say it, but I know he wants more independence, and that's what they focus on here.

"Here's the check for the first, last, and deposit," I tell her, sliding a cashier's check over the counter towards her.

I've written checks this size, but usually, it's a client's money to pay a vendor or a location.

Never have I paid a lump sum this large for something personal. Though I guess I'm not the one paying for it, Ryker is.

She slides the check over in her direction and then she exchanges it for the contract.

"Go ahead and sign on the three spots where I left a 'sign here' sticky. Then you'll be all set. I have an available move-in date on... " She leans to her left to the wall there and looks at the calendar. "A week from today if that works?" she offers.

That's quicker than expected but will work well since I leave the next day for Vancouver with Ryker. I'd like to have Jerrin settled before I go.

"That sounds perfect," I say, signing the three spots on the contract and then sliding it back over to her. I can hardly believe this is happening, and I have Ryker to thank for making it possible. "Could you call me with the exact move-in date? I need to leave now to avoid being late for another appointment," I ask, looking at the time on my phone.

I have enough time to get to the immigration office, but you can never be too sure with unruly traffic.

"Sure thing Ms. Di Costa. Thanks again for letting us know. I'll give you a call once I've confirmed that his apartment will be ready," she says, pulling the signed contract off the reception desk.

"That would be great. Talk to you soon," I tell her.

"You bet," she says back.

I turn and head for the glass automatic doors that I had come through a few minutes before.

The second I walk back through the sliding glass doors of the center, I realize that Ryker was right. I blow out a breath and the feeling of so much weight on my chest has vanished.

Without having to concern myself about losing Jerrin's spot, I can now focus one hundred percent of my energy on the fiancé visa interview that we have in forty-five minutes.

> Juliet: All done. Headed for the office.

> Ryker: Me too. See you soon.

CHAPTER ELEVEN

Ryker

Seeing her text gives me reassurance that she didn't get cold feet last night and decide to bail on me today.

She's already on her way while I sit in my car in the parking garage a couple blocks from the immigration office.

I had nowhere else to go after practice this morning, and I wanted to get here as soon as possible. You never know what kind of traffic you might hit driving through downtown, and this isn't the kind of appointment you show up late for.

I wait in the parking lot until I see her SUV pull into the parking garage a few rows away from me. I get out and head for her vehicle so we can walk in together.

"How did the lease signing go?" I ask, my voice echoing off the cement ceiling and walls.

She smiles when she looks up and realizes it's me making my way to her across the cement parking lot structure.

"You waited for me?" she asks, stepping down from her SUV.

She looks beautiful and well put together, like always.

Her long, dark, silky hair is styled in a professional bun. She's wearing another peacoat, though a light pink instead of the tan one she was wearing on the ice when I proposed, a white blouse, black leather pants, and a set of dark pink pumps.

She looks sophisticated yet approachable in all the pink.

Against my slacks, button-up shirt and blazer... skipping the tie, I have to say, together, we look like a well-dressed couple.

"I had to make sure that you found the place ok," I say, sticking out my elbow for her to grip onto my arm for stability in those heels.

"Is it that or did you want to make sure I showed up?" she asks with a teasing twinkle in her eyes.

"It might have been a little of both," I admit.

She lets out a chuckle as we walk toward the exit of the parking garage.

"The signing went flawlessly, thanks to you. You were right. Completing the paperwork just now... I feel so much calmer knowing Jerrin is taken care of. I didn't realize how unsettled I felt until the second she gave me a move-in date."

She pulls closer to me to avoid a passerby walking in the opposite direction as us down the busy sidewalk of Seattle.

"I'm glad to hear that issue is settled for you."

She pulls out her phone from her pocket and her fingers start briskly texting back with one of her arms still wrapped around mine in case she trips.

I want to lean in a little further to see who's talking with but we're still getting to know each other and it doesn't seem like any of my business. The idea of some guy hitting up my fiancée puts a pang of jealousy in my chest, and I clench my fist.

She notices my eyes on her and looks up from her phone after she sends off the text and tucks it back in her pocket.

"It's from Autumn. I guess you have an alumni event coming up in two weeks that Shawnie and I need to plan."

Oh right, alumni week is coming up.

"The Hawkeyes like to ramp up for the championship games so they start doing more spirit week-type stuff in the weeks before to get the crowds excited. Alumni week is when we bring in one or two ex-Hawkeyes players for every home game that week to do the coin toss."

"Oh, I see," she says.

"Is this going to be your first event for the Hawkeyes?" I ask, not remembering her saying she's planning anything else yet.

"Yes. And I want it to be perfect."

"It will be. You're planning it."

She shoots up a look at me. Her perfect white teeth and pink lips stretch into a wide smile.

She's fucking stunning and if all goes well during the meeting, she'll be my wife.

A few minutes later, we walk into the building.

It's the typical grey, stark existence of a government building with the slightly stale smell of an older building but I'll settle for a few hours in a dingy building over the circumstances I thought I was going to end up in.

We ride the elevator up to the second floor where I was told the immigration office is located in my appointment confirmation email.

The elevator doors open directly into the lobby. Walking into the large space, there's an L-shaped layout of navy-blue padded chairs and a coffee table with old magazines stacked for reading.

A reception desk sits with glass plating between the lobby and reception and a wooden door stands near the window. I'm guessing it leads to a hallway full of offices.

"I'll check us in."

Juliet nods and walks over to one of the chairs, taking a seat and checking her phone. Probably another text from Autumn.

An older woman sits on the other side of the glass partition. She doesn't look up at me but she must see me coming in her peripheral vision because she hits the intercom.

"Name," she says, smacking a piece of gum between her teeth.

When I get closer, I see she's reading a detective thriller and hasn't taken her eyes off it once.

"Ryker Haynes. I have an appointment with Frank Bishop."

She hits the intercom button that must go to Frank's office.

"Your appointment is here," she says, and then lets off the button before a response comes from the other side. "He'll be out shortly," she says, still reading her book with no eye contact at all.

"Great... thanks."

I think.

I head back to sit down in the lobby with Juliet but before I even reach the chair, I hear the wooden door open and my name being called.

"Mr. Haynes! What a pleasure to be meeting the legend in the flesh," a booming voice says behind me.

I spin around to find a slightly overweight, balding man in a suit and glasses. He has a coffee stain on his white undershirt, which is mostly covered under his blazer and tie.

From here, I can't tell if the stain is from today or if he forgot to get this particular shirt dry-cleaned and walked out the door in it this morning.

Based on his gambling predicament, I have to wonder when the last time he bought new work attire was instead of betting his money on a sports game.

"You must be Frank. Thanks for meeting us." I feel Juliet walk up beside me. "This is my fiancée, Juliet."

"Nice to meet you both. I'm glad the scheduling worked out. If you two will follow me, we'll make our way to my office," Frank says.

We follow him down the hallway. The nerves of whether we're going to pull this off, prick at the base of my skull.

I know that Frank is the one helping push this through for his own gain, but he assumed I proposed to the woman I had been dating for a number of months. Not a woman I only met days ago.

A few doors down, Frank offers up his hand for us to enter first.

The small office is as bland as I'd expect an immigration officer's office to be. Beige walls, a small desk, and a black pleather rolling office chair that looks as though it should have retired years ago. On the other side of the desk are two navy blue paddled chairs that match the ones in the lobby—one for both of us. I offer my hand to usher Juliet in front of me, letting her enter first. She does and takes the seat in the farthest one, leaving the outer chair open for me.

I sit next to her as Frank comes in last and plops down in his chair. The pleather groans at his weight.

"So, I hear we have a wedding coming up. Congratulations. I saw the proposal on the ice. That was quite the spectacle," he says, giving me a nod of approval.

"Thank you. I'd been meaning to propose for a while—" like the night I met her in the parking lot "—and what better time than Valentine's Day? We want to get married as soon as possible," I say, reaching out for Juliet's hand and taking it into mine.

I smile at her, and she smiles back, though her smile is guarded and coated in professionalism. Not that Frank would know the difference in her smile but I'm getting better and better at reading my future wife.

"Well, let's get some more information. How long have you two been dating?" he asks, pulling a yellow legal notepad and pen in front of him.

"Our relationship has been a bit of a whirlwind. But when you know, you know," I say.

"I suppose you're right." Frank chuckles. "And Juliet, is your family excited about the upcoming nuptials? How do they feel about you marrying into a legendary hockey family and to a soon to be two-time Stanley Cup winner?" He gleams, sending a wink my way.

If only he knew that what I do for a living is one of the reasons Juliet almost didn't agree to this arrangement. And it's the sole reason why her mother doesn't approve of me.

I can see Juliet swallow hard, her hand unintentionally squeezing mine a little tighter. "They were surprised," she says honestly. "But my brother is now Ryker's biggest fan."

Frank looks down at his legal pad as he jots down a note.

I glance over at her and give her a reassuring squeeze of my hand. I know very well that her mom isn't happy about this but she's doing well to hide that fact.

"And Ryker, how about your family? How do they feel about your wedding plans?"

"They're ecstatic. We're headed to go celebrate our engagement next week in Canada. My mom can't wait to meet the woman who finally got me to pop the question," I tell him.

"Very good," Frank says back with a nod, again writing our answers to his questions. "As you know, we have to conduct these interviews to ensure that your relationship is on the up and up. And that you're not just getting married for a green card to stay in the country," he says, looking at Juliet and then me.

"No sir, we're very much in love."

I pull her hand up to my lips and kiss the top of her hand in a show of affection.

"And where will you two be residing?" he asks.

"In my penthouse downtown. Juliet is moving in just after the wedding. Her family is old-fashioned, so we've been waiting until after the wedding to live together," I say.

"Sure, I see. We don't want to piss off the in-laws early on. Smart," he tells me, jotting down another note. "And when do you two plan on tying the knot?" Frank asks, still staring down at his legal pad as he writes.

I don't want to seem too eager by standing up to look over the desk, though I wish I knew what he was writing down.

"As soon as possible. I want her last name to match the one on the jersey she wears to my games," I say.

"Your contract with the Hawkeyes is up in four years. You've mentioned possible retirement after this last contract if you win a Stanley Cup. If you retire, where will you two reside then?" he asks.

"We'll stay in the United States until after retirement. Then we'll move back to Canada to start a family."

Juliet snaps her head toward me, her eyebrows raised as if taken aback by my answer. I want to remind her that this is all fictional and that we'll be divorced before I retire but now isn't the time. Juliet's reaction to moving to Canada to start a life with me is Amelia all over again, and every other woman who hasn't wanted to make it work living a split life in both countries.

Juliet and I never had the conversation about my plans for retirement—that I intend to move back to Vancouver and coach my dad's team, the Vancouver Vikings. At least until I fulfill my father's legacy and bring them a championship at the hands of a Haynes coach. Something he never quite accomplished while he was alive, though they made it to the playoffs many times before.

This is the way I'll honor my father and everything he's given me.

The love for hockey.

"I see," Frank says. "That sounds like a great plan."

He jots down a few more notes and then he drops his pen down on the pad and pushes it out in front of him.

He leans back into his pleather chair. It tips back for him and again groans at his weight.

"Okay, now that we've covered the essentials," he says with a grin. "What do you think the Hawkeyes' chances of winning the Stanley Cup are this season?

A Cheshire Cat smile stretches across his lips. He crosses his right leg over his left knee and his fingers fold over the top of each other, resting in his lap.

I knew this was why he was helping us. And usually, I could talk all day about hockey, especially the Hawkeyes' potential for a championship victory. But I'd like to know what Juliet and my chances are of getting approved for the K-1 visa. If he could just get to the point, that would ease the tension tightening Juliet's grip in mine.

I've been in a lot of high-stakes situations in my life while playing competitive sports. But this feels like the biggest long shot of my life, and the upside could come with a worse downside if someone figures out our arrangement.

Deportation and ineligibility to ever apply for a U.S. visa again seems like a harsh punishment for the offense. But Juliet's consequences might be considered even worse.

That's why we go for broke or we don't go at all. And at this point, we're in too deep to turn around now.

Not to mention that I owe this to my team. Bailing out on them now, right before it means the most, is something I'd do anything to avoid.

I know I need to give a little and appease Frank to make sure this goes through without any issues that could cause a raised brow.

"I think with the way our team is playing, how the season is going, and who we're up against next means we have a clear shot in the championship. That is of course if the Hawkeyes don't lose their captain and center," I say.

Yes, that was a plug for getting Juliet and me the approval we need, but I'm ambitious enough for one last push.

"Right. No, of course. The Hawkeyes need number 19. I agree one hundred percent, which is why you're here," he says. "I think you two are a perfect example of love and commitment. I'm approving your application and signing off on your paper-work."

He writes one word in large lettering at the bottom of the notepad, large enough for both Juliet and me to see.

APPROVED.

I feel her hand relax a little in mine.

"I'll get the approval documented and you'll be set to go. Congratulations. Welcome to the United States," he says, and stands out of his office chair.

I release Juliet's hand and stand.

Frank offers his hand and I reach out and shake it. Relief washes over me that the hardest part is over.

Juliet stands next and Frank takes her hand to shake it as well.

"How soon can we get married?" I asked him.

"Usually the paperwork takes a little time but I know you're in a time crunch with the playoffs coming. I'll personally push it through today. You can get married as early as tomorrow afternoon."

I whip a glance over at Juliet whose jaw seems to have dropped just a little as she stares back at Frank.

Then she turns to look at me, wide-eyed. She knew we would get married, but I don't think she thought it would happen so quickly.

"We're leaving for Canada next week and it would be good to have the wedding certificate done and filed with the state before we leave," I tell him.

"Sure. I'll add notes in your file to make sure reentry into the US goes smoothly."

"Thanks, Frank. We appreciate all you've done to help us," I say.

"Yes, thank you," Juliet says.

She finds that professional smile of hers again and plasters it on.

There she is.

I was worried there for a minute, but I knew the confident, take-on-anything Juliet would reappear... and she did.

"It was a pleasure meeting you Ryker, and you Juliet. I look forward to seeing you dominate and win the Stanley Cup. The Hawkeyes are due for a win. And so are you," he tells me.

I know he really means, "Win me a fat payday for my troubles," but I'll take a vote of confidence instead.

Juliet turns and takes a step toward me. She's ready for this interview to be over and I don't blame her. I take a step back and wrap my arm around her back to guide her past me toward the exit.

"I appreciate you getting us in on short notice."

"Anything to help the team. I'll be in touch. And remember, you have to be married for two years before you're an official resident."

"Right, we understand."

I'm also ready to leave this office and hope never to have a reason to come back.

Even if we had said anything questionable, Frank probably would have ignored it and signed off on us, anyway.

I don't know how much the man has on the game. But from how quickly he approved us, I'd say it's more than the man can afford to lose.

Juliet and I walk out of the office and down the hall, neither of us saying a word. We walk through the lobby that we checked into not that long before and I push the elevator call button.

The elevator doors open almost instantly. We both walk in, neither of us saying a word until the elevator doors shut.

"That went well," I say as the elevator begins to descend to the ground floor.

"Tomorrow?" she asks, staring at the elevator doors in front of us.

"Is that going to be a problem?"

"No." She shakes her head and drops her eyes to the ground for a second before returning them to the elevator. "This is what I agreed to. And you've already fulfilled both of your parts of the arrangement. If you want to get married tomorrow, then we'll get married tomorrow," she says, finally locking eyes with me.

I see the sincerity in her face.

It caught her off guard, which I can relate to, but she's not getting cold feet.

"We'll keep it simple. Just a quick courthouse wedding and then we'll be married."

The elevator doors open, and we walk inside. I press the lobby button and the elevator starts moving down to the ground level.

"We'll each need a witness at the courthouse. Do you have someone you can ask?"

"Yes, my friend Shawnie will come. She already agreed."

"What about your mom? Will she want to be there?"

"No." She shakes her head. "I don't think she'll come."

Her reluctance to share more information doesn't surprise me, given her mom's disapproval of her marrying an athlete.

The elevator doors open and we walk out into the lobby and head for the exit to the bustling sidewalk of downtown Seattle.

"Are you still moving in tonight as we planned? Tomorrow we'll head to the courthouse and get married before I leave town for our away games. And then when I get back, we'll leave for Canada."

I push the exit door open for her to walk through first.

"Where are we staying once we get there?"

"I have a house in the suburbs. It's close to the charity event and my mom's. We'll stay there."

Juliet isn't giving much in the way of facial expressions. I can't read if she's getting cold feet now that all of this is happening, but asking questions is a good sign.

"What does your mom think about me?" she asks.

"She'll love you. She loves everyone. But mostly, she's going to love you because you're the one who got me down on one knee."

Juliet grins as we walk down the sidewalk. It's the first time I've seen a real smile since we walked into Frank's office and I'm happy to see it back.

"I should prepare you for the offspring question. While we're there, it's probably all my mom will talk about," I say. "And you'll get to meet my brothers and my sister, along with my niece and nephews, who are all great."

I consider warning her about my sister. She's the hardest sell. But my sister's smart and she's going to see that Juliet is different to other women I've dated in the past.

"Do you need any help with moving your stuff?"

"My SUV has plenty of room in the back. I'll be able to get it all in one trip."

"Why an SUV?" I ask.

I would have pegged Juliet for driving a sleek two-door BMW instead of the large SUV that she has to climb into in heels.

"Party planning requires a lot of décor and supplies. It's just easier to have my own form of transportation for balloons and anything else I need that isn't getting delivered by the rental company."

"I can lend a hand with setting up at any of your events, whether it's bringing in a bouncy house or hanging decorations up high," I offer.

We're only a block away from the parking garage as I see it come into view.

"Thank you, Ryker. I appreciate that. I'll keep that in mind for the next birthday party I do. Do you do clown impressions?" she asks.

I glance over to find a smirk across her lips. She's teasing me and that humor of hers has me thinking that the next two years are going work out just fine.

Chapter Twelve

Ryker

Juliet: I'm a few blocks away.

Excitement pulsates through me unexpectedly.

I grab her key for the penthouse and her parking permit for her spot downstairs off the kitchen island and head out my door.

The ride down the elevator is quick and I walk through the garage to the gated entry. I see her headlights waiting on the other side of the garage gate. I scan her new parking permit and the gates begin to slide open to allow her access.

It works... good.

I want to make sure that everything is in working order when she's here. I don't want Juliet to have any issues accessing the apartment building, especially when I'm out of town.

I walk up to the passenger side door and she hits the unlock button to let me in.

"It's official," I say, putting her parking permit lanyard over her rearview mirror.

It swings back and forth and she stares at it for a second but then moves through the gate since it has a timer and it's already beeping a warning that it will close soon.

I point out turn-by-turn directions through the underground parking garage to her new parking spot. The three penthouses on the top floor have premium parking right next to the elevator.

"Right here." I point at the spot closest to the elevator. "This is your spot now."

"This is my spot? Then where is yours?" she asks.

I point to the black Maserati parked next to her.

"I'm parked to the left of you."

We both get out of the SUV and head to the back. She clicks a button, and the automatic open starts to lift the back gate.

She said she can fit a lot in the back and she wasn't kidding. The back seat of her SUV is packed full.

I should be happy that she took my request to move in seriously, and I am. This is more than I thought she would pack and it has to be most of her wardrobe at home.

"Is this all of it?" I ask.

"You're the one that wanted me to move in. Can you not handle me, Haynes?" she asks.

"No, I can handle you just fine."

She does not know just how well I'd handle her.

Juliet starts to grip her hand around the handle of a large black rolling luggage.

"Don't worry about it. I got it. I'll get everything out and then you can roll up a couple."

"Thanks," she says, and then takes a few steps back to give me room to pull everything out.

I pull down the first two large pieces of luggage and then a smaller one for her.

"Here, can you pull this one?" I ask, handing it to her.

"You know I loaded all of this myself."

"I do but now you're with me. The rules just changed."

I turn and pull two more bags that I crisscross over my chest. I can feel her staring at me after my comment. I don't know if she finds my chivalry endearing or annoying but she'll have to get used to it because that's what she's getting for the next two years.

I start pulling the two large pieces of luggage behind me toward the elevator.

She clicks the close button on her key fob and follows behind.

"It's going to take a couple of trips to get it all but you should have enough here to start unpacking," I tell her, looking down at the biggest pieces of luggage I've ever seen, packed to the brim.

I smile to myself.

The more stuff she moves in, the clearer the sign that she's going to make this work.

The elevator door opens and we ride up to my penthouse on the eighth floor. When it opens, we both exit with our luggage in tow.

"There are three penthouses up here?" she asks.

"Yeah, one belongs to Lake Powers and his girlfriend Tessa, who you met in the Owner's Box, and the other one is Coach Bex's. The last one is mine."

"Do they live here all year round?" she asks.

"Nope. Bex goes home to the UK. I go home to Vancouver, and Lake goes home to Colorado."

"Wait, none of you stay in these penthouses during the off-season? They're just vacant that whole time?"

"The offseason isn't that long when you count when we have to be back for training. It's only a few months' break and then we're all back. I won't be able to leave during the next two years for extended stays though until my green card is approved. I'll have to take shorter visits home instead."

"So you'll be around during the offseason?"

"Yeah. Is that a problem?" I ask.

We glide the luggage in through the front and I look behind me to find Juliet cataloging the layout of everything she sees.

"The kitchen's to your right. Feel free to load whatever you want in the fridge. It's too big for me to fill on my own."

She looks to find the large kitchen built for a restaurant.

"This place is beautiful," she says. "And you only live here during the season?"

"I have a house in Vancouver near my family. Whenever I have time off, that's where I am."

Her eyebrows stitch together in a look of concern that washes over her face as her attention switches from looking over the house to glancing up at me.

"Wait, I don't have to go with you to Canada for the off-season, do I? We never discussed that as part of our agreement."

I get she has a business that she couldn't be away from for an entire summer, but the look on her face has me wondering if there's something else she doesn't want to be away from that long.

"I won't be leaving for the off-season. I can't spend that much time out of the US during the next two years while the K-1 visa is under review."

"Ok good," she says.

My answer seems to put her back at ease, and she begins to survey the penthouse again.

"Is there a reason you couldn't leave with me for an extended stay if something came up?" I ask.

Since me living in two countries has been an issue in past relationships, I'm curious to hear her answer.

Her eyes meet mine again. "My business is taking off right now. And even if Shawnie could manage it all herself... my brother—I can't leave him for that long."

I never made it clear to Amelia that Canada is always going to be a part of my future, but with Juliet, I want to make sure she understands.

"When my contract is over in four years, I plan to move back to Canada, where my family lives. I just thought you should know."

She doesn't seem phased in the least by my information.

"We'll be divorced by then, right?" she asks, though it's not really a question.

It's more of a polite way of reminding me that this relationship is temporary.

"Right," I say back.

Again, Juliet shows her willingness to put her brother's needs before hers. Not that she needs me or has any desire to move to Canada. But even if she did, she wouldn't consider them because her brother is her priority.

"This penthouse has two masters and two guest bedrooms. You'll have your own ensuite bathroom and the room is spacious, but you're welcome to use any part of the penthouse. This is your home now, too. I want you to feel comfortable in it."

She follows me down the hall, and I turn to our left into the first bedroom, which is the second and slightly smaller master bedroom.

We walk in and she looks around the space for a moment, her gaze wide-eyed.

"This is bigger than my apartment," she says.

I know that can't be true but I chuckle anyway.

"It's a large room. It should give you plenty of space. The bathroom and the walk-in closet are through that door," I say, pointing to the double doors. "And if you want, this room is big enough for a small office space. I'll buy whatever furniture you need for in here. Or you can take one of the guest bedrooms down the hall for an office space. Unless you already have—"

"No, I don't have an office space. Shawnie and I have talked about it but Seattle's office space rent is outrageous. We just work on our laptops wherever we meet up. An office space would be... amazing."

If I had known the office was such a big deal, I would have mentioned it sooner when I asked her to move in.

"You're going to be here for two years. You might as well have a space to work in."

"Thank you," she says, spinning around to face me, a sparkle in those violet eyes that have me almost offering to buy her office furniture.

I'd better leave and head back downstairs before I offer up the penthouse.

I push the two pieces of luggage closer to the bed and then pull the straps off over my head from the bags I brought up. "This should be a good start. Why don't you start unpacking while I bring up the rest?"

"Thank you, Ryker. This is more than I expected."

I want her to like it here. I don't want her to feel as though the next two years are that much of a sacrifice.

"I'll be back with the rest."

I turn and head for the door, closing it slightly behind me to give her a little privacy, even though I'll be back soon.

It takes two more trips to clean out the back of her SUV. Every piece of luggage is packed to the brim. I'm pretty sure the last one only has shoes in it.

On my way back up with the last of the luggage, I hear her on the phone.

"Mom, it's my wedding day. I know... I know that you're not happy. But you don't have to support us. Just please come. Be there for me," she says. "I know you think he's going to ruin my life. But he's not. I promise you. It's all going to be fine. And we get to move Jerrin in next week."

I turn around and leave the luggage by the door to give her space.

Her mom won't come.

I already knew she wouldn't, but I was hoping maybe with the fact that we were getting married tomorrow she'd change her mind... for Juliet's sake.

I know my family would be here if I told them I was getting married. The guilt of keeping this from my family gets heavier the closer Juliet and I get to saying our vows, but coming clean about why Juliet and I are getting married isn't smart.

The fewer people who know, the better.

CHAPTER THIRTEEN

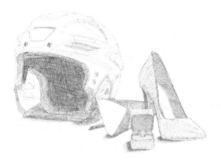

Juliet

I hear the text notification buzz on my phone.

> Shawnie: Which apartment number are you? I'm coming up.

I told her that Ryker's apartment was in The Commons so I shouldn't be surprised she's showing up.

> Juliet: Apartment number 803.

> Juliet: Why are you coming up?

Shawnie: Because you're coming with me to get ready. He can't see the bride until you walk down the aisle.

Oh, Shawnie and her belief in wedding traditions.

Now is not the day for them, but I'll go willingly, or she'll just drag me out kicking and screaming. Besides, no matter what this is, fake or "real", this is the first time I'm getting married.

Moving into Ryker's last night was a pleasant surprise. Not just because of the nice amenities but also because of how welcoming he's been since the moment I walked in.

The call with my mother, on the other hand, left me fighting back tears after we got off the phone.

Angry tears or sad tears, I can't be sure because I never let them drop. Her lack of support hurts but I know she feels she's already been down the road I'm about to travel and she wants to stop me from going through the same heartache she endured with my dad.

At the end of the day, her absence at the courthouse won't prevent me from keeping my word to Ryker. She can be upset with me but I know what I'm doing is right for my brother and for the man I've committed the next two years to.

The smell of bacon and eggs permeates throughout the house as I exit my bedroom. Though I usually don't sleep well the first night in a new place, whatever mattress Ryker bought for that bed is pure magic. I slept like a baby... even after the argument with my mother.

I walk out to the kitchen to find Ryker making breakfast... shirtless, in only a pair of navy sweatpants riding low on his hips.

"Good morning," he says, glancing over his shoulder at me emerging from the hall.

His back is to me as he finishes stirring the eggs and then piles them up on a plate.

"Morning," I say back.

I try my best not to stare at the bare, broad shoulders of the man I'll be sharing a roof with for the next twenty-four months.

I distract myself by dropping my purse and shoes by the front door for when Shawnie gets here.

"It smells good in here," I say as I reenter the kitchen.

"Are you hungry? I made enough for both of us."

"Yes, please. Shawnie is coming up. She's demanding I go to her house to get ready."

I pull out a barstool and take a seat at the island.

He's flipping pieces of bacon, standing at the stove with his back to me and I stop myself from giving all six-plus feet of him a full scan without his noticing.

Seeing him like this—domesticated and making break-fast—somehow puts him in a new light. He's not just a hockey player. I'm marrying him to help him get his green card.

He's a roommate.

A luggage carrier.

A skilled cook.

And an underwear model.

And in a matter of hours... he's going to be my husband.

It feels like the image I have of Ryker in my head and the way I feel about him is constantly changing by the day. I just hope the musical chairs stop at some point so that I can get my head on straight.

"Are we still going down to the courthouse together?" he asks, dishing up a plate.

He walks over with a plate of eggs and bacon and sets it down in front of me.

Seeing him this close-up, I realize he looks even better now than in that underwear campaign. Those few little freckles scattered along his pecks and that light patch of hair forming a happy trail aren't photoshopped away.

I clear my throat when I realize I'm staring at his chest. There's no way to pretend I wasn't looking. But he said I was allowed to look while we were on top of Oakley's two nights ago.

When I look up, he has a knowing smirk on his face. Is he doing this on purpose?

Avoidance is best used in these circumstances.

"I'm not sure. Shawnie is taking me hostage."

He nods and then walks back to the kitchen. "Want ketchup with your eggs?"

"I'll take some if it's no trouble."

He grabs a bottle off the countertop and flips it up, catching it casually back in his hand. If he's trying to impress me... it's already working.

Though I need to resist.

"No trouble for my bride on our wedding day," he says with a cheesy grin.

I can't help but smile back when he smiles like that at me.

He walks over to the island, squirts a silver dollar size of ketchup on my plate, and then returns to the stove to dish up for himself.

His helping size is more than four times what I could eat in a sitting but I've seen the man play a hockey game. I'm sure he needs every calorie of energy he can consume.

The nerves almost make me not want to eat but I know I should eat something.

He walks over to the island and sits down, his arm grazing gently along mine as he sits on the barstool closest to me.

"Are you doing that on purpose?" I ask.

He turns and looks at me, his eyes locking onto mine. "Doing what on purpose?"

"Trying to seduce me?"

His eyes dart between mine. "I don't know... is it working?"

A knock on the door cuts the moment like a knife.

Ryker stands up to head for the door but I grab his arm to stop him.

"Don't you even think about it," I warn.

"What? I can't answer my own door now?" he asks, tossing up his hands.

"Not like that you can't."

"Is this the jealous side of Juliet?" he asks with a devilish grin.

"No. It's not that. If she sees you like this," I say, motioning to his shirtless torso, "she'll never stop hounding me about living with the playgirl centerfold."

He laughs. "You're kidding?"

"No... I'm not."

I slip off the barstool, grabbing my plate of food because now that sexual tension has me starving and I'm taking my breakfast with me.

Another knock sounds at the door. This time, it's a little more impatient than the last.

"She's here. I have to go. Thank you for breakfast," I say, running to the door and debating how I'm going to keep my nosy friend from barging in here to see what's going on between us.

"Don't you need to take anything with you?"

"No. I'm sure Shawnie has everything we need," I say, knowing that my best friend is probably over-prepared as usual.

I slip on my shoes and grab my purse before opening the door.

Shawnie beams, holding an iced coffee in her hand for me.

"You'd better caffeinate for what I've got in store for you," she says as I try to shut the door behind me. "Hey, don't I get to see the place before we go?"

"No," I bark.

"Bye Shawnie," Ryker says, barely catching Shawnie's eye before the damn soft shutting door cuts out her view inside.

"Oh my God, you horn dog. You couldn't even wait until your wedding night?" Shawnie says to me, loud enough that Ryker hears it.

I hear him chuckle before his footsteps take him away.

I grab Shawnie's arm, balancing my plate of breakfast in the other.

"Come on, we're going," I demand, leading her to the elevators.

"You ready to get married?" she asks with glee.

"As ready as I'm ever going to be."

CHAPTER
FOURTEEN

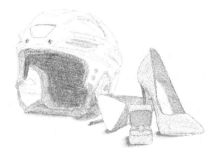

Juliet

After an elevator ride and a thirty-minute trip to Shawnie's apartment, we head up to her door.

My belly is now full, and I thoroughly explained to Shawnie that the only thing I did last night was argue with my mother about this very wedding and color coordinate my shoes in the closet I only filled halfway.

The minute Shawnie opens the door to her apartment, she starts in. "Before you freak out, I need you to know that I'm your best friend, and I refuse to let you make a mistake on your wedding day."

"What did you do, Shawnie?"

I walk through her front door as she steps to the right and out of the way.

The white dress we tried on at the mall, which fit me like a glove, hangs from her window sill.

It's as beautiful as I remember, hanging in the morning light of Shawnie's apartment. A pair of silver pumps that I tried on with it at the shop sit just below it.

"Shawnie... you didn't," I tell her, my voice tinged with a mix of gratitude and resignation.

I can't decipher whether I'm happy or irritated with her.

"You're wearing this dress and you're going to look drop-dead gorgeous. And Ryker is going to keep you forever."

I want to argue with her.

I want to refuse to wear the dress.

I want to tell her to get her money back.

But I can't do any of that because... for the first time since I hung up with my mom last night, I'm excited to show up to the courthouse today in that dress.

Shawnie knew I would need this boost of confidence to get me through today.

It's amazing what you can get through when you feel incredible in yards of white organza. But also, I can't deny the thrill in the idea of Ryker seeing me walk down the aisle in this dress.

It's the kind of dress more fit for a red carpet than a fairytale wedding, but that's exactly what this wedding calls for.

I walk over to the dress and touch it gently with my hand. I'm out of words, which isn't like me.

"I knew you'd love it once you just let it happen."

Maybe she's right but I'm not happy that she paid for this.

"I'll pay you back," I assure her.

I also look over to the silver shoes she purchased and find a pair of white panties lying over the side of the shoe box. I pick them up and read the butt.

Mrs. Haynes.

"What are these?" I practically spit out.

She can't be serious and expect me to wear these. Yes, I've seen dozens of brides wear something under their dresses before, and I thought the idea was cute, but those couples were in love.

"Just stop your wailing and come do your hair and makeup. The least you can do is appease me after all I did," she says, walking into her open-concept kitchen.

Shawnie is a master of guilt-tripping me when she needs to and it's working wonders now.

"No panties... no dress," she adds.

I look over toward her kitchen to see that she has a curling iron and every piece of makeup she owns out on display for our use.

I do as she asked and sit in the seat, drinking my coffee.

"Thank you for this," I tell her softly... minus the panties.

She rubs my shoulder with one hand for a second while her other keeps the curling iron in my hair.

I don't know how I would get through today without her and even though I resisted this at first, dressing up, even for a courthouse wedding, makes this feel important.

And it is.

Ryker staying in the country and helping his team win the championship is a big deal and I get to be a part of that. That's how I need to see this. Like Ryker said, this is real if our goal is to help each other reach our goals.

However, the fear of being found out still sticks at the back of my mind. How will I keep my brother's new lease paid if I end up in jail for defrauding a K-1 visa to help Ryker? I have to push that out of my mind for today to make it through these vows.

After both of our makeup and hair are done, I slip into the dress. Shawnie zips me up and the minute the zipper touches the end, I know I'm ready to get married.

Shawnie slips into a dress of her own and then hands me a bag from the lingerie store in the mall.

"You didn't give me a chance to give you a bachelorette party. So at the very least, you need something for tonight."

Something for tonight...

My wedding night with my husband.

I never imagined that I would spend the night after my wedding alone, but this thing between Ryker and I is uncharted territory and the last thing I want to do is complicate an already complicated situation.

I open the tissue paper and pull out the first piece—a beautiful silky white teddy with just barely-there triangles covering the nipples.

It's beautiful.

It really is.

And if I were getting married to the love of my life, I wouldn't be able to wait to wear this for him. Then I look down to find a red lace teddy that's completely see-through.

"You shouldn't have done this," I tell her. "These won't get any use over the next two years."

"I just saw your shirtless fiancé; I wouldn't make those claims so quickly. Just be open-minded, Juliet. You're marrying a man who's so far taken very good care of you. I don't think you should be as glum as you are about the situation."

I put the white, silky teddy back into the bag and wrap the tissue paper back over it.

She's right, though I hate to admit it.

He's given me the money that I need for my brother and offered to pay to put an office in his apartment for me to be able to work from home. Anything I've asked for, he's given me... and even things I haven't.

The more time Ryker and I spend together, the more I enjoy his company. He's funny and kind, and maybe if things had been different and he had not been a professional athlete, he would have asked me on a date, and I would have said yes.

She looks down at the time on her cell phone.

"We need to go. Grab the lingerie bag and let's get out of here," she says.

I bend down, reaching for the short train behind me and pull it up so that it doesn't drag on the ground. I grip the ribbon strings of the lingerie bag and walk behind her towards the door.

We load into Shawnie's car and she gets us to the courthouse with more than enough time to make it to our scheduled appointment with the judge.

Shawnie finds a parking spot and then we head into the courthouse. We find our floor level, and as we exit the elevator to the courtroom, I see Seven standing outside of the double doors.

"He asked me to exchange the rings. He wasn't sure if he's allowed to see you beforehand," Seven says.

"He's not," Shawnie interjects quickly.

Seven offers her up the gold band for Ryker and the moment that the ring hits her hand, I realize how serious this is. Ryker bought himself a ring.

A symbol of the vows we're about to make today.

This is real.

I pull the diamond ring off my hand. It's the first time I've taken it off since Ryker slipped it on my finger. I've been too scared to lose it and giving it to Seven still makes me nervous.

"Is there anyone else in there?" I ask, holding onto the last glimmer of hope that my mom decided to show up anyway.

"No. Just us," Seven says.

I nod.

I knew it wasn't likely she would have a change of heart, but it was worth a shot.

"Start whenever you're ready," he tells me.

He walks through the door and closes it behind him.

Shawnie pulls out her phone from her bra in her dress and cues up a song. A song I told her years and years ago when we were in college that I wanted to walk down the aisle to. I can't believe she remembers it now.

The song streams around us as she and I both tug on one of the doors together. The double doors open and the moment my eyes latch on Ryker, I know this isn't the wedding I thought it would be.

Ryker

I stand at the head of the courtroom in a black suit with the minister and Seven. My hands clasp together in front of me as I wait patiently for Juliet.

I haven't seen her since this morning when Shawnie showed up and yanked her out of the house.

I have no idea what she'll be wearing.

A pantsuit?

A dress?

One of my jerseys as a joke?

I don't have long to wait because, within seconds, the heavy, solid oak double doors open. Juliet is in full view, arm in arm with Shawnie as they clear the doors and start walking down the aisle toward me.

My mouth goes dry at seeing her in a full white gown. She looks beautiful with her hair down in loose waves.

The minute our eyes meet, I know I made a mistake.

Juliet deserves a real wedding, fake or not. Maybe I should have given her the ninety days we have on the visa to plan something better. I thought fast-tracking this would suit us both.

Now, I'm not so sure I won't regret giving Juliet a courthouse wedding to remember me by when all of this is over.

Classical harp music echoes into the courtroom from Shawnie or Juliet's phone, filling the silent void around us.

The full-length spaghetti strap dress has me unable to take my eyes off her. It fits tight from the low-cut top down to the full curves of her hips. A slit comes up the left side of her dress and stops high on her thigh.

I can't help but imagine what it would feel like to let my hands wander past the slit of her dress and allow my fingertips to roam over the soft skin of her thighs.

She's fucking gorgeous as she makes her way toward me. My hands itch in anticipation of reaching out to take hers into mine.

I feel Seven leaning closer behind me.

"You sure about this?" he asks, low enough that no one else hears it.

My eyes don't leave Juliet's, and hers don't leave mine.

This might be temporary, but the minute I saw her in that white dress, I realized that I've never been more sure of anything.

"I'm sure," I tell him, keeping my sights on my bride.

We only agreed to two years, but no matter when this ends, Juliet is my wife until she signs on the dotted line and divorces me.

"Who gives this woman to be married?" the officiant asks when Shawnie and Juliet stop just short of my reach.

"I do," Shawnie says.

Shawnie pulls her arm from Juliet's and looks to me to take her best friend.

I know she did this.

She made Juliet the bride she deserves to be.

Her hands are soft as they slide into mine and I pull her up the one step with me.

We face each other as the judge continues.

"You two have opted not to exchange vows. Is that correct?" the officiant asks.

"That's correct," I tell him, though now rushing through this might have been a mistake too.

"Very well," he says, seeming unmoved by our decision to want a speedy ceremony on what should be the happiest day of our lives.

He doesn't seem as though he cares either way. Officiating our wedding is probably just one more task he has to fit in today between a sea of other responsibilities, like passing judgment in traffic court issues and landlord-tenant disputes.

He'd just as soon move on to the next task of his day.

"We are gathered here to bear witness to this man, Ryker Haynes, and this woman, Juliet Di Costa, entering into a commitment of marriage. They both have come here of their own free will to be united under Washington state law," he says, just barely a cadence to his monotone voice. He's probably done this a thousand times and could recite it in his sleep. "Do we have rings to exchange?"

"Yes, we do," I say.

Seven leans over and hands me Juliet's ring... with the added wedding band I slipped him to combine.

"Ok then, repeat after me," he says, turning to me.

I keep my eyes focused on Juliet as I repeat every word that the judge instructs.

"I, Ryker Haynes, take you, Juliet Di Costa, to be my lawful wedded wife. To have and to hold, in sickness and in health until death do us part. With this ring, I thee wed."

I slip the ring back on her finger and with it, the wedding band I bought yesterday when I went to pick up my ring.

She looks down at it, noticing that there's a new component to her ring.

She doesn't say anything since we're in the middle of our vows, but her parted lips say she wasn't expecting it.

Then the judge turns to Juliet.

"Repeat after me," he says.

Shawnie hands her my ring and then her eyes lock on me and I listen to every word she vows to me.

"I, Juliet Di Costa, take you, Ryker Haynes, to be my lawful wedded husband. To have and to hold, in sickness and in health, until death do us part. With this ring, I thee wed."

She slips on my wedding band, the cold metal against the heat of her fingers causes a tingling sensation as they brush against my skin.

"By the authority vested in me by the state of Washington, you may now kiss your bride," the judge tells me.

I lick my lips and smile down at her.

I take a step closer and she leans into me. She wants this kiss too and I plan to make sure she never forgets it.

I dip down and press my lips to hers. I pull her against me, my hands gliding over her ass and pulling her tighter.

The first kiss is testing but then I slide my tongue over her lips, and she opens for me.

I know I shouldn't make out with my wife on the steps of the courtroom with an impatient judge but fuck it. When we head home, I want Juliet to remember who she married.

CHAPTER
FIFTEEN

Juliet

Leaving Seven and Shawnie at the courthouse and riding up the elevator with Ryker to his penthouse has me wondering how tonight will end.

Will I end up alone in my bed... or naked in his?

He's already told me that the ball is in my court. If I want something to happen, I'm the one who has to initiate it.

That kiss in the courthouse has me thinking about how much I want to explore that thing further. And the lingerie bag that Shawnie made sure I didn't leave the courthouse parking lot without feels heavier in my hand than the thin teddies should weigh. The fear of breaking that boundary and getting closer, only for this all to end in two years, makes pursuing this with Ryker feel like a dangerous choice.

The elevator reaches the eighth floor and we step off together, heading for the door.

Ryker stops just shy of the door and swings his arm under my ass while the other arm wraps around my back, pulling me into a cradle hold.

I squeak out a noise and quickly wrap my arms around his neck to hold on, the small white lingerie department bag smacking against his back. The tissue paper inside crinkles from the collision. "What are you doing?" I ask.

"I'm supposed to carry you over the threshold, aren't I?" he asks, continuing toward the door.

"That's the tradition. But this marriage is anything but traditional."

Still, the gesture is sweet and I don't want him to put me down.

He releases my back while I tighten my hold around my neck as he fishes out his key.

Once inside, Ryker doesn't put me down right away. His green eyes lock onto mine, and then they dip down to my lips for barely a second. If I hadn't been watching, I would have missed it. Is he thinking about that kiss in the courthouse like I am?

I want to lean in and kiss him with his mouth so close and this is the perfect opportunity to initiate something between us. But giving into these feelings will only complicate things further.

"Where should I put you down?" he asks.

I don't know if he's giving me the opportunity to tell him to take me to his room or if it's just a simple question. So I opt for the safest route.

"Right here is fine," I say inside the entry. "I should probably change out of this dress and into regular clothes. I'm sure I have emails from clients and vendors that need responding to."

Not that I want to take this dress off. I'd wear it all week if I could. Sleep in it and bathe in it too. And getting right back to work as usual less than an hour after getting married feels weird, but what else are we going to do in this penthouse all afternoon on our wedding day?

He doesn't take my instructions. Instead, he walks me through the penthouse, down the hallway, and then he sets me on my heels right in front of my bedroom door.

He waits to make sure I have my footing before he completely releases me. Once he's sure that I'm stable, he tucks his hands into his pockets like he's trying to keep from reaching out to touch me any more than he already has.

"Welcome home, Mrs. Haynes," he says. "Let me know if you need anything. I'll be down the hall taking off this suit."

He turns and heads back down the hallway toward his bedroom.

The title of being a Mrs., but moreover, his Mrs., is a reality check. This is real. We're married, and now the clock for the next two years begins. A full two years of living as roommates with a man I'm very attracted to. What could possibly go wrong?

I walk into my room and stare at the wall in front of me. Did I make the right decision to tell him to drop me here? Or should I have told him to take me where he wants?

Would he have taken me to his bedroom?

The strings of the department bag still lay against my finger-tips, and I look down and watch the bag sway back and forth.

Fake marriage or not, sleeping alone on my wedding night just feels strange. Does he feel the same?

There's only one way to find out.

I take a deep breath, mustering up all the courage I can before tossing the bag onto the bed and turn back to head out of my room.

"Ryker?" I call out, walking down the hall to his room.

I walk up to his door that he left open.

"Yeah," he says, walking out from his ensuite in only a pair of slacks that are unbuttoned and unzipped. His pants hang low on his hips, his bare torso displaying the ripples of every muscle out on display.

My eye follow the dark hair of his happy trail to where it disappears beneath the elastic band of his boxers.

"Can you help me with this zipper? It's a little hard for me to reach on my own. Shawnie had to zip me into it," I tell him.

It's true that she did zip me in but I'm skilled enough at this point in my life that I can unzip myself pretty much out of anything.

But I need an excuse for walking in here and it's the first thing I could think of.

"Yeah, come here," he says, stepping further out of his bath-room and heading straight for me.

I turn my back to him, pulling my long hair out of his way so he can access the zipper better.

His fingers connect with the top of the zipper and I inhale sharply at the warmth of his skin against my back.

He starts to unzip me slowly. The only sound I can hear is our mixed breathing and the sound of the teeth of my zipper slowly releasing me from the dress.

He's close.

So close that I can feel his body heat radiate behind me.

The top of his open slacks brush against the top of my ass, creating a tingling sensation across my skin.

I know we're less than an inch away from connecting and it has me fighting the urge to push back against his solid body to feel him behind me.

He bends over my shoulder just slightly. "You should know that you're the most beautiful bride I've ever seen," he says, the deep timber of his voice tickling against my ear and creating a flutter of excitement low in my belly.

The warmth of his breath spreads against the side of my neck creating goosebumps everywhere it touches.

"Thank you," I say softly, over my shoulder.

When the zipper finally nears the end, I know what Ryker will find.

He stops the moment the zipper reaches the bottom of my ass, the dress opening for him.

"What are these?" he asks.

His hands rest on either side of my hips as his thumbs glide over the writing on the white cotton panties that Shawnie got me. A shiver shoots down my spine at his touch.

"Mrs. Haynes," he says, his voice low, reading the words on my panties.

"Do you like them?" I ask.

"I think I found my new favorite place to see my name on your body."

My heart thumps against my rib cage at his admiration.

"You're unzipped, Juliet. Anything else you need?"

I already know and the thought of being bare before him sends a flutter of excitement through me.

I turn to face him, my dress only hanging on by the thin straps and my right arm holding the bodice up against my breasts.

"I never thought I'd sleep alone on my wedding night."

His eyes lock onto mine and my attention dips down to the large bulge in his pants.

His eyes follow mine to his hard erection pushing against his slacks.

"I want to fuck you Juliet, I can't hide that fact. But nothing happens unless you want it to."

I hold his attention as I pull the spaghetti straps from my shoulders and drop the dress to the ground.

The dress pools at my feet, and with no bra or any other undergarments under my dress, I stand in front of Ryker in only a pair of white panties and a pair of silver stilettos.

I hear a rumble in his throat as he takes a full scan of my body.
"Fuck."

He takes a step closer, towering over me. His hands slide over my hips, his warm fingers gliding over my panties.

My hardening nipples are so close to brushing against his rib cage.

I run my hands up his bare chest until they reach his pecs. He's hard everywhere and the thought that his cock is erect and hard for me gives me a thrill I haven't felt in so long.

"Can I stay with you tonight?" I ask.

"You can have anything you want from me, Juliet. I won't say no."

He pushes back a strand of my hair and tucks it behind my ear.

My attention breaks away from the light scattering of freckles on his skin and reaches into his green eyes. He's watching me admire everywhere my fingers explore.

"And if I want to sleep with you?" I ask.

His hands squeeze against my hips and I let out an involuntary moan.

Every little thing he does has me eager to be under his control. To feel his power and to give myself over to the tension that's been building slowly since we met.

"Spell this out for me. I don't want to misunderstand. Are we consummating our marriage right now?"

I suck down on my lip and then push up on the tips of my high heels and wrap my arms around his neck, pressing my naked breasts against his chest, and my lips against his.

He growls low into our kiss while his hands slide over my ass and grip tight. His fingers dig into my skin as he pulls me up his body.

The way he picks me up so effortlessly has me craving more of his touch.

I wrap my legs around his waist as he walks us back to the bed and gently sets me on top of his grey comforter, laying me down on my back.

His eyes wash over my body as he pulls down his slacks and discards them out of his way.

Usually, I'd feel a bit of self-consciousness laying out like this for him, the stream of light coming through the closed curtains. It's still the afternoon and there's no darkness to hide in.

But I don't want to hide.

Not with the way he looks at me.

His erection is no match for the thin fabric of his boxer briefs as it strains against the material. His cock is rock-hard and impressive from what I can make out, just like the rest of him.

The look in his eyes is carnal, but there's also a promise in them that tells me he'll take care of me.

"If you want to stop or you change your mind, you have to tell me. I can't read your thoughts and my cock is too hard to process subtle cues."

I nod and then he puts one knee on the bed and bends over me. His arms flex to hold his weight over me, his abs tightening as he hovers above my almost naked body.

He bends down and kisses me, his lips sucking and pulling against mine while his tongue slips into my mouth and tangles with mine.

This is so much more demanding than the kiss at the courthouse and it's exactly what I was waiting for the entire drive back to his penthouse.

I thread my fingers through his hair to pull him closer. He groans in approval.

He pulls back and begins to kiss down my neck and then across my chest.

Every move he makes has my body warming in anticipation, but I can't shake the one thing I need to ask. The one thing I need to know is whether he has the answer to.

"Ryker?"

"Huh?" he says, his mouth still expertly working down my chest between my breasts.

"Are we doing the wrong thing?" I ask, voicing my concern of screwing up and making this more complicated than it needs to be.

His lips pull off my body for a second and his arm pushes him up to look at me.

"The wrong thing?"

"Yeah. Like are we making a mistake and complicating things between us?"

There's a softness in his green eyes where a moment ago was pure lust.

He drops to his elbows, bringing himself eye-to-eye with me.

"What's complicated about us? You're my wife Juliet... you're the only women I should be fucking," he says, his eyes searching mine. "But if you don't want—"

He begins to lift himself further off my body.

"No!" I say quickly to stop him, pulling my arms around his neck tighter and bringing him closer. "Don't leave."

He could easily break through my hold if he wanted, but he doesn't, he stays close—debating his next move.

"What do you want from me right now? I need you to say it."

"I want to know what it's like to be with you," I tell him, pulling him closer.

He wraps his arms around me and holds me close as we tangle back up together.

He slides his powerful thighs between mine, forcing my legs to stretch to accommodate his wide body... so much bigger than mine. His hard cock presses against the top of my cleft. My center clenches at the instant pressure of him.

His hand trails down my body and his fingertips glide over my panties.

"You're wet, Juliet. Tell me that's for me."

Of course, it's for him.

I can't deny how badly my body wants him.

And now he feels the evidence.

Ryker

"Yes... yes, it's for you," she pants through our kiss.

I look over the woman lying in my bed. Her silky black hair splayed out over my sheets, every inch of her warm skin and mauve nipples calling for me to taste her. That sweet smell of cinnamon and vanilla, now mixed with the smell of her arousal.

I wasn't expecting this side of Juliet. I knew there was a possibility that it existed but I didn't think she'd ever let her guard down enough to let me see it.

I slide my index finger past her cotton panties and run it through her slick, wet heat. Her eyes flutter closed at my touch.

I thought, at best, we'd be good roommates.

I never thought she'd let me this close.

But now that she has, I'll spend every minute of this time she's giving me to make sure I give it to her better than she's ever had it.

I want her coming back for more... I want this woman addicted to what I can give her, because fuck, I'm not all that far from it myself.

She whimpers as my finger swirls through her slit, adding pressure against her swollen clit. I swallow every moan and sigh that passes her lips, knowing that she's making those noises for me.

"How does that feel?" I ask.

"Good," she says, her voice trembling. "So good."

I push down on the side of her panties, and she reacts to my signal by lifting her perfect ass so I can take my favorite panties off her.

Note to self: Buy Juliet a lifetime supply of cotton panties in every color under the sun and have Mrs. Haynes printed on every pair. Then, throw away her thongs.

No amount of see-through lingerie could have gotten me as hard as seeing her with my name written across her perfect backside.

All I ever want to see her in from now on... are these.

I push her panties down over her ankles and then I pull my lips off her mouth, sinking down further on the bed to see the last piece of her body hidden from me.

Her hands grip around my wrists as I descend.

Is she nervous? Does she not like oral sex?

"Are you scared of what I might do?" I ask her, looking into those violet eyes that have had me hypnotized since the minute I met her.

"No, I trust you," she says.

I like that she said it out loud and I hope she means it because she can trust me—especially to make her come.

I glance down at the slit between her thighs.

"My wife has a pretty pussy," I say, licking my lips.

I bend down and run my tongue through her folds.

She bucks against me and whimpers out my name. I could get used to hearing her say my name like that. My tongue swirls around her clit as Juliet's fingers dig against my scalp. The feeling of her desperation pulling me closer, needing me deeper, has my cock throbbing uncomfortably in my boxer briefs. I don't know how much more I can take before I combust from the sounds Juliet is making for me.

My tongue dives into her center and her little ass squirms against the sheets of my bed, her sobs of ecstasy echoing off the walls of my bedroom.

Every night should be like this with her, and if she lets me, they will be.

"Ryker... please," she says, pulling on my hair, her breathing labored.

I release her sweet pussy and glance up to find her staring down at me, watching me devour her.

"I want you inside me," she says, her chest heaving as she tries to catch her breath. "Now."

I need to sink inside her as badly as she wants me to. I need to slide inside her wet heat and feel her center squeeze me as she comes. I need to bury myself into the woman I haven't stopped thinking about since I saved her from slipping on the ice on the Hawkeyes parking lot.

We both need this.

Connection.

Release.

Busting through the boundaries of keeping this arrangement untouched by physical connection. There's no way we can go back now... is there?

"There's nothing I'd rather do than be inside you," I tell her, pushing up toward her face again. "I need a condom first."

I lay a demanding kiss against her mouth and she takes everything I give her, giving me little needy noises that I consume as quickly as they pass through her lips.

I reach over her for my nightstand, not taking my mouth off hers. My fingers find a condom and I pull it out of the drawer. I push down my boxer briefs until my feet can kick them off the bed. I discard the foil wrapper to the floor and then push the rubber over my engorged cock before settling back between Juliet's thighs, my lips not leaving hers for a second.

"Hurry," she says against my lips.

I press my tip against her entrance, and she takes in a swift breath, her eyes finding mine.

"Don't worry, I'm going to fill you. Just like you asked."

This is her chance to stop me. This is the last stronghold of self-control I have left and then it's gone. I've never wanted someone as badly as I want her but I didn't think this was possible. I didn't think she'd let me touch her.

The minute Juliet's tight pussy wraps around my throbbing cock, I'll be a lost man. Primal need takes over until the sheets of this bed are wet with sweat and sex, and our sated bodies are struggling to catch our breath.

"I need it," she begs.

I won't make her beg again.

I thrust into her, and she gasps as she takes me. I hiss at the sensation of the first contact with her tight warmth, my teeth gritting so hard to keep from coming that I could break a tooth. She encourages me further with her whimpers as I advance into her, an inch at a time until every inch of me is buried deep and I'm fully seated.

I feel more hot liquid coat my cock from her body. She's fucking turned on and nothing could get me harder than knowing I do it for her. This woman turns heads in every room she walks into, but right now, I'm the one turning her into mush in my hands. There's no bigger ego boost than that.

"Oh God, you're so big," she moans, rotating her hips and matching my every thrust.

She's not complaining about me being too big... no... she wants more. She likes the way my cock stretches her and so do I.

"Yeah, but you take me so good, beautiful," I whisper against her ear, grinding down deeper and pressing her into the mattress.

Her hands tighten around the back of my neck as she holds me close, her legs wrapping around me and her heels digging into the low of my back, just above my ass.

My thrusts become more frantic, penetrating deep and ramming her against the memory foam each time. Her moans become louder with every stroke of my cock.

Hovering just barely above her, I watch between us as her full breasts bounce under me. Her mauve nipples have my mouth watering and I won't miss my chance to taste all of her.

"Ryker..." she moans out, her eyelashes fluttering. "I'm close."

"Yeah? Come on my cock, Juliet... I want to feel it."

I want to spend the whole day finding every way I can bring Juliet pleasure but my self-control to keep from coming is wearing thin and I don't think I can take much more before I lose my grip and come first. And that is the one thing I refuse to let happen.

Juliet comes first... always.

"Dig those heels in harder and come," I tell her, picking up my pace and bending down to suck her nipple into my mouth.

"Oh..." she moans as I twirl my tongue around her hard nub.

She grinds harder against me, matching my rhythm, until I hear her scream my name, her pussy pulsating around me. Her fingernails claw into my back as she rides out her orgasm.

I release her nipple from my mouth to watch Juliet's face as she comes. I want to remember what she looks like when she loses control... just in case she never lets me touch her again.

Watching her come ignites the knowing signs of my own orgasm that threaten to hit me and I can't stave this off anymore.

"Are you...?" she asks.

"I'm right there. I had to make sure you got off first," I tell her.

Her sated smile is all I need in this world. Maybe it's the sex talking, but fuck, I've never witnessed anything as gorgeous as Juliet after she's been satisfied.

"It's your turn. Come in me," she says, with a sex kitten voice I haven't heard before.

"Fuck," I say, burying my mouth against her neck and inhaling her in.

I pump a few more times until my own climax breaks loose and I groan out my orgasm against her neck. I empty everything I have into the condom buried deep inside of my wife.

My wife...

I lay there between her thighs for a moment as I come down, both of us trying to catch our breath and process the fact that this marriage just changed in a matter of moments.

I slip off the bed and head for the bathroom to get her a cloth to wipe down with.

I help her clean herself up and then I dispose of the washcloth and lay back down next to her.

She finally kicks off her heels and turns toward me.

"Did we just make a mess of things?" she asks but the look in her eyes isn't fear or dread like it was when she asked earlier.

She wants reassurance that we'll continue everything as planned.

I don't know how to tell her that nothing is the same now, and that everything has changed, but that won't help me get any closer to her. And since I'm leaving for a few days for away games, the last thing I want is her alone in her head until I can get home and we can talk them all out.

I make a show of looking around my bed.

"No… I think we just made a mess of the bed."

She laughs and I pull her into me. She comes willingly, laying her hand against my chest.

"Should we do that again?" she asks.

"Hell yeah."

CHAPTER
SIXTEEN

Juliet

Ryker left early this morning, which was probably for the best, considering my menstrual cycle started when I woke up. By the time he returns, I should be nearly done with it.

Meanwhile, Shawnie and I have a busy week ahead with two birthday parties, a corporate event, and a gender reveal to set up for. Additionally, we need to finalize our plans for the alumni night at the stadium that's scheduled for the week after Ryker and I return from Canada.

The next few days are definitely going to be hectic for me and not having the distraction of a gorgeous 'fake' husband walking around the penthouse will allow me to get everything I need done.

> Ryker: Getting on the Hawkeyes jet now. Have a good day today. Are you going to watch tonight's game?

> Juliet: I wouldn't miss it. I have my jersey laid out on my bed for later.

> Ryker: Good girl.

I can't stop the warming of my cheeks when he calls me a good girl. I can even hear the deep timber of his voice in my head when he says it.

I think I might have a crush on my husband.

Is that going to be a problem?

Ryker

It's been two days since I left Juliet in my bed so I could catch the jet with the team.

In last night's game, I took a hit that knocked me on my back and I'm still feeling it today even though I slept on ice packs. Juliet's texts had me smiling last night before I went to bed.

> Juliet: I know I'm new to hockey, but aren't you supposed to stay upright and on your skates?

Though Juliet can flick me shit as good as my teammates, I'd rather get it from her any day. I like it when she gets feisty. But whether she can take it as good as she can dish it... remains to be tested.

> Ryker: You take a slide swipe from a two-hundred-and-fifty-pound Russian, and you try to keep your ass from hitting the ice.

> Juliet: Maybe next time, ask him not to hit you again. Otherwise, your wife is going to track him down and yell at him.

I knew she was kidding, and we both knew I wasn't going to ask.

Petrov, who skates for Houston, isn't going to be intimidated by my five-foot-four-inch Italian wife, though he'd definitely try to hit on her.

> Ryker: Sure. It's worth asking.

> Ryker: Are you still at the corporate retirement party?

> Juliet: It's winding down but I'll tell you what, no one can party longer than a person who doesn't have to go to work for the rest of their life.

> Ryker: I'd celebrate too. Don't stay out too late. Text me when you get back to the penthouse.

Juliet: Okay.

Two hours later, the light of my phone illuminated my face in the darkness of Seven and my hotel room.

Juliet: Home. Goodnight.

Ryker: Night wife.

This morning, I woke to the sound of a knock on my door.

I look over to find that Seven's queen-sized hotel bed is empty. He's probably already downstairs in the hotel gym lifting weights.

I stumble to the door.

When I open the door, I see Briggs in running gear.

"Hey, want to go for a run before our flight? We have a couple of hours before check out."

"Sure. Let me get my stuff," I say, keeping the door open for him.

He enters the hotel room, standing just inside.

I walk to my bag lying open on the ground under the window. I pull out my sweats and slip them on and then a T-shirt. Next, I lace up my running shoes and head toward him, grabbing my room key and cell phone off the table.

Once we get outside, we start stretching for a minute.

"How's married life? Autumn said you two had a quick wedding down at the courthouse," Briggs says. "Thanks for the invite, asshole. You're going to be one of the groomsmen in my wedding, but I don't even get to watch yours?"

Of course, his fiancée would tell him what's going on between Juliet and me.

"Seven was the only person I asked. Don't get your thong in a twist. My mom wasn't even there."

We both stand up straight after we finish stretching and line up along the sidewalk outside of the hotel. My back is killing me but my muscles crave a good workout in the morning and we have time before our flight.

I open the running app on my wristwatch to account for our time.

"Ready?" I ask.

"Let's go," Briggs says back.

It takes a few seconds to get our stride in sync but once we do, Briggs continues.

"Don't trip me for asking, but... did you marry Juliet for a green card?"

What the fuck?

He didn't beat around the damn bush with that one.

"Are you kidding me? Did you talk to Seven?" I ask.

Seven is usually good with a secret, but maybe I overestimated him this time.

"Seven? What's the point in asking the human Fort Knox? I'd be better off asking a rock, it would tell me more."

He is right there. Seven is impossible to get any information out of, top secret or not.

"Where is this coming from?"

"It just seems between the timeline of you and Amelia breaking up... and then you getting married, inviting none of your friends—"

"Seven was there," I argue.

"... and you didn't invite your own mom. Not to mention that I know your visa is due around now."

The timeline of everything spells a lot of this out. My four-year-old niece could probably put this puzzle together, but what Juliet and I do is no one else's business, and that's how I plan to keep it. The fewer people who know, the better.

Juliet and I aren't even close to being out of the woods yet, and though getting deported for a length of time and possibly never getting to apply for another visa for the rest of my life is a serious risk, Juliet's possible prison time is the reason that keeping the list low is crucial. This arrangement is on a need-to-know basis. Everyone else can read it in my autobiography when I'm dead.

"Ok, what's your point?" I ask, my breath starting to labor as we push ourselves for every step.

"Just that if you need anything," he says, trying to catch his breath. "I'm here to listen."

"Thanks, Conley, I appreciate it," I tell him.

The rest of the run we do in silence as we push our bodies to make good time before circling back around to the hotel.

I get his concern, and keeping this from my friends isn't what I want to do. But I'm doing this to make sure I can stay with the team for the championship and fulfill my four-year contract.

I know that any of my teammates would do whatever they could to help me, but hopefully, it never comes it that.

CHAPTER SEVENTEEN

Juliet

> Ryker: Going to be home tonight. Will you be home or do you have an event?

> Juliet: Nope. I'm free tonight. See you at home.

> Ryker: I like it when you call it home.

"Knock knock," I say as I open the door and head into the commons room on my brother's floor.

It's a large room with light grey walls and a couple of different areas to sit with sofas and TV's. There's a communal fridge and microwave, though it seems to be used mostly by family coming to visit since remnants of birthday cake and abandoned soda bottles seem to be all that's in the fridge whenever I look inside.

And I don't know if popcorn is just the snack of choice or if someone burned a really bad bag one time, because I swear this room always smells like buttered popcorn. Not that I mind. I love buttered popcorn.

Since Jerrin has a roommate, we usually take our card game to the commons room, which is often vacant anyway and has a bigger TV than the one in his room.

My brother usually has something on as background sound. I'm not surprised to find him streaming an old Hawkeyes game from earlier this season.

He's already sitting at a table with his cards out, prepping for our usual Texas Hold'em game. He looks up at me for a moment, his eyes registering it's me.

His eyebrows rise which is usually the closest thing I get to a smile, but that's fine with me. My brother doesn't have to fit any social norms to suit me. As long as I know he's happy and that he wants me here, it's all I care about. Based on the fact that the card game is set out, he's looking forward to our game.

"I bought a little treat for us today," I tell him.

"What?" he says simply, not looking up.

"Turkey and cranberry panini and mango smoothies."

Another one of the things my brother loves, and when I get a chance to spend the afternoon at the park with him, that's always the place he wants to go for picnic supplies.

"Are you ready for our game?" I ask, unwrapping his sandwich and grabbing his smoothie.

"You ready to lose?"

I laugh at his typical response.

"I'm always prepared to lose when I'm playing with you," I tell him, dropping his sandwich and smoothie next to him on the table and pressing a kiss on the top of his head, feather soft as to not disrupt his focus.

He gives a small snicker, which is a win for me, since you don't get that many from Jerrin.

I grab my own sandwich and smoothie from the bag when I hear the bathroom door open.

It's my mother.

She showed up because she knew I'd be here.

This is a special time for me and my brother so I'm a little frustrated that she came in to ruin it with more talk about how I'm going to regret marrying Ryker.

"Hi, Mom."

My brother doesn't seem to mind our conversation. His head is down, his eyes on his task at hand, setting up our first game.

If the kid went to Vegas, he'd be considered a card shark. His ability to count cards is remarkable.

"How'd it go yesterday?" she asks.

"Well... I'm married."

She rolls her eyes and looks out the window at the courtyard below, folding her hands across her chest.

"I know you're not happy about this, but it's already done, and Jerrin gets to move into the new center next week."

Jerrin's eyes pop up quickly to look at me.

"The new center?" he asks.

We've talked about this for months. I knew I had to prepare my brother. I've driven him by the new building a few times just to get him familiar. And we even walked into the lobby to check the place out. His eyes lit up when he saw the baby grand sitting in the corner. I knew they would.

I know change is hard for him but this change is going to be good. And he seemed okay with the idea of it.

"They're going to set you up with an occupational therapist that loves Texas Hold'em," I tell him.

Jerrin nods but keeps at his task at hand, not touching his food or smoothie, but he doesn't usually like distractions when he's playing cards.

"I told you he doesn't need this new center," my mom says.

"Can we not do this right now?" I ask, gesturing to the card game I'm about to take part in.

I haven't seen Jerrin all week with my full schedule and my mom knows it.

I can see her eyes soften. She knows she's cutting into my time with my brother and that this isn't the time to have this conversation.

"Of course," she says. "But we're not done talking about this."

"I'm sure we're not," I say back, not taking my eyes off my brother starting to distribute the cards.

My mom sits down quietly in a corner on the sofa. Pulling out her tablet, she starts reading some book... quietly at least.

I'm glad we can be in the room together, the three of us, without this being an issue.

As my brother and I start to play, I can't help but feel as though my feelings for Ryker are starting to change. I don't know what that means, considering everything's temporary. Maybe the next two years will be better than I expect.

We didn't get much of a chance to discuss how our wedding night might affect our relationship going forward but knowing that he'll be home in a couple more hours has me anticipating his arrival.

After Jerrin and I play our game, I head back to the apartment. Ryker gets back from being out-of-town and I have that lacy red lingerie sitting unused in the department store bag that Shawnie got me, though it seemed like the thing he loved the most was that underwear with my married name on the back.

The minute I push through the penthouse door, I hear classical music playing but I don't remember leaving the music on when I left this morning. I walk in a little further to find a bouquet of red roses in a vase on the island and take out Thai food with candles lit all over.

I look toward the hallway to find rose petals leading all the way down to the hall.

Is Ryker home already?

Did he do this for me?

My heart leaps at the thought.

For him to go to this much trouble after just getting home from a couple of really hard games out on the road is the sweetest gesture.

But then I hear a female voice.

"Ryker. Honey, is that you?"

I pause.

Panic setting in.

I quickly debate the possibility that I walked into the wrong penthouse, but I must not have because I don't have a key to the others and this is obviously Ryker's place.

I think about turning on my heels and running out of the front door before I see something I can't unsee, but then I realize that I live here now too. And he's the one who told me that we can't see other people. So it doesn't feel right that I should feel chased out.

A woman finally emerges from the hall in lingerie.

Jealousy and rage bubble up in me instantly. The thought of my two-timing father and how I might have just married the same man has me ready to pack every article of clothing I have in this house and leave, telling Ryker I'll see him in two years when our time runs out. But I need answers.

And I want them now.

She jumps a little at the sight of me. She must not have been expecting Ryker's wife to be standing in the kitchen.

"Oh, you must be Ryker's wife." She smiles.

But the smile almost seems contrived and who the hell smiles at someone's wife while standing in lingerie waiting for her husband?

"Who are you and where is Ryker?" I demand, not offering the same pleasantries.

"He's not home yet. I didn't realize you lived here."

"Why wouldn't I live here? We're married. And what are you doing here, barely dressed for my husband?"

"I'm Amelia. I was Ryker's girlfriend before you got engaged," she says, walking out of the hallway and heading closer to me.

Who told her to come closer? I sure as hell don't want her anywhere near me.

The name Amelia brings up a memory. Tessa had some choice words for her in the Owner's Box the night Ryker and I got engaged but that night was such a whirlwind I didn't ask any questions.

"Ok, then if you know he's married, what the hell are you doing coming into our home dressed like that?" I ask.

"Because I know it's fake between you two so I figured he might be interested in a girlfriend if he doesn't have a real wife."

"Excuse me?" I say, my voice raising in shock and anger that this woman would think she can come in and offer Ryker anything like that when he's married to me.

Did he tell her that our marriage is fake? She didn't realize that I live here. Did he tell her that we don't live together and that she's welcome to be here?

Ryker is still a stranger to me and I have no idea what to think.

But I do know that the sexy reunion that I thought I'd have in bed with Ryker tonight is definitely not going to happen.

Yes, I was originally fine with an open marriage, back when I thought we'd get married and then I wouldn't see him again until we had to sign divorce papers. But after our wedding night, things have changed. Or at least I think they have.

"I have to give it to you, though. You made out with a better proposal. He didn't propose to me with a ring."

"He proposed to you? Why aren't you the one married to him instead of me?"

What is going on?

Did he propose to two women?

When did this happen?

"He proposed to me first but without a ring," she says, her eyes casting down at my left hand.

"Oh my God," she says, taking quick steps toward me.

My body gets rigid as she gets closer to me, and I consider taking steps backward away from her until she reaches out and grabs my left hand with a strong grip.

"He got you a three-carat diamond? I only asked for two carats," she whines.

Honestly, who the hell is this woman and why isn't Ryker married to her instead if they dated before he and I met... and he proposed to her?

"So then why are you not wearing this ring instead of me?"

The idea that I was the second pick kind of hurts, even though I didn't even know him before we ran into each other in the parking lot.

"I didn't want to live in Canada," she says. "But now you can stay married to him for two years while he and I still date. Then when he becomes a resident, you two can get divorced and he and I can go back to our life together. Everyone wins."

Everyone wins?

Ryker never mentioned a girlfriend on the side or a woman that he planned to date after our divorce.

He was very specific.

We aren't allowed to see other people. This just doesn't add up.

I hear the door open behind me and I can only imagine who it must be. The door closes and I hear Ryker's footsteps behind me, labored, no doubt because of the scene playing out in front of him.

"Ryker, honey! You're home," she says, and it takes all the self-control I have, and desire not to go to jail for assault, not to slap her for calling Ryker 'honey'.

The nickname grates on my nerves to hear her say it for the second time.

He's not hers anymore... right?

"Amelia, what are you doing here?" he asks, walking up to us. "Did you let her in like this?" he asks me, standing beside me.

Now with Ryker in the penthouse, I hate that Amelia is still in lingerie and that her body is perfection.

It really adds insult to injury.

"I was just telling your wife here that we could have an arrangement."

"How did you get in, Amelia?" he asks, his voice low and threatening, ignoring what she just said.

"Ryker, I made a mistake breaking up with you. But now that you're married, in two years' time, this won't even matter anymore. You'll get divorced and you'll be a US citizen."

"What made you think you could come up here and make yourself at home? I have a wife. I have a new life."

"You asked me first, but you didn't even ask with a ring," she says, pointing a finger at me. "What's so special about her that she got a broadcasted proposal and a ring bigger than what I asked you for?"

I'd maybe feel bad for her if she wasn't such a spoiled brat... and didn't come up here to seduce my husband.

"You didn't have any problem dumping me and moving on the next day with the safety for the Seattle Sonics," he says back, but from how it sounds like this breakup played out, I'm surprised Ryker even wanted to get married at all.

"I made a mistake, Ryker. I know that now."

"Mistake or not, I'm glad your answer was no. Now leave your key and get the hell out of my penthouse. And if you harass my wife again or come within a hundred yards of her, I'll have a restraining order issued."

Ryker walks back to the front door and opens it for her to exit.

Her eyes go wide.

I don't think this woman has had anyone say no to her, let alone threaten legal action.

She stomps off to the kitchen, tugs on her knee-length jacket, and grabs her key off the kitchen island.

She slaps her spare key into Ryker's awaiting hand.

"You're going to regret turning me down in two years when she divorces you," she says.

"The only regret I have is proposing to you at all."

She makes a huffing noise and walks out the door. Ryker closes it behind her.

"Juliet, are you ok?" he asks.

I don't say anything as I walk down the hallway.

I hear Ryker make his way into the kitchen quickly and start blowing out all the candles. She probably lit twenty in there and it's a major fire hazard he needs to handle first.

I don't even know what to say. I know this isn't his fault, and yet, on some level, she must have thought she had hooks in Ryker deep enough to show up like she did.

Ex-girlfriends... new girlfriends, my father had them all.

I follow the rose petals down the hall and to his room. I take the steps inside to find candles lit and rose petals all over the bed that we had consummated our marriage a few days before.

The way I view this room has changed, as stupid as that is. I'm going to blame it on the hormones since I'm at the tail end of my menstrual cycle, though that's a cop-out.

Nothing's changed. It's the same. But now I have the memory of the woman who was here before me and I've seen what she looks like.

Ryker isn't the same man as my father, I know that. But Ryker is also still a stranger. A professional player with women vying for his attention every day.

Ryker walks up behind me.

"Hey," he says. "I'm sorry that happened."

"Why did she think she could come up here?" I ask.

I just need to know if he gave her any reason to believe that there was still something between them.

"I have no idea. But she's gone now, and she won't be coming back."

The fact that he threatened her with a restraining order doesn't sound like a man holding a door open for an old flame.

"She's pretty."

"Not as pretty as you," he says, taking a step closer.

I turn to face him. I'm tired of looking at this room covered in rose petals and candlelight. A room that feels like a stranger broke in and drew graffiti all over something sacred.

"You didn't tell me you proposed to someone else before me."

"She and I dated for six months. When I found out that I needed a fiancé visa, I proposed. When I told her that if I got deported that I would lose my Hawkeyes spot on the team, retire and move to Canada, she refused that life, claiming that she didn't want to be married to an old has-been hockey player who lives in Canada." He scanned the bedroom for a second and then his eyes meet mine again. "She doesn't want me, Juliet. She wants Haynes #19, Captain of the Hawkeyes and US resident."

I think about how hurtful it must have been for him to have proposed to someone only to have them turn him down because of money and fame.

"Stay with me tonight," he says. "I've been gone three days."

"I'm on my period."

"Good. I love shower sex."

I blush a little at the fact that Ryker isn't squeamish about my time of the month.

"I don't think tonight," I say.

"Then just sleep next to me."

I look over the bed.

"It's tainted."

Just saying the words makes me feel silly.

Makes me feel like a jealous wife.

But that's what I am and there's no point in hiding it. I'm a jealous wife who's jealous of the woman who was here before me. If I didn't care for Ryker at all, it wouldn't bother me. But our wedding night changed so much.

He walks over to his bed, flipping the sides of the comforter inward toward the rose petals and pulls it all up and off his sheets and then flings his comforter out into the hall.

"Please stay with me. We don't have to fuck, just lay next to me and tell me everything you did while I was gone."

Coming home to find a woman in my husband's house hit a little too close to home for me.

"I think I just need this one to air dry overnight. I'll see you in the morning, ok?"

He stands there with his hands on his hips, studying my facial expression.

I can see the disappointment on his face but I need the night to regroup my thoughts and bring me back to what we're doing this all for.

CHAPTER EIGHTEEN

Ryker

Last night was shit.

I didn't sleep more than a few hours, too busy debating whether I should knock on Juliet's door and try to talk this out with her or leave it be.

I came home looking forward to spending the night with my new wife and instead got blindsided by my ex-girlfriend dressed in lingerie in my kitchen and looking to burn the penthouse down... in more ways than one.

A pop of bacon grease hits my bare stomach, but it's a small price to pay for not ruining every shirt I cook breakfast in. I swat at the grease and wipe it off my skin with one hand as I hold my phone to my ear talking with security downstairs.

"Yeah. Can you just make sure that when the moving company gets here, they bring the bed up?" I ask.

I've called security downstairs about the new king-sized bed I just ordered. If Juliet won't sleep with me because of the bed in my room, then it has to go.

I can't blame her for feeling like the bed is "tainted".

If I had to sleep with her in a bed that she's had for over six years and several boyfriends, I'd probably take a chainsaw to the damn thing.

I want Juliet in my bed as often as she'll allow it and if a new bed eliminates undue strain, it's a small price to pay. The cost for the new bed set won't make a dip in my bank account, anyway. And even if it did, she's worth the investment.

"No problem Mr. Haynes. You want to make sure the bed goes to your master bedroom?" he asks to clarify.

"Yes, exactly."

"Do you want them to move the other bed to storage?" the head of security asks.

"No need. They can donate it or trash it."

I add more strips of bacon to the frying pan.

"Very good, sir. I'll draft up a memo for the rest of the team just in case the furniture company shows up when I'm not on shift."

"Thanks," I tell him, and then hang up the phone.

I called up the furniture shop that I bought everything for this penthouse from this morning and asked them to send me their most popular in-stock king-sized bed set and deliver it to my house before I get back from Canada.

I hear Juliet's footsteps emerge from the hallway as I lay my phone on the countertop and continue stirring the eggs.

"Did I just hear you say you ordered a bed?" she asks, sliding onto one of the barstools at the island.

"Yeah. It should be here and set up when we get back from Canada."

I don't turn around. I don't want to make this a dramatic moment. It's simple. The woman I want in my bed doesn't feel comfortable in it, so I ordered a brand-new one that neither of us have slept in with other people.

"Did you do that for me?" she asks.

I have the option of a yes or no answer but honesty seems like the only way to go here.

"Yes," I say simply. "Do you want eggs and bacon?"

I hear her slide off the barstool and walk around the island toward me.

She leans up against the countertop to my right.

"I'm sorry about last night," she says. "I mean, not how I reacted to Amelia but how I closed you out after. Seeing another woman in the penthouse when I walked in... was..."

"You thinking that your mother's prophecy was coming to fruition?" I say, because this is what I thought it was about.

"Yes... I guess so." She nods, glancing down at her platform Keds sneakers. It's the only time I haven't seen her in heels besides barefoot, but I won't get stuck on that when we have bigger things to discuss.

It's not that her pulling away didn't have anything to do with me. It's just that it had more to do with her father and the fear she has that I'll do the same thing. That what her mother tells her is correct.

I get it. Which is why the bed has to go.

"You didn't need to buy a new bed," she says. "Trusting in this area is just hard for me, especially faced with a woman from your past standing in the hallway in lingerie."

I clamp my eyes shut for a second, wishing I could erase that moment between us, but I can't.

If the roles were in reverse and I walked in on a guy practically naked, waiting for my wife to show up, I'd probably have beaten the guy until he was unrecognizable.

I'm just glad I showed up when I did to kick Amelia out before Juliet formed any other ideas about what was going on.

I stop stirring the eggs and drop the spatula on the countertop.

I turn to her and wrap my hand around her hip, pulling her in closer to me. Now getting a good look at her, she's dressed more casually than usual too.

"The new bed is going to be good. It's a clean slate moving forward."

She nods up at me.

"Are you hungry then?" I ask.

"Actually, I have to go. I'm moving my brother in today before we leave for Canada tonight."

Oh shit... right. I forgot about that with my out-of-town schedule and then the shit show of Amelia's surprise visit.

She looks down at her phone. "Oh! I'm going to be late—I have to go. I'll see you later?" she says, and then doesn't wait for my answer.

"Yeah, I'll see you later."

The door closes before I get the words out.

I reach for my phone and fire off two text messages.

If Briggs wants to help, I've got just the thing.

Juliet

It's moving day but I think the person most excited is me.

I walk into my brother's apartment to find most of his things already packed, my mom still shoving as much as she can into the few backpacks that aren't already stuffed to the brim.

Both centers provide the furniture. This makes moving simple since all Jerrin needs is his clothes and the bin in which he keeps all his hobbies.

My brother is sitting watching a televised replay of last week's game.

It's a game in which that Russian defender flattened Ryker, and it's always hard to watch him go down like that.

I anticipate the hit as I look over my brother's shoulder but even knowing it's coming doesn't prepare me for it.

My brother and I both wince the second the hockey stick comes across Ryker's body, and he falls back, hitting his head on the ice.

Ouch.

I'm glad he's home now and gets a few days to recover before he has to play another one, though the stakes are getting higher and higher as the season progresses.

I hear a knock on the open door and turn to find three large men walking through my brother's apartment doorway.

The moment my eyes connect with Ryker's, my heart thumps against my rib cage, my pulse elevating within seconds.

"Hey, are we late?" Ryker asks.

He's dressed in gym sweats and a zip-up hoody. A far more discreet image than the bare-chested man I left this morning in his kitchen.

I watch as Seven and Briggs trail behind him in similar attire, all of them carrying Hawkeyes gear in their hands.

"Hi," I say, my heart racing at the unexpected sight of Ryker showing up here this morning. "What are you doing here?" I ask, smiling up at him.

My head whips quickly to see if my brother just saw who walked in or if he's too immersed in the TV, but when I glance over at him, he is staring at the three hockey players that he watches almost every day.

"I thought you might need some help moving so I brought a couple of guys from the team. We can move couches or a bed... whatever heavy stuff you have."

"We only have a few backpacks left to pack. The new center has all the furniture so we're basically done. But thank you for coming," I tell him.

I can't believe he showed up like this without being asked. He just called his teammates, pulled in a favor that wasn't even for him and showed up.

"You're sure?" he asks.

I nod with a smile and then glance over at my brother.

"Jerrin, do you see who showed up to help us move into your new studio apartment?" I say, though my brother is wider-eyed than I've seen him in years.

Ryker does not know what he just did for my brother and my heart wants to burst with gratitude to the man who keeps showing up for me in one way or another whenever I need him.

Whether I know I need him or not.

"We also brought some housewarming gifts," he says.

Seven and Briggs step forward with not just any Hawkeyes gear but signed jerseys and a signed hockey stick.

"Jerrin, come check this out," I tell him.

He gets up for the sofa and heads for us.

"This is my brother Jerrin and my mom Theresa," I introduce.

"Mom, Jerrin... this is Ryker, Seven, and Briggs."

"Hello," the three men say in unison to my mother.

My mom offers a quick smile but keeps to her far space against the back wall of Jerrin's apartment.

Seven hands my brother the hockey stick, covered in signatures from all the players.

"This is the official one that the Hawkeyes use to play out on the ice," Seven tells him.

"This hockey stick is for me?" my brother asks.

Jerrin looks to Seven, who nods, and then to me.

I give him a reassuring smile.

My eyes wander over to my mother to see if she's witnessing what Ryker and his teammates have brought Jerrin. I see her still packing but these three men, whose presence couldn't be ignored even if you wanted to, have her eyes wandering over occasionally.

Next Briggs steps up with a stack of three official jerseys.

One for Haynes.

One for Wrenley.

And one for Conley.

Their signatures are written across their number on each one.

"These are for you too. Maybe you can take turns wearing them when your sister brings you to a game," Briggs says, handing Jerrin the jerseys that I can guarantee my brother will be wearing one of every day for the rest of the year.

"If you come out for practice one day, we can take you for a tour of the locker room," Seven offers.

"Could we?" My brother turns to me to ask.

"I don't see why not."

I've never considered taking my brother to a home game because he typically doesn't enjoy loud noises and boisterous crowds. It's not that he couldn't handle it if he wanted, but he's never had an interest. The idea of getting my brother to willingly participate in an event like this has me over the moon.

I could kiss Ryker right here and now.

Throw my arms around him and tell him how grateful I am for what he's done for my brother today.

And what he's done for me.

I look to Ryker, who is the last one with his gift. It's a bouquet of mixed flowers. He has a tendency to bring me flowers, but these are a little different.

"Here, Theresa," Ryker says, taking steps toward her. "These are for you."

He outstretches his hand to her, and she takes the bouquet of flowers with a little reluctance.

But once they're in her hands, she can't resist pulling the fragrant flowers to her nose.

She takes a deep inhale of the gorgeous bouquet and then gazes over its arrangement.

"Can we talk for a minute?" he asks her.

Her eyes break away from the flowers in her hand and she studies him for a second.

She doesn't look to me or around the room at any of us.

My mother is one of the most confident women I've ever known and Ryker's request doesn't intimidate her in the least.

She nods in agreement, "Sure."

Ryker turns directly around and heads for the door of my brother's apartment.

I reach out to him as he passes.

"What are you—?"

He reaches out and squeezes my hand quickly.

"Don't worry, I got it," he says, and then releases my hand, his eyes back on the exit with my mom directly behind him.

He steps out of the doorway and into the hall. My mom follows, pulling the door closed to just a crack behind her.

If I know my mother, she's closing the door because she has some choice words to share with Ryker, too, and she either doesn't want me or Jerrin to hear them.

Seven watches the door shut and then turns to Jerrin.

"Hey, the game's on. Mind if we sit and watch it with you?" he asks my brother.

"Yeah, that would be ok," my brother says, laying the jerseys on the back of the couch and pulling Wrenley's jersey over his head and over his thin hooded sweatshirt.

The three of them sit on the couch together, Seven and Briggs on either side. Seven and Briggs give Jerrin a play-by-play of what it was like being out on the ice that day and inside information on other plays on the Hawkeyes.

My brother is on cloud nine and my heart couldn't be any fuller, even with the anxiety of Ryker and my mom out in the hallway.

I take a few steps closer to the closed door.

I know I shouldn't eavesdrop, but I can't help but want to know if their conversation is calm and level or if they're at each other's throats.

It's hard for me to imagine Ryker getting that worked up with my mom. He always seems to stay so level-headed, other than during the fights on the ice. Even kicking Amelia out, he kept calm. My mother, on the other hand, could rip into Ryker with ease if she felt the need to, and I can't let that happen.

If Mom goes off on him, I need to be able to rush out and break it up because I can't let her scare him away.

I hear Ryker's voice first.

"I know you don't like me, Theresa—"

"It's not that I don't like you. And it's nothing personal Ryker, it's just that professional athletes are all the same. You have short attention spans and big egos."

"That's not true. We're not all like that," he argues calmly.

"My daughter is the prize now, but that shiny penny wears off eventually. And what happens when your career ends before you're ready? You can honestly tell me you can turn off the lights on your career and a quiet family life with my daughter will satisfy you? You'll want the spotlight again, and you'll sacrifice her happiness to get it wherever you can with whoever will give it to you."

"You don't know me yet, but if you give me a chance, I'll prove to you that I'm different. I promise you, there is nothing I want more than to make your daughter happy."

I can hear my mother tsk at his response.

"I won't give you my blessing but I won't stand in your way either. My daughter has made her decision and now all I can do is hope that this ends in two years with my daughter not in tears on my living room couch. Can you at least manage that?"

"I can," he says simply.

"Her father did enough damage to her for a lifetime. I don't need her to have more reasons to lack trust," she says, her voice becoming more relaxed like she's sharing a concern more than a warning.

"I won't let that happen. You have my word," he tells her.

"We'll see, won't we?"

Then I hear her footsteps return toward the door and I jump back.

My mother pushes the door open and walks through, her flowers hanging by her side. She doesn't glance up at me as she heads back to her spot against the far window of the apartment to finish backing my brother's last backpack.

Ryker walks in, several feet behind her and not as quickly. Was that conversation defeating? Is it making him rethink things that have happened between us?

My mother made me sound fragile, and though my father has broken my heart worse than anyone else, I'm not made of porcelain.

He gives me a somber smile and then turns to the guys.

"You guys ready to go?" he asks.

He slides his hands into the pockets of his jeans as he turns his eyes on the TV and watches himself score that goal at the end of the third period to win the game. This was even after that huge hit earlier in the game by Petrov.

I remember jumping off the couch and screaming in the living room of his penthouse, wearing my Haynes jersey.

"Yeah, we're ready," Seven says.

Briggs finishes explaining what a breakaway is and how Ryker is one of those rare players who always seems to find a way to get himself alone with the goalie.

Pride bubbles up in me that my husband is one of the best in the league at what he does.

Seven stands up and then so does Briggs.

"We'll see you around, OK?" Briggs tells my brother.

"Get your mom or your sister to bring you out at the end of practice one day and you can hit some pucks with us... if you want," Seven offers.

Ryker walks over to me and slides his hand over my left arm.

"We have to put in some time at the gym. Are you sure you don't need help bring anything down?" he asks.

Seven and Briggs glance around the apartment to see if there is anything they can help with but my mom and I have already been taking down trips to my SUV with my brother's things.

We have two backpacks left to load at most.

"I'm sure."

I turn to Seven and Briggs. "I appreciate you both for coming and bringing Jerrin gifts. This was the best moving day surprise we could have asked for."

My mom pipes up from across the room. "You've made our week," she says.

My mom isn't an ungrateful person and I know she sees what these three men just did for my brother. She's just cautious.

Seven and Briggs walk out first and then Ryker follows behind.

I walk out of the door and into the hallway with them.

"Hey, Ryker?" I say, waiting for him to turn around.

"Yeah?"

I take a couple of steps toward him until I'm flush against him and then push up on my platform Keds and wrap my arms around his neck.

"We'll meet you down at the car," Briggs says, seeing me plastered against Ryker.

Ryker just nods, his hands wrapping around my back. His thumb glides over the hollow of my spine.

"You don't know what you just did for my brother," I say, holding back the emotion I feel for someone taking the time to understand him. "And what you did for me."

"I told you Juliet... this is real, no matter the timeline. I'm here for you when you need me. Just ask me to show up for you and let me prove to you that I will."

I nod, and then he lowers his lips to mine and sets a soft kiss against my mouth.

"Are you packed to leave tonight?" he asks.

"Yes. I had a lot of thinking to do last night so my bags are packed and waiting in my bedroom," I tell him.

I still don't feel great about the way I handled things last night but I can only move forward.

"How many are there?" he asks with a teasing glint in his eye. "Should I have rented a plane just for your luggage?"

I'm happy to see the playful side of Ryker hasn't been squashed by my mother's inability to support us and me shutting down on him last night.

"Can you not handle me, Haynes?"

"I think I proved to you on our wedding night that I'm more than capable of handling you," he says, his eyes hooding and dipping down to my lips again.

"Juliet, these two backpacks are ready to take down," my mother calls out.

Her voice breaks the moment, but I know he and I have a lot to do today before we can leave town tonight so it's just as well that we part ways now.

"Coming, Mom," I tell her.

"I'll see you later."

I release my hold around his neck and his hands graze over my hips as he pulls back.

His slow, lingering touch sends tingles down to my toes.

"Bye," I say.

"Bye, wife."

Then he turns and heads down the hall.

It's my turn to prove to Ryker that I'll show up for him. And I'll do this by going with him to Canada.

I know this trip is important to him, and that he wants to give me a glimpse into this part of his life means something.

CHAPTER NINETEEN

Ryker

Checking in for our flight took less time than I anticipated, mostly because Juliet packed lighter than I expected. Not that I would have cared if she had brought her entire wardrobe. Whatever she wants to bring to make this trip enjoyable for her is fine with me.

After we make it through security, Juliet heads to the coffee shop in the terminal and I head to the bathroom.

My phone rings as I pass through the men's bathroom opening.

I pull my phone from my back pocket to see James's name incoming.

"Hey, James. What's up?" I ask, walking towards the commercial-grade bathroom sinks.

"Have you heard anything from Immigration recently?" he asks, the sound of concern coating every word.

It's not like James not to start a phone conversation with a pleasant greeting before jumping right into business. That might be more concerning than the tone of his voice.

"No, why?" I ask, glancing back at my reflection in the bathroom mirror.

"Because Frank wasn't at the poker game last night, and he hasn't missed a game in years."

That's it?

A gambling addict didn't show up for one poker game?

Maybe it's unusual for Frank's behavior but I wouldn't consider it a cause for concern regarding our visa.

"Why would you think that has anything to do with Juliet and me?"

"I heard some whispers that he's on unpaid leave due to a conflict of interest on a Fiancé visa he pushed through."

Now, that might be a reason to be on alert.

"Did they say who the visa was for?" I ask.

"No. But you'll tell me if immigration reaches out to you?"

"Yeah, I will but—"

"I have a client walking in. I have to go. I'll keep my ear to the ground to listen for what I can find out. Don't forget to call me if they contact you."

Then the phone goes dead on his end.

What the hell?

Where is this coming from?

And how would anyone in immigration suspect that our K-1 visa is fake? I can only hope that the visa he's on leave for is for someone else. If Frank was willing to bend the rules for us, who knows who else he has bent the rules for?

Still, if this has to do with us, we could be looking at criminal charges. And though I don't want to get deported, I'll never forgive myself if Juliet ends up doing prison time for this.

The biggest question here is, what evidence could they have against us?

And I don't want to admit to her that I based our entire arrangement on an immigration officer with a gambling habit and his own motives for pushing us through.

A detail that I chose not to share with her from the beginning.

Until I know all the facts, I don't won't alarm Juliet.

I take a pee and finish up in the bathroom. Thoughts swirling in my mind of anything that we said in our interview that could have been a red flag. The only person I told was Seven and I know he wouldn't say anything to anyone. Could Juliet have told someone who would have called Immigration on us? Or did Frank say something to someone about pushing my visa through so that I can play in the championship?

There are too many possibilities to be sure of where the information leak came from. I'll have to wait and hope that James finds out that Frank's leave has nothing to do with us. That's the best-case scenario.

I wash my hands and then head out of the bathroom to find Juliet.

Heading towards the coffee shop, I spot her walking out with an iced coffee and a big smile on her face the second she sees me. I can see her beginning to trust me finally. I got her into this mess so it's my responsibility to make sure no harm comes to her.

If it comes down to it, I'll do whatever it takes.

Juliet

It's just past ten o'clock at night when we touch down and get my luggage from the airport carousel.

The flight to Vancouver from Seattle was a short one... really short, and Ryker couldn't believe how light I packed for this trip.

I made it my personal goal to bring the least amount of clothes that I've ever brought on an overnight stay. With only three nights away, it isn't like I need to bring a lot.

Ryker told me he lives in a suburban house in Vancouver, but he failed to mention that it's far bigger than his already large penthouse and is situated in a gated community.

"Thanks for the lift," Ryker tells our rideshare driver as we exit his car.

Ryker walks to the back and pulls out my only large rolling luggage while I bring a small bag I carried on with my laptop and a few other things in case I have time to work while I'm here.

"This is nice," I tell him as we walk up to his house, the cool wind blowing all around us and a light dusting of snow still hidden between the blades of grass in his yard and on the roofs of all the houses around us.

The snow doesn't look fresh though. Maybe from yesterday or the day before but even in the darkness of the night, the snow on the mountain tops around Vancouver sparkle in the moonlight.

"Thanks," he says. He inputs the security code to the house into the pad and then the door unlocks. "It feels good to have roots planted here."

He pushes the door open and then walks into the dark house first. It's one of the first times that he hasn't had me enter a room before him but since there's always a possibility that a burglar is in the house, it's better he goes first.

He walks in and turns on the foyer lights for us to see our way around.

The floors are beautiful and made of some kind of stone while the ceiling in the entry reaches to the second story.

The house is mostly open concept on the bottom floor with a living room, dining room, enclosed den, and kitchen all within view from the entry. A large staircase sits just beyond and I assume that's where the bedrooms are.

With all the excitement of today with my brother's big move, and then flying, I'm exhausted and ready to go to bed.

But the question is, whose bed?

I yawn as I look around at the space.

"Are you tired?" he asks.

"Yeah. I could use a pillow and a comforter about now."

I almost fell asleep on the plane ride over but the wind was tossing us around so much that as soon as my eyes drifted closed, the plane would jolt, making me grab Ryker's wrist a few times.

He smiled over at me each time, the picture of cool and calm.

"We have a big day tomorrow and I'll be skating all day so bed is probably the right call."

I follow him up the flight of stairs while Ryker carries my big bag with him.

"My sister came by the house earlier to turn the heat on and put a few things in the fridge for the morning. If you're hungry or anything, you're welcome to whatever is downstairs."

"Thank you but I should be sleeping like a baby in about five minutes."

We walk down a long hallway with at least six different doors, though it's too dark to know if they're guest bedrooms or bathrooms.

Ryker stalls toward the end of the hall, a door on either side of him.

"What's wrong?" I ask.

"I'm not sure if I should put your things in my room to the right, or the guest bedroom to the left."

Today was the last day of my cycle but just to be safe, I'd want to wait until tomorrow anyway, and we both need our rest for the full-day tournament tomorrow.

Though I'll admit that I haven't stopped thinking about our wedding night.

"We're going straight to bed, right? So does it even matter where I sleep tonight?" I say, making an argument for it not being a big deal if we sleep separately.

"No, I guess you're right... it doesn't matter where you sleep," he says, turning to his right and into his room with my luggage.

I grin to myself as I follow him into his room.

He sets my luggage on the bed for me so that I can get all of my things.

I unzip my bag while I listen to Ryker in his walk-in closet undressing.

I grab one of my old favorite pairs of pajama bottoms, an old t-shirt I've been wearing for eight years. Then I pull out my travel makeup bag with my toothbrush and makeup remover and head to the bathroom to get ready.

Ten minutes later, I emerge, clear-faced, with peppermint breath and no period in sight.

Ryker turns when he hears the bathroom door open, likely waiting his turn in only a pair of basketball shorts and no shirt. Does this man not own a t-shirt? But I know he does.

His eyes dip down my body until they stop at my breasts. I shoot a look down my body as well, wondering if there's some gaping hole where my nipples are poking out or something, but everything appears fine.

"Is something wrong with my shirt?" I ask.

"University of Washington Men's Rowing," he reads.

Oh... right.

"It was an ex-boyfriend. He left it at my place and it's so comfortable that I turned it into my pajama shirt."

But I can't remember the last time I've even thought of Oliver when wearing this shirt.

Ryker turns and walks away, back into his walk-in closet, and emerges with a black Hawkeyes t-shirt.

"What's that?" I ask as he comes closer.

"A new pajama shirt. This one is going in the trash," he says, staring at the grey UW crew shirt I'm wearing.

Jealous, is he?

I have to admit that after the Amelia incident, it's nice to see that Ryker feels as warm about my exes and I feel about his.

"But I like this shirt," I argue.

"You'll like this one more," he says, offering the black shirt with turquoise writing over the front.

I lift my arms in the air and dare him to take my shirt off.

He eyes me for a minute and then licks his lips. Tossing the new shirt he's giving me on the bed, he grips the old college t-shirt at the bottom of the hem and pulls up. In one swift action, he has my shirt off and his eyes connect to the thin sleeping bra that I'm wearing underneath.

The sparkle in his eyes dims a little the minute he realizes that I'm not bare underneath.

I giggle as I walk around him and grab the shirt off the bed that he pulled from his closet.

He walks up behind me and snakes an arm around my middle, pulling my backside against his front.

"That wasn't very nice. You set me up for that," he says, though I can see in the floor-length mirror on the opposite side of the wall that he's grinning.

He knows I got him as punishment for making me toss my favorite shirt, but the look on his face made this a fair trade.

I pull the new shirt over my head and push my arms through. The shirt even smells a little like him, plus the smell of fresh sheets. I take a deep inhale and now I'm even sleepier than before.

"I'd say we're even now."

I pull out of his hold and crawl into the side of the bed that Ryker doesn't use.

He watches me get under the sheets and then he turns back to the bathroom and closes the door.

I listen to the sounds of the toilet flush and then his electric toothbrush, until finally, I'm out cold.

My dreams fill with an alternate ending to Ryker pulling off my shirt.

One where I wasn't wearing a sleep bra.

And one that *comes* with a happier ending.

CHAPTER TWENTY

Ryker

This morning was a mad rush to get out of the house so that we had enough time to go through the coffee shop drive-through for breakfast and Juliet's coffee.

We pull up to the outdoor rink for the charity event.

Banners and balloons hang all around the outdoor space.

"Looks like they went all out this year," I say, opening my truck door and sliding out.

"This is a bigger event than I pictured," Juliet says, her eyes wandering over the parking lot to see the hundreds of cars filling the massive ice park grounds.

"It's grown over the years since we first started. There should be over a thousand spectators here today."

This is one of the biggest parks in the city, and during the winter months, the city puts in three full NHL-sized rinks.

The city hosts peewee hockey tournaments, ice skating competitions, and a city curling league that meets a few times a week.

In addition to all of that, they host the boys and girls club hockey tournament that a lot of ex-pro and semi-pro players from all around the area attend to bring in sponsorship and money for the kids. Its popularity pays for almost the entire year to keep the boys and girls center open for after-school programs and grants for families that can't afford to pay.

It's a program my dad believed in and he had us kids playing in the tournament as soon as we all were old enough to clear eligibility. Now, me and my siblings still play in honor of my dad.

I walk to the back of the truck and get my duffel bag out. I sling the bag across my chest and then grab my hockey skates and close the door.

Juliet is already out and waiting for me at the end of the truck, her iced coffee in one hand.

Seeing her in jeans, stylish snow boots with faux fur lining, a puffy down jacket and a beanie with a matching fur ball on the top has me smiling. With the mountains of Vancouver as her backdrop, I can't help but want to ask her again if she could see herself living here one day. But she and I haven't agreed to anything more than the next 730 days until my green card is official.

Jumping ten steps ahead with Juliet will only make her leerier, and I already know her stance on it. Her wide-eyed expression in the immigration office when I mentioned starting a family here someday after retirement made it clear.

Still, my chest tightens at how natural Juliet looks like she fits here.

How she fits with me.

I walk down the side of my truck and she follows next to me as we head for the park.

"Anything you should prepare me for when it comes to your family?" she asks.

"Only that my mom doesn't know that this is temporary so if she starts making plans years in advance, just go with it. And if she asks when we're going to start a family... which she will," I say, lifting a brow at Juliet. "... tell her it's not in our plans until after I retire. That will be the easiest way to get her off your case and it keeps us on the same page."

It's not far from the truth. If I was going to have kids, I'd like to wait until my four years are up and I'm back in Canada, anyway.

"And if she asks how we met?"

"Just tell her the truth. Tell her we met in the parking lot outside of the stadium and I caught you before you slipped on your ass. You fell for me instantly," I tease.

She slaps my arm with the force of a fruit fly and then giggles.

"Right, because who couldn't resist your obvious charms?" she says sarcastically. "You practically threw a fit when I didn't know who you were."

I can't wipe the stupid smile from my face as we walk through the parking lot. We've come a long way since the first time we met. It's crazy to imagine that only a week ago, I ran into a gorgeous raven-haired woman in the middle of the night outside of the stadium. And now she's in my hometown, about to meet my family.

"That's not true. It just seemed unlikely since you sat in the stands, and I played a full game in front of you. Plus, you were wearing a jacket with my jersey number on the back," I remind her.

"Well, if you're going to be a stickler for the details..." she jokes.

I can already see the stands from here and the first of the three ice rinks up ahead.

Four figures stand out in our team colors. The same colors we've worn since my dad picked them out years ago. Only now, the back of our jerseys say: "In loving memory of Coach Haynes."

My sister and my three brothers stand facing each other, waiting for our game to begin.

"Hey," I call out, raising a hand to get their attention.

Juliet and I step up over the sidewalk and head through the short chain link fence that surrounds the large park.

My youngest brother Austin sees me first and gives a nod, and then Camden, Everett, and Harper all turn their heads to see us walking up.

"If it isn't the prodigal son," my oldest brother Camden says.

"Wasn't he the favorite?" I toss back.

"You wish, big shot."

We embrace as Camden pats my back. "Good to have you home, brother," he says.

And then Harper squeezes in for a hug next.

I make my rounds through my siblings quickly.

"So you must be Juliet? I'm Everett," my second oldest brother says, walking over and hugging her too. "We hug in this family. Didn't Ryker warn you?" he asks.

She hugs him back and I can see her genuine smile over his shoulder.

She looks over to me when he releases her. "No, he didn't but I like a good hug myself."

I'm relieved to see that Juliet is already warming up to the family.

"That's Camden, Austin, and Harper," I tell Juliet, pointing to each of my siblings.

Before any of my other brothers or Harper can get a hug in next, we're interrupted by my mother's voice.

"What about me?" she asks behind the wall of six-foot-plus tall Haynes men.

My mother, barely five foot two inches, pushes through a crack between Austin and Camden and comes barreling at me like a freight train.

"And that's my mom, Annie," I tell Juliet quickly before I get assaulted in a bear hug.

"Ryker!" she says, wrapping her arms around my middle and giving me the Annie Haynes signature squeeze, her head laying against my chest as she does with all of my brothers as well.

"It's good to see you, Mom."

"I'm so glad you're home," she says, pulling back to look up at me. "Now where is my new daughter-in-law you brought me?"

My mom's eyes are lit up like a kid on Christmas morning.

"He didn't pick her up at from the department store on his way over, Mom," Everett quips.

My mom ignores him. She's gotten good at selective hearing with five kids.

She searches around us and the minute her eyes latch onto Juliet, she gasps.

"Oh my gosh," my mother says, walking over to Juliet. "You're gorgeous." My mother beams.

"I know, right?" Harper says. "Now you can be honest Juliet, was my brother wearing a bag over his head when you agreed to date him? Or did he catfish you into thinking he's a looker before you agreed to marry him and then you felt too bad to hurt his feelings so you went through with it out of pity?"

Everyone laughs except for my mother, who grabs Juliet's free hand. She has plans for my wife and none of us are invited.

"Ignore these baboons and come sit with me and your sisters-in-law," she says, tugging Juliet with her.

I'd wondered where Camden, Austin, and Everett's wives were but it makes sense that they're probably already sitting down, getting my niece and nephews settled with snacks before we get started.

Harper's husband is in Toronto on a work trip so he'll be the only one Juliet doesn't get to meet but Harper and her husband are in Seattle a few times a year so she'll get her chance.

Juliet sends me a wide-eyed look as my mom pulls her back through the space between Austin and Everett, but at least it's accompanied by a smile.

"Bye, new sis," Camden calls out.

They all chuckle at my mom's blatant show that we're all old news to her. She has a new shiny daughter-in-law, and I guarantee she's about to show her off to all the ladies in her garden club who have come to everything my family and I have done since we were kids.

"Mom! I don't get to say goodbye before you take her away?" I call after them, but my mom has already disappeared toward the bleachers set up for the mass of visitors, all filling up at all three ice rinks.

"I don't think Mom reacted that way with any of our wives," Austin says.

"Told you... prodigal son," Camden says.

"Did you mean protégé son?" Harper says, coming to my defense with a smirk.

Camden and Everett made it to the minors and played for a while. On the other hand, Austin had different goals and went straight on to become a heart surgeon. The asshole is brilliant and I'm glad he didn't take the pressure our father applied on him. He probably could have made it to the NHL with me if he wanted.

Camden's buddy from his college hockey days starts heading our way from across the ice. Our sixth player and our goalie—the position my father used to play.

The announcer asks the two teams to prepare, and I head over to the bench to tie up my skates.

A few minutes later, I skate out to do the coin toss with a member of the opposing team.

My eyes search out the beautiful woman in the crowd who's wearing my ring.

I find her quickly and see that my mom has the two of them cuddled up under a pile of blankets with my niece and a warm thermos of hot cocoa that she must have brought from home for each of them.

Juliet is crowded by a gaggle of older women all probably hitting her with rapid-fire questions about us and our plans, but from here she's smiling... and so is my mom.

I see my nephews all running across the top of the bleachers and my sisters-in-law all trying to wrangle the three small boys.

Damn, it's good to be home.

Juliet sees me watching her and sends out a little wave.

I wave back.

Having her here to support me is exactly what this marriage should be about. We take turns showing up for one another and that's how I hope things continue from now on.

A few minutes later the referee tosses the coin, and the game is on.

Chapter Twenty-One

Juliet

Seeing Ryker out on the ice, playing with his family—I've never seen him laugh so much.

He's in his element here and I get now why being home is so important to him. Why being without his family is so crucial to his happiness.

After every goal he makes, he skates by close to me and smacks his hockey stick against the sideboards to let me know that he sees me. Butterflies break out every time he lets me know that he's watching me too.

As the tournament goes on, Ryker's team continues to advance up the bracket. Depending on who they play next, we move from rink to rink to watch them, taking a break in between to stop at the snack shack with Ryker's niece and nephews, adding the occasional potty break to mix things up.

Getting a chance to meet Sienna, Arie, and Kali—Ryker's sisters-in-law—gives me more of a glimpse into how caring and inviting his family really is.

I have no idea how many people I met while watching the tournament. However, it felt like I barely got to see any of the games with the influx of people that Annie introduced me to.

Their excitement to see Ryker settled is heartwarming and I'm starting to see the appeal of a place that has such a loving community around it.

Annie and I wait in our spot on the bleachers at the end of the last game as visitors start to usher out to their cars in the parking lot.

Our team lost the last game by a single goal in overtime, but they played well the entire day.

The sun is settling now over the beautiful mountains, and it will be dark in less than an hour.

Finally, Ryker emerges from the bathroom after changing into jeans and boots.

"Do you want to head to the bar? It's where all the players from today are heading and it has great BBQ. It's sort of a tradition."

"Sure, that sounds fun. And I could use some dinner."

Annie and I head down off the bleaches and follow Ryker out to the parking lot.

We say our goodbyes since Annie isn't coming to the bar and opting for a warm bath before the 'craziness of tomorrow'.

Her words have me a little concerned since today seemed pretty crazy to me. What could tomorrow bring that requires her to take a long bath first in preparation?

We climb into the truck and then head for the bar.

"My sister will already be there, but the guys are going to meet us after they drop the wives and kids off at their houses."

"Your family is great. I don't think I've ever been around such a big family that seems so close."

Now, seeing his family in action as they show up for one another, I have a better understanding of why being here is so important to him.

"I got lucky and I won't take family for granted again," he says.

I know his guilt about the time he missed with his father is still something that weighs on him heavily. But I'm sure if his father could see the legacy he left behind in his kids, he'd be proud of Ryker.

Pulling into the bar parking lot, it's already plum full, but Ryker finds a parking spot and we head inside.

The building is free standing, with wooden sides and a rustic feeling. A set of cow long horns adorn the front door. I'm guessing this is a cowboy style bar.

And guessing by the loud country music that could be heard as far out as the parking lot, line dancing is probably in full swing.

Ryker opens the door for me and I'm assaulted by the smell of peanuts, beer and BBQ. I take a step into the dimly lit bar as Ryker takes a step in behind me.

The bar's rough-cut wide plank floors and matching walls with old western saddles, cowboy ropes, and all sort of other decorations give this bar an obvious identity.

In the middle of the bar is a large square space with overhead lights where a few dozen people are all dancing to the same line dance.

"Come on, let's find Harper. She probably already got us a table."

He opens his hand up for me to take to keep me close in this packed bar, and I do, happy to get to touch him.

The second our fingers touch, my hand tingles everywhere his presses against it.

I mindlessly follow him, not even bothering to look for Harper. I'd blindly follow this man wherever he leads and maybe that's something that should scare me, but right now it doesn't.

He catches sight of her and pulls me with him.

"Did you order starters yet?" he asks her, pulling out one of the barstools for me around the six-top table that Harper saved for our group still on their way to meet us.

"Yeah, an order of fried pickles and two orders of garlic bread knots."

I take a seat and then he pulls out the barstool next to me and takes a seat.

"Have you heard from any of the guys yet?" he asks.

"Camden is on his way, Everett is getting the boys to sleep first, and Austin is bailing because Kali is having really bad Braxton Hicks from being on her feet all day."

I noticed that Kali seemed pretty far along. She said it was their first, and that Austin is a bit of a helicopter dad already. From my point of view, considering my father doesn't even want to see his kids, a helicopter dad is better than no dad. But I also get that when you're the one that's pregnant, getting bossed around to sit more and drink more water can get on your already fragile nerves.

Harper's name gets called over the loudspeaker for a food order pickup.

"I'll get it," Ryker tells her. "Just relax. You played a good game today, little sister."

This is the part of Ryker that I see so much at home. The Ryker that carried all of my luggage up when I moved in and the one that opens doors and shows up at my brother's apartment with gifts.

Seeing it here again is evidence that it's not just something he does for me... it's who he is.

He turns to me next. "I'm getting a beer, want something?"

"Water to start would be great."

"One water, coming up."

He turns and heads behind us to the pick-up window.

"How do you like Vancouver so far?" Harper asks over the music.

"It's beautiful, and it feels a lot like home," I tell her.

With Seattle being less than three hours away, and Vancouver also being on the water, it's not surprising that it feels so similar here.

"I like Seattle too. I'm there a lot to curate art shows for my company's clients," she tells me.

"You're an art curator? That sounds like a pretty cool job. How did you end up in that field?"

Seeing her in full hockey gear, I wouldn't have guessed that's what she does for a living.

"I fell in love with art during an art history elective course my freshman year," she says, taking a sip of her red wine. "What do you do… besides put up with my brother?" she says with a grin behind her glass.

"I'm a party planner. Mostly weddings and birthday parties, but we just got a new larger account doing events for the Hawkeyes."

Her eyebrows raise for a second, seemingly impressed with the new addition to my portfolio, though I'm sure she assumes that Ryker got it for me… which he did.

"So, you do corporate events?" she asks.

"We can do anything."

Between Shawnie and I, we can pull off any event, and with the new Hawkeyes event coming up, I'm looking forward to showing off our new skill set.

"Would you be interested in art gallery openings?" she asks. "It wouldn't be every time I have a showing but occasionally my boss wants a big media splash for an artist and he likes to go a little bigger with the party."

She's asking me to decorate for an art opening? This is right up Shawnie's alley and when I tell her, she's going to be thrilled.

"We would love to," I tell her, reaching for my card in my purse and handing it to her.

"Great. I have an event in a couple of months that I need help with, so I'll be in touch."

"Hungry?" I hear Ryker's voice over the music as he comes up behind me with plates of hot food.

Ryker pushes the plates to the middle of the table and Harper and I immediately dive into the fried pickles, the oil from the fryer still a little too hot to eat.

The music from the DJ all of a sudden starts to lower as the last song ends.

"I've got a request tonight from one of the bar guests who tells me we have a set of newlyweds in the house that eloped and didn't get their first dance..." the DJ says over the mic.

A few whistles and claps ring out around the bar.

Instant shock sets over me as my stomach feels like it just lunged into my throat. I cough at the tiniest piece of fried pickle that I just inhaled down the wrong tube.

I smack my chest twice and then shoot a look at Ryker.

Did he put the DJ up to this?

But he returns the same look of raised brow bewilderment so it couldn't have been him. He searches the room like he's expecting to find another newly married couple who eloped, but I'd bet money that there's only one.

Us.

"...if I can have everyone exit the floor, for one song we'll bring them out and play them a little something special."

My hands turn instantly clammy and perspiration forms across my forehead. Somehow, when it comes to Ryker, I keep getting pushed into the spotlight. The first time when he proposed on the ice in front of screaming fans, and now again, in front of drunk hockey players.

I'm so much better behind the scenes, running around and making other people shine on their big day.

"Can I get Mr. and Mrs. Ryker Haynes out on the dance floor?"

"What good fortune you two have," Harper says.

I whip a look around to see her grinning devilishly back at us.

"You did this?" he asks Harper.

"Every bride deserves her first dance, and you took that from her. Now you're giving it back," she tells him.

My hands begin to shake a little at the thought of dancing in front of all these people in the middle of the dance floor, but the idea of being in Ryker's arms when I'm doing it calms me. He's the only one I want to do this with.

"Come on, wife," Ryker says, holding out his hand. "Dance with me."

His eyes are warm, not a stitch of nerves in his gaze, but he plays in front of a packed stadium several times every week. This is his bread and butter. And he loves it. He might be a hockey player, but I've seen him play to the crowd—he's also an entertainer.

He pulls me gently behind him and out onto the dance floor.

Flutters of excitement break loose at the thought of our first dance. Harper's right, we didn't get one. There are a lot of firsts and wedding traditions that Ryker and I skipped.

Brett Young—In Case You Didn't Know starts playing the minute we reach the middle of the linoleum flooring.

The lights above us make it feel like we're under a spotlight with the people in the bar harder to make out.

Ryker pulls his right hand around my left side and then takes my right hand into his as he begins to sway with me. I let him lead as my left hand travels up his right arm and settles on his shoulder.

I exhale at the sensation of being held safe in his arms. The safest place I've felt in so long. I just hope my heart is safe here too.

His eyes lock onto mine and everything around us drowns in a sea of black. In only a second, Ryker changes an uncomfortable experience into a moment I'll remember as our first dance.

We find our groove as Ryker sways me back and forth in a slow circle, his eyes not breaking from mine for even a moment. He's a good dancer, but that doesn't surprise me. What surprises me is how much I don't want this song to end.

"Did I ruin everything?" he asks softly.

The question takes me off guard. Did he ruin everything? If anything, he's made everything better.

My business.

My brother's living situation.

"How could you have ruined everything?"

"I should have given you a real wedding, Juliet. You're not the kind of woman that I should've hidden away in a courthouse with two witnesses. I should have done this right from the beginning."

There's almost sadness in his eyes as he speaks. A regret for how he handled our nuptials. But I don't see why he should feel that way when we had agreed to it.

"We agreed to a courthouse wedding. It's ok—"

"It wasn't ok... and it's still not ok. My sister was right."

"It was just a wedding. It was supposed to be fake," I say, but the minute I say it, I regret it.

He flinches at the word fake, and I don't blame him, because now... nothing about us feels fake.

"Does this marriage still feel fake to you?" he asks.

"No," I say. "Nothing about us feels fake anymore."

He searches my eyes for a second and then asks another question.

"Do you like being my wife, Juliet?"

This answer only requires one tiny word, but the word means so much.

"Yes."

Ryker lowers his head and kisses me, releasing my hand and wrapping both of his arms around my back to pull me closer to him. I press into his kiss, giving back as much as I receive, running my hands over his shoulders as he continues to sway us in a circle.

Finally, the song ends and the crowd cheers.

Ryker pulls his lips reluctantly from mine. My eyelashes flutter open to find him waiting for me patiently.

"Congratulations, you two," the DJ says. "Alright, you crazy people. Let's get back on the dance floor and get this party going."

The music returns to its high energy as people rush back onto the dance floor, passing us as we head for the dance floor exit.

Ryker leads me back to our table where Harper is no longer sitting.

We both look around and find Camden, Everett and Harper pouring over the BBQ menu.

"I'm going to order us some food. Do you have anything specific you want?" he asks, a smile still on his face.

I don't know if that permanent smile is from our kiss or from my answer but it looks so good on him, I hope it stays.

"You know this place best, and I'm not picky. Whatever you get will be fine."

He leans in and gives me a chaste kiss before heading toward his siblings who are standing by the ordering window with menus in their hands.

I turn my barstool back to the dancing patrons and tap my toe to the music. I take a fried pickle and dip it in some delicious homemade fry sauce.

Yum, these are so good. I've always passed over the fried pickles at pubs I've been to in Seattle but now I'll have to give them a try in the future.

"Hi," I hear a voice say just to the left of me. "Is this seat taken?

CHAPTER TWENTY-TWO

Ryker

"You two looked good out there," Harper says as I walk up.

"Thanks for that," I tell her honestly.

She's like the best damn wingman that I didn't know I needed.

She lifts an eyebrow like she's surprised by my reaction.

"Happy to help."

Then she turns to my brothers. "Are we just going to order a bunch of different things on the menu and share?"

The guys all nod and start listing things on the menu that sound good.

A text dings on my phone, and I reach in my back pocket and pull it out.

> **Amelia:** You're crazy if you think this little scheme of yours is going to work.

Goddamn it... why the hell does she keep popping up?

> **Ryker:** There's no scheme. And lose my number.

I text quickly back. The last thing I need is Amelia causing problems between Juliet and me.

> **Amelia:** You forget that I know too much.

Shit, I guess she does.

My chest starts to tighten when I think about what Amelia might decide to do with that information. It wouldn't get her far with me, but if she's vindictive enough, she might use this to get me deported.

I don't give a shit about what happens to me, but if my ex ends up sending Juliet to prison for this, I'll never forgive myself.

At this point, it's Amelia's word against ours. Yet somehow, that doesn't bring me much comfort.

> **Ryker:** Is that a threat?

> **Amelia:** Only a reminder.

> **Ryker:** You can say whatever you want about me, but if you come after my wife, you'll wish you hadn't.

I block her number and then slide my phone back into my pocket.

I'm no longer hungry and the idea of losing Juliet to divorce has shifted to the fear of losing her to prison.

With Frank on leave and no new information from James, this text message from Amelia has me even more on the edge.

The need to be close to her—to show her how much I want her—to get her under me, blazes through my body.

When I look over to the beautiful woman waiting for me to return to the bar table, I see someone else at the table I don't recognize. And I don't like the way he's looking at her like he thinks he has a shot at taking her home.

A primal instinct to claim and protect what's mine from Amelia and the asshole sitting too close to my wife burns in my chest, and before I can think, I start making my way toward the table. I'm ready and willing to toss her over my shoulder and haul her out of here to get her alone.

The threat of losing Juliet feels too real.

Juliet

"Oh I'm sorry, I'm married," I say, lifting my hand to show him the ring.

Though I'm not sorry at all. He may be a good-looking guy but he's no Ryker.

He pulls the barstool out that Ryker was sitting on before our dance and takes a seat. "That's fine, I don't mind."

Yuck.

"Well, I'm sure he'll mind. And you're in his seat," I tell him, hoping he'll get the hint that my husband is in the bar and should leave before Ryker sees him.

But he grins instead.

"You're the most beautiful woman in this bar. All I want to do is come by and say hi. Is that a crime?"

"Depends on what country you're in." The deep timber of my husband's voice comes from directly over my shoulder.

I look back over my shoulder to find Ryker staring daggers at the guy sitting in his spot, his sage green eyes darkening to a deeper hue than I've ever seen before.

I've seen Ryker angry on the ice, but I've never seen it up close. He always seems so calm, even when he's upset. Like when he kicked Amelia out of the penthouse.

"She told you she's married. I think it's best you leave."

"We were just talking, man," the guy says, putting up his hands and standing up from the bar stool.

He finally got the message. However, Ryker had to deliver it.

"Don't come anywhere near my wife again," he warns.

"Fuck... ok, I got it," the guy says, and starts walking away.

Ryker stands in the same place, and even in the dimness of the bar, I can see his heart beating wildly at the pulse point of his neck.

I put my hand on Ryker's arm.

"Ryker, it's fine. Just come sit with me," I say.

But he ignores my request.

"Come with me," he says back.

"Where are we going?"

"Just come with me, please," he says, opening his hand and offering it up for me to take.

The vulnerability in his eyes has me lifting my hand off his arm and placing it in his.

He guides me carefully off the barstool and then leads me through the bar, past table after table until we near the bathrooms.

He turns into the alcove where the men's and women's bathrooms are.

"We're going to the bathroom?"

He pushes through the men's bathroom with my hand still in his.

"Anyone in here?" he asks.

No one answers.

He pulls me in further and then closes the bathroom door, sliding the thin metal lock across the door to keep everyone out.

"Ryker, what has gotten into you, and what if someone needs to use the restroom?"

"They can piss outside. The drive home will take too long." He barely gets the words out before he turns to me, cupping my face in his hands, his warm full lips descending onto mine and sealing our mouths together in a kiss more possessive than any kiss he's given me before.

I grip onto his wrists on either side of my face as he backs me up against the bathroom sinks. He lifts me up and sets my ass on the bathroom counter, not breaking our connection for a second as his tongue demands entry between my lips.

The smell of his spicy deodorant, mixed with the sweat from today's tournament, and the taste of the IPA beer he was drinking, floods my senses with him and only him.

My thighs open and he steps between them, pulling my ass toward him, and plastering me hard against his erection.

"You're beautiful, Juliet... so fucking beautiful," he says between his kisses. "And seeing someone think they can take you from me drives me fucking insane."

Hearing him say those words... that someone taking me from him is an unbearable thought, warms my body all over. Wet heat dampens my panties at how he wants me.

"He couldn't take me from you. I wouldn't have gone," I assure him against his mouth, lifting my hands to run through his hair, gripping tight to pull his mouth closer to mine.

I wasn't done with that kiss out on the dance floor and I don't think he was either. Having this moment with him is all I want, though I wish we were back at his house in the suburbs instead of in the boys' bathroom.

But that won't stop me from letting him take whatever he wants from me right now ... and I hope it's everything.

I can feel his hard cock between us as I begin to rock against him.

He growls at the friction as he pushes harder against me, dominating my mouth as he shows me how he'd fuck me if we didn't have clothing between us.

"I need to get inside you, Juliet. I need to have you," he begs. "Right now."

A shiver cascades down my back at his admission.

"I need to know that you're mine," he says against my lips.

"I am yours," I say. "Until this is over, I'm only yours."

The idea of this being over in a matter of two years is a painful thought but that conversation can be had another time. I don't want to veer away from what's happening between us. I don't want to break this spell that's come over him.

I love that he wants me so badly that he couldn't wait one more minute. And that the drive home would take too long, though it couldn't be more than twenty minutes.

Right now, all I want is for Ryker to do what he's begging me for. To take me against the bathroom counter and show me who I belong to.

I'm desperate for him and he's the only one that can satisfy this craving to be overtaken until I'm gasping for oxygen and pleading for release.

"I couldn't fucking think when I saw him sitting next to you. How the hell am I going to survive seeing you with someone else when you leave me in two years?" he asks.

He's struggling with this too. I want to tell him to toss out the agreement, that this feels as real as he told me it should, but that conversation shouldn't be had in the men's bathroom of a bar while we're dry humping on the countertop.

"Don't think about that right now. Just be with me. Stay in the moment."

I tug his hair tighter, bringing him as close as physically possible, but there's no way for us to get any closer, not without him burying his hard cock inside of me.

A loud thud echoes inside the bathroom. And I instantly grip onto Ryker tighter, flashing a look at the door to make sure it didn't open.

An unsuspecting bargoer is trying to use the restroom.

"Bathroom closed for cleaning. Go outside," Ryker yells, and then his mouth descends back on me, working his way down my neck.

His hands release my jaw and clutch the hem of my shirt.

I'm reluctant to suggest going home but I feel a little guilty taking up the bathroom when people are three beers deep.

"Maybe we should go home and let people use the bathroom," I say, halfheartedly.

"Not until you scream my name and I make you remember who you belong to. After that, no asshole is going to confuse that you're taken and well fucked."

He continues working his way down my neck and toward my chest. His hot, wet mouth and teeth leave a delicious trail of marks on me as he goes.

"I didn't tell him he could sit."

I feel it's important to clarify that I never wanted the guy to stay. I never would have entertained his advances. Ryker needs to know that.

"The next time a man tries to sit next to you... just ask him if he values his life."

A pang of desire fills my panties with more wet arousal until I know they're dripping wet for him now.

Besides tonight, I've only seen Ryker lose his cool on the ice. But seeing him take out an ice hockey player in past games already tells me that although Ryker is even-keeled most of the time, there's a sharp edge to him if someone causes undue harm and messes with something that's his. And that sharp edge... cuts.

"I'll be sure to tell them that my husband doesn't play nice with others," I say.

"That's a good girl." His deep timber voice is low and sexy.

I watch as Ryker hooks a finger into the top of my black long sleeve underlayer and pulls it down over my chest to get access to as much skin as possible. The shirt gives enough to offer him a view of the top of my breast. I'm happy that I wore my best push up bra today even though I planned on being under layers of clothing all day.

He groans as his mouth finds the swell of my breast but it's not enough for him... or for me. I need more.

More friction between my thighs.

More of his hot mouth.

He reaches for the hem of my shirt and I lift my arms, letting him pull the wicking material up over my head.

He discards the shirt on the counter and then hooks a finger into my bra, yanking it down until my nipple pops free. He launches forward, taking my hard nub into his mouth—swirling his tongue over and over until I whimper in agony at the pulsating of my clit.

"I need your cock," I sob. "Please, Ryker."

His finger releases my bra but his mouth remains as his hands reach for my jeans.

With expert precision, he gets my jeans unbuttoned and un-zipped. In one fluid motion, he yanks my pants down to my boots.

He doesn't even bother to look between us—he knows my panties are soaked and my body is ready for him. Instead, he keeps his mouth on my nipple, ringing out pleasure from between my lips.

He pulls back for a second, the coolness of the air around us chilling my wet nipple. He reaches for his wallet and takes out a condom, pushing his wallet back into his jeans pocket.

His mouth returns to driving me crazy as my head falls back—my eyes fluttering closed to the sensation.

I hear his pants unzip and the foil of the condom ripping open.

I reach down to feel him and find his cock covered in latex. He hisses as I grip ahold of him, feeling his power in my hand.

"How does that feel?" he asks.

"So good," I pant, my heartbeat almost through my chest at how close I am to feeling him stretch me open again.

"How bad do you want it?"

Another person attempts to open the door with a loud thud but this time I'm too entranced to care.

"Get lost, we're busy in here."

"But I gotta shit," the voice says, muffled behind the door.

"Invest in adult diapers," Ryker shoots back.

Ryker's mouth connects back with mine and then he reaches around the base of his cock. I release my hold on him as Ryker presses forward toward me.

He reaches down between my thighs and notches his thick tip against my center. I gasp as he rolls himself through my arousal, coating his cock so that it slips in easily.

I don't think that anyone has ever gotten me as wet as Ryker has. My body is addicted to him like nothing I've ever experienced.

"Answer the question, Juliet. How bad do you want it?" he asks, holding his cock in place at my entrance.

"So bad that I'll do anything you ask if you give it to me."

His eyelids hood and his eyes lock onto mine.

"Then promise me, no one else," he says.

"No one else," I repeat, my voice shaky with need.

He grants me my wish and presses into me. I moan out as I feel his girth fill my entrance. He doesn't give me a little at a time like the first time we were together. I don't think he has the willpower for slow this time and I feel the same.

In a matter of seconds, he's thrusting so deep that he's almost completely inside of me. My body opens for him like it knows him—stretching to accommodate his size.

"Promise me," he says, as he gasps for more air.

"I promise, Ryker." I pant, gripping around his shoulders as he buries himself from root to tip.

He groans out as his jaw clamps down and his teeth grind trying to keep his composure.

His thrusts are aggressive as he pounds himself into me each time. His pelvis assaults my clit with every advance he makes. The arousal and pain mixed together cause tingles to burst at the back of my skull.

I know my body won't take much more. The anticipation of this moment builds to the point that something has to give way.

I tighten my arms around his neck even tighter to keep me anchored closer to him, my ass squirming against the slick countertop. I'm going to come at any second but I don't want this to be over. Unfortunately, my body is making all the rules and I have no choice.

"I'm almost there," I whimper.

"Take it then. This is yours," he grunts.

He continues to pound into me. With every stroke of his cock, he brings me rushing toward the cliff. I can't resist it—I can't stop it—I can't even slow it down.

I cry out as one last thrust of his hips pushes me over the edge. I free-fall into my climax, gasping for air as the inner muscles of my center pulsate and contract around his girth.

"Jesus," he growls. "Your pussy's squeezing me. I can't..."

His voice cuts off as he tries to hold it together.

"Come with me," I say with the last bit of energy I have left.

He grips around my back with one hand and then grips my left ass cheek with the other. He moves me in rhythm with him, his eyes fluttering closed as he grunts out his pleasure.

"Fuck, fuck..." he says until he groans out and empties himself into me.

He keeps rocking as he reaches the end of his orgasm, unloading every last drop.

I feel the tip of his cock start to twitch and spasm deep inside of me.

"Holy hell," he says as he regains his breathing.

He dips down and kisses me again, my arms still locked around him. I take every kiss he gives me.

"Do you feel better?" I ask with a grin.

He pulls back from our kiss and looks down at me.

"Yeah... do you?"

My body feels better but my heart and mind are more confused than ever.

Between the fear of abandonment, the fear of getting caught for our fraudulent marriage, and that I am falling for my fake husband faster than should be possible... I'm not sure if I'm ok.

It's a problem to solve tomorrow because tonight, I'm going to enjoy the man who just claimed me in so many ways.

"Yes. So much better," I say.

"Are you hungry? My sister probably already ordered us food."

"Starving."

Chapter Twenty-Three

Juliet

Last night, after walking out of the bathroom only to meet—to my utter and complete mortification—a long line of angry men needing to use the restroom, we spent the rest of the night eating BBQ. Camden, Everett, and Harper made a game of who could outdo the other with bathroom sex puns.

Was I embarrassed by their little game?

A little.

Would I do it all over again if given the chance?

Yes.

Seeing that possessive side of Ryker was the hottest thing I've ever witnessed a man do for me. If I had to pick one moment in time to re-live over and over again for the rest of my life... it would be that one.

The rest of the night, Ryker found ways to touch me and I leaned into it all. I don't know what will happen when we get back home but I want to stay in this bubble for as long as I can.

"Morning." I hear his voice behind me.

I turn to find him stretching his arms up over his head and a smile across his lips.

"Morning," I echo.

He's so sexy in the mornings with his hair all messy from sleep and his bare chest with that six pack that somehow always looks like he's flexing.

"Are you ready for this today?"

Today?

He means breakfast at his mom's... which sounds amazing. I am already falling in love with his family and it's been less than 24 hours. But breakfast leads to the lesser-known Haynes Family Sledding Competition. Something I know nothing about, and something that Annie felt she needed an entire night last night of relaxation for.

"There isn't enough snow to do it, is there?"

"We don't need snow. Camden just wets down the grass and we use inner tubes."

Somehow that's not reassuring.

"I wish you would tell me more about this competition today. How do I get ready for this? What am I supposed to wear?"

I almost prepare myself for him to tell me 'bubble wrap', but he just turns over onto his side to face me and wipes a strand of hair off my face.

"If I told you, you'd fake the stomach flu," he teases. "But I promise it's fun and you'll be happy you did it."

I know that Ryker takes my safety seriously and that he wouldn't put me in a position to get hurt. I have to let go and just enjoy this adventure with him. The last thing I want to do is be the weak link in this family. Especially since I witnessed his five-foot-three-inch sister checking a player almost twice her size into the sideboards at yesterday's tournament. This family can smell fear and I'm going to have to grow a pair and rise to the occasion if I want to fit in—and I do want to fit in.

I've never wanted to fit in with a group of people more in my life.

After we both get ready and stop for coffee at the drive-thru coffee shop, we pull into Ryker's mom's house. There are several other cars here already, one of which is a minivan with a bumper sticker on the back that reads, "Don't laugh... you're next," with a cartoon picture of a mini-van on it. I'm guessing that means Camden or Everett are here with their kids.

It's an updated ranch-style home, with bricks that have me guessing the home was built in the 70s and perched on a large lot with a sloping backyard. This is where I'm guessing the deadly sledding competition will commence.

Though there isn't much snow left to sled on, the temperatures are certainly cold enough for it. I'm happy to have dressed in several layers for the sledding event.

We both get out and head for the door, Ryker not bothering to knock as he opens the door and walks straight in.

"We're here!" he calls out in the entry.

We both start slipping off our shoes in the entry, next to the dozens of other shoes that are also sitting right inside the door. Ryker takes off his jacket and hangs it on a hook and then takes mine and does the same.

The smell of baked goods, syrup, and something salty fills Ryker's childhood home.

"In here!" I hear Annie's voice call out, though I can't see her.

The clinking of dishes and the hum of voices suggest that they're all in the kitchen already.

I follow Ryker as we head through the entry, past a sunken living room to our right and a hallway to what I'm guessing would be bedrooms, to our left.

In front of us are a set of glass double doors where a large two-story play set is covered with the Haynes offspring having a blast. All of them are zipped into puffy down jackets.

The second we round the corner, we're met with the whole Haynes adult crew.

The Haynes brothers are all standing around the island as Austin seems to be looking up an answer to a group question while Camden and Everett hover over his shoulder.

Sienna and Kali are chopping fresh fruit while Arie is making up a fresh batch of coffee in the U-shaped kitchen.

"Oh good. You two are here. Breakfast is just about ready," she says.

The breakfast spread is already forming on the granite countertop. Two large egg and cheese quiches, a good sized glazed ham set on a wooden cutting board, and an entire waffle station with a tower of steaming hot waffles, mixed fruits, and syrups to go on top, all are laid out in a row like a buffet. Plates, silverware and napkins are already lined up at the front of the buffet. It's crazy how much food has to be made up to feed this family.

When Ryker said they couldn't have an animal because his mom was too busy taking care of them... I'm starting to understand why. But the smile across her face as Ryker dips down and kisses her temple as he reaches for the knife for the ham, I can see that this isn't work for her, it's a labor of love that she does proudly.

I want this too. I want this life... with Ryker.

"Juliet, honey, go take a seat at the island and relax. Ryker, your brothers are useless. Can you slice the ham up for me?" she asks as she pours more pancake batter into a hot waffle maker.

"Sure, Mom," Ryker says, sliding his hand down my back to tell me to head to the island.

He turns and heads for the knife butcher block but I can't sit while everyone works.

"I'd like to help. What can I do?" I ask.

Annie looks over her shoulder and gives me a smile of appreciation.

"How about telling Harper and the kids that breakfast is ready? We'll start dishing up as soon as Ryker gets the ham sliced. This is my last waffle to make."

So that's where Harper is.

I nod, happy to be of help.

I walk back around the kitchen and head for the glass double doors. I see Harper at the top of the two-story play set with an eye patch and sword.

"You'll never take me alive," she says in a pirate voice and then jumps into the enclosed corkscrew slide until she is spat out with all the grace of an adult using a child's play set.

"Hello." I laugh as Harper lies at the bottom of the slide and grunts in pain.

I imagine she'll need a chiropractor after that stunt.

"Oh... hi," she says in surprise, picking her injured body off the slide and limping toward me. "You made it."

"Of course, we wouldn't miss it."

I'm a little confused as to why she thought we might not come.

"After last night, I half expected Ryker to lock you up in that house of his and never let you out." She snickers.

I can see why she would think that considering he locked us in a bathroom at the bar. It wouldn't have surprised me if he'd decided to stay in bed all day.

"Yeah, well, we discussed it, and we figured we had to eat sometime," I tease.

She chuckles at my joke. My chest fills with a little pride in getting Harper to laugh.

"Breakfast is ready. Your mom wanted me to tell you," I say.

"Yum, ok. The kids will be happy to hear it," she says, and then turns around, putting her hands on either side of her mouth, and yells, "Food is ready! The last one to the kitchen walks the plank of doom after breakfast."

She watches over her shoulder to make sure the kids heard her and are all getting off the play set and then she follows me back into the kitchen.

A few minutes later, the kitchen is packed with noisy bodies all moving around the space. Some family members grab drinks out of the fridge while others start working through the well-thought-out buffet line.

We eat while twenty different conversations are taking place at once. It's loud as everyone talks over one another and children run around our feet… and I swear I'm holding three conversations all at once, but this right here… this is bliss.

A completely different kind of bliss to meeting Jerrin's triumphant gaze as he wins another round of poker. Or the bliss of sitting with my mother at her kitchen table, talking and laughing and sharing secrets late into the night.

But bliss all the same.

After breakfast, I walk in to find that all four brothers have cleaned the entire kitchen. Ryker and Austin finish hand washing the last plates and Camden and Everett are putting away condiments and wiping down the countertops.

I have to give it to Annie, she trained them well.

Camden finishes putting away the salt and pepper and then walks past me to the dining room where the rest of the family are sitting.

"All participants of the sledding competition," he starts. "It's time to head out to Haynes Hill."

"Haynes Hill?" I turn to ask Everett, who's the closest to me.

"It's the hill in the backyard. Our dad coined it Haynes Hill to make it more exciting."

"Did it work?" I ask him as he finishes wiping down the island next to me.

"Dad made everything more exciting." He nods with his head down, finishing his task.

"I wish I could have met him," I say.

"He would have loved you," Everett says back, looking up at me for a moment.

That simple statement. So minor—so few words, but the impact of it hits me. The thought that Ryker's father would have loved me even though my father didn't is something I never knew I needed to hear.

I can feel Ryker's eyes on me from the sink. He heard what his brother said.

Ryker's eyes lock on mine, and he nods in agreement to Everett's statement. I swallow down the emotion that wants to show itself in the form of moved tears.

"Everyone out to the yard," Camden announces.

Ryker and Austin wipe their hands off with dish towels and then everyone starts to head for the glass double doors.

Ryler heads for the entry and grabs our coats first.

We stand at the top of Haynes Hill, snowless but still freezing outside. The grass glistens with water from the hose that Everett turned on as soon as we got out here to help the inner tubes slide easier down the hill.

Ten black inner tubes are blown up and set up against the side of the house. This family must do this a lot to have ten inner tubes on the ready.

"Since Juliet is new to the family, and we have a couple of cheaters in the group..."

"Harper," Austin coughs out.

"Hey! I don't cheat." Harper says, shoving Austin's arm.

"... I'm going to go back over the ground rules," Camden says. "We will split up into teams. Since Kali is pregnant, she's sitting this one out and she'll be the official referee and judge today."

"Go Kali," Austin says. "Husbands get preferred treatment."

"Shut up Austin, Camden's talking," Ryker says.

But Camden seems unfazed by everyone's interruptions.

"That means we have an equal number of men vs. women, so that's how we'll divide the teams."

"Wait, that's not fair. You guys push harder than us," Sienna, Camden's wife, objects.

"Yeah, but we're lighter than these sasquatches so we don't have to push as hard for us to go faster. This is good... this is what we want," Harper says.

"The object of the game is to get all of your teammates down to the end of the hill by pushing them as hard as you can and attempting to knock the other sledder off their inner tube. If you are knocked off your inner tube, you must run back up the hill, get back to the end of the line, and try again." He looks over at Harper. "You cannot jump back on the inner tube where you were kicked off."

Wait, we have to try to bounce people off their inner tubes?

"I didn't fall off the inner tube. I was still in play," Harper objects.

I chuckle at these siblings squawking with each other.

"You were out, Harper. Ryker practically bounced you into old man Jones's yard at the end of the fucking block," Austin says.

"Damn it, shut up Austin," Harper growls.

"Language you two," Arie, Everett's wife, warns. "There's kids out here."

"The team with all of their teammates down first, wins. Everyone got it?"

Harper nods and then walks over and grabs an inner tube off the house and lines up at the top of the hill. The rest of the wives and brothers grab their inner tubes, too, and then start lining up next.

I pull my wedding ring off my hand and store it in my jacket pocket, zipping it up for safekeeping. I have a feeling things might get slippery and I can't stand the idea of losing this ring in the grass if it slipped off my finger.

Ryker grabs us both an inner tube and hands me one.

Since I don't want to be the reason we lose, I wait and line up at the very end. I want to see everyone's technique before it's my turn.

I'm an amateur, I just don't want to look like an amateur.

Besides Harper and Austin who take the first spot at the top, obviously, with an ongoing sledding rivalry to settle, the rest of us end up paired with our significant others.

I guess if I had to bounce someone off their inner tube, I'd rather it be the man who couldn't keep his hands off me last night.

I watch as Harper and Austin make their run. Harper's inner tube smacks into Austin's but he stays on.

Arie is already belly down on her inner tube and the second the hill is clear, Sienna gives Arie a big push while Everett jumps and belly flops onto his inner tube.

He wobbles a little out of control from the big flop but he manages to stay on.

"Ok, Juliet. Do us proud," she says, running and jumping onto her inner tube, Camden doing the same thing.

"You're going to do great. But hold on tight because they don't call me the Bounce Master for nothing," Ryker says.

I laugh at the most ridiculous nickname I have ever heard. It's the least threatening moniker a person could have besides Kitten Whisperer.

"That's a terrible name," I tell him.

"Take it up with Everett. He gave it to me when I was six so it hasn't aged well. But I'll have you know that back then, the name set fear through all the neighborhood kids who dared to sled against me."

We walk up to the edge of the hill and watch Sienna and Camden.

Camden hits Sienna's inner tube hard and her black tubes spin out of control at the bottom of the hill but she's still on when she makes it to the bottom.

I won't be the one to lose this for the team so as soon as Sienna clears, I belly flop onto my tube and start sailing down the hill. The freezing air hits my face, but it feels like victory.

I can't see Ryker, but I can see the finish line and the girls jumping up and down cheering—until all of a sudden, I see Arie grip Sienna's arm in horror.

I feel Ryker's inner tube rather than see it.

And before I know it... I'm sailing through the air without my inner tube.

Wack!

A branch slams against my body, and I'm confronted by the smell of pine trees and wetness under me as I lay on soggy, freezing grass.

"Ouch..." I groan.

I'm in a bush. Ryker slammed me into a bush.

"Shit... Juliet." Ryker calls out, jumping off his inner tube and barely getting his footing as he starts running to me.

Harper and Sienna get to me first and grab an arm each to help out of the plant.

"Juliet... are you ok?" Harpers asks.

"Yeah, I think so," I say.

They get me to my feet and the second Sienna sees my face, she grimaces.

"Austin, come quick. She might need stitches," Sienna says, her eyebrows downturned.

She squints at something above my eye.

"Stitches? What's wrong?" I ask, my eyes bouncing between the two women, but neither of them says anything as they both study something above my eye.

Ryker comes up next and then Austin behind him.

The girls release me to let Austin get a closer look.

"Damn it, I'm sorry Juliet. I couldn't slow the inner tube down. I didn't mean to launch you like that," Ryker says while Austin assesses whatever Sienna and Harper were looking at.

The cold wind swirls around me. It penetrates through my clothes to my skin, everywhere that the wetness has sunken in.

I shiver for a second and run my hands up and down my arms while my teeth start to chatter a little.

"No, stitches but Mom has band-aids in her first aid kit. Wipe her up and get her warm, she's freezing," Austin tells Ryker. "You didn't hit your head, did you?" he asks, checking both my pupils.

"No," I tell him.

"Ok, good. It'll be a little bruised tomorrow, but you'll be fine," Austin says.

"I'm going to take her up to the house," Ryker says, wrapping an arm around my shoulders in an attempt to warm me up.

"Feel better, Juliet," Sienna says behind us as we walk back up the hill.

"I'm sorry. I didn't mean to hit you that hard," Ryker says as we walk back up the hill and toward the house.

"I'm fine Ryker, I promise," I try to assure him.

"One more round?" Camden asks the rest of the group from a ways away.

They all agree and head up toward the house.

We pass by Annie who's outside with the kids on the playground.

She looks up with a smile at us and then sees the gash I'm assuming is on my forehead. "Oh my gosh, are you ok?" she asks, standing quickly out of her chair like she's about to run after us but then she looks toward the playground.

"Yeah, I'm ok. Just cold," I say quickly.

"I'm going to take her in and get her bandaged up," Ryker tells her.

"Ok... band-aids are in the hall closet. Call me if you need me. And get a blanket on her," she says quickly.

I can see in her eyes that her mother's instincts are kicking in and she's struggling not to come with us but she has littles to watch and Ryker can take care of me.

We head into the kitchen and Ryker lifts me up and sets me next to the sink.

He takes off his jacket and lays it over my wet jeans. The body heat from the inside of his jacket goes a long way to warming me but I'll need to get out of these wet clothes to warm up.

He grabs a paper towel, wets it, and then starts to lightly pat the wound.

I hiss the second the wet towel meets my cut.

"Here, I'll be right back. I need to get a band-aid and some antibiotic cream for it."

"Ok, thanks."

I watch as he heads out of the kitchen and down the hall quickly.

He comes back with a white and red first aid bag and sets it down next to me.

He pulls out the cream and squeezes a little on his finger.

"I'm sorry I rammed you that hard. I only meant to push you out of bounds."

The guilt in his voice is so sweet but he shouldn't feel so badly. I already told him that I'm fine.

Besides, it was all for fun and at high speed on inner tubes, there isn't a lot of control you have to change direction. It wasn't really his fault. I know he wouldn't hurt me on purpose.

"You were just threatened that I was going to beat you," I say with a devilish grin.

He chuckles and looks up at me.

"Is that right? You think you were about to beat me on my home turf?"

He finishes patting the antibiotic ointment on my cut and then reaches for the band-aid, carefully pulling the two tabs apart to open it.

He pulls off the backs of the band-aid and then lays it over the cut on my forehead.

"I was about to beat you. Worried that you might have met your match?" I ask.

"Oh... I know I've met my match," he says.

He takes a step closer, his hand reaching up and wrapping around the back of my neck, pulling my mouth closer until our lips meld together and all I can taste is him.

He tastes like strawberries and syrup with a hint of ham from breakfast.

The glass door opens, and Ryker pulls his mouth off mine.

"Hey, don't stop on my account," Harper says. "I just came in for bottled water."

"How did round two go?" Ryker asks her, straightening back up.

"The girls won." She smiles. "But now it's a husband and wife pissing match, so I decided to come in and check on Juliet. How you feel champ?" she asks.

She gets to the fridge and opens the door, pulling a bottle of water out of the side door.

"I'm fine. But I'd like to get out of these wet clothes," I say.

We hear the door open again and Annie peaks her head in.

"Ryker, can you help with the pirate flag on the top of the play set? It just blew off and I'm not tall enough to put it back."

"Sure, Mom," Ryker says.

He turns back to me. "I'll be right back. Are you ok here for a minute? Then we'll find you dry clothes, ok?"

He walks out of the kitchen and out the glass doors.

Harper leans up against the island and takes a pull from the bottle of water in her hand.

"He's in love with you, you know?"

"I'm sorry?" I ask, confused by her question.

But the serious look on her face has my palms in a cold sweat even though I'm already freezing.

"Ryker. He's falling in love with you. I can see it in his eyes. He's never looked at any woman that he's been with the way he looks at you. I think you might be one of the only women he's brought home since high school."

He's in love with me? My stomach does a little flip at the thought of it being true.

She takes a small sip of her water again and then screws on the cap.

"Right... well... we're married so he looks at me differently, I suppose."

"No, it's not that," she says, shaking her head. "What are you getting out of this deal?"

"You're going to have to be more specific. I have no idea what you're talking about," I say.

I should be getting warmer under the collar at this conversation, but instead, I begin to shiver harder as Harper practically corners me about her brother and our marriage.

I wish Ryker would come back in right now. I have no idea how to handle this situation and I have no idea what Ryker told her.

I'm looking at jail time if our arrangement is found out so opening up to a stranger in my fake husband's childhood home isn't something I'm prepared to do. Whether it's his sister or not.

I have no idea if she can be trusted with this information, or how much Ryker wants her to know about it.

"I know you're probably not going to tell me because, from the looks of things, my brother has decided to lie to all of us, which is fine. If this is a need-to-know basis, I get it. Except the moment he gets his green card and you two get divorced, my mother will be devastated." She shifts her weight and leans toward the glass doors to make sure no one is coming to interrupt us.

Where the hell are you Ryker?

"Though I'm not in favor of what you guys are doing, I think that my brother deserves to get to play out his contract, and he already told me that his other visa was about to expire."

"Harper, I don't know what your brother told you but—"

"He didn't tell me anything. It's just that the timeline of Amelia, the visa expiring, and your shotgun courthouse wedding, I put two and two together."

"I care about him," I say quickly.

"I can see that, too. But if you care about him and are not committed to "until death do us part," you need to stop doing what you two are doing in public bars and stop letting him think there's a chance you won't leave at the end of all this. He's only going to fall harder from here."

The door opens from outside and she and I both whip our heads to look at who it is.

"I'm back," Ryker says, walking around the kitchen and heading for me. "A hot shower will warm you up. What do you think?"

"A shower sounds good."

...and a minute to myself after what Harper just said.

I already know how I feel about him, it's just that the thought of forever is scary. Not the act of being with Ryker forever—I already know I want that. It's the fear of setting my hopes on forever and having them yanked from me like they were from my mom.

But I have to trust at some point and see where the chips fall. I can't be guarded forever, or I'll find myself alone one day. And if there's anyone who's worth trying for, it's Ryker.

If we stay together long-term, we would need to discuss Ryker's desire to live in Canada after he retires. I can't, in good conscience, leave the country until my brother feels settled and feels secure. I also need to see him making progress with the Occupational Therapist.

"I have a pair of sweats and a hoody in my old bedroom that I left here in case. I'll put them in the hall bathroom for you," Harper tells me.

"Thanks, sis," he says, his eyes still on mine.

Harper turns and heads down the hall, and Ryker takes his jacket off my legs, lays it down next to me, and grips around my waist, pulling me off the kitchen counter and putting me back on my feet.

I follow him as he leads me out of the kitchen and down the hall.

Harper walks out of one room and then Ryker turns into it.

"Have a good shower," she tells me as she passes by.

I know she's protective of her brother, I get it. I would feel the same way if this was happening to Jerrin, and he was falling in love with a woman that I knew may or may not love him back.

I watch as Ryker turns on the shower for me and I start to peel off my jacket and my sopping wet pants.

Standing in only my underwear and my thin camisole shirt, my legs feel like icicles, and my panties are still wet with lawn water.

Soon enough I'll be under the warm spray of the shower.

Ryker pulls back his long-sleeved shirt and reaches in past the curtain, standing there for a moment waiting for the water to turn from cold to hot.

"It's warm," he says.

Relief hits me and I can already feel the warmth of the steam from the hot water filling the small guest bathroom.

He pulls his hand back and walks to the cupboard, giving my body a once over before walking around me to pull out a towel.

"You look freezing. I'm sorry I didn't get you in here sooner."

"It's ok."

It gave Harper and me a chance to chat.

He hands me a towel and I take it, my left hand on top of the towel and my right underneath.

He looks down at my hand and his eyebrows furrow instantly. He clamps down on the towel, not letting me have it.

"Where's your ring?"

"I took it off for sledding. It's safe, I promise."

"Where is it?" he asks, his eyes narrowing on me.

Is he honestly not happy that I took it off for one afternoon?

"In my jacket pocket," I tell him.

He finally releases the towel and trudges over to my jacket that I put on the bathroom vanity.

He unzips the jacket pocket and pulls out the ring before turning back to me. He pulls my left hand gently from the towel into his and then slides the ring back on.

"This ring belongs on your finger, where other people can see it and know you're taken," he says.

There's that sexy possessive side of him again that gets me worked up.

"I didn't want to lose it in the grass today," I tell him.

"It never comes off, Juliet. Promise me that this ring never comes off your finger," he says, backing me up slowly until my ass hits the wall next to the shower.

"But what if I lose it?" I ask.

He slides his arm around my back and his chest plasters against my body.

"Then I'll buy you a bigger one next time. Promise me," he says and then presses his lips to mine.

I kiss him back, the heat from his mouth and the billowing steam from the shower starting to warm my frigid body.

"I promise," I say.

He loves me.

He hasn't claimed it out loud, but Harper's words keep echoing in my head that I need to stop leading Ryker on by making him think that I want more than these two years. But I'm not leading him on, because I do... I want "until death do us part".

And I want it with him.

Chapter Twenty-Four

Ryker

Our hands tangle into a mess of uncoordinated need and desire. Grabbing and pulling. Kissing and sucking. Neither one of us can seem to get enough of the other.

I pull the thin white camisole up and over Juliet's head and then I unlatch her bra, letting it fall to the ground between us. Anything that keeps me from her body has to go. I stare down at her perfectly bare body. There are so many things I want to do with her and if I get what I'm after, we'll have a lifetime to explore it all.

Juliet tugs at my t-shirt. If she wants me naked, I'm more than happy to oblige. I follow her lead and pull my t-shirt from my body.

I unzip my pants and push both my jeans and my boxer briefs down in one fluid motion. My hard cock springs free of its confines, looking for Juliet to sink into. The only woman I've wanted since the moment we met—the only woman I'll *ever* want.

The only thing left between us is her panties and the agreement of our fake marriage. I wish we would have written that agreement up on paper just so I could burn it.

"Let's get you wet," I tell her, hooking my thumbs into her underwear and tugging down until they drop to her ankles.

The second she steps out of her panties, I lift her up and guide her to wrap her legs around my waist. I know she needs to be warmed up, so I pull her off the wall and step over the bathtub ledge.

The minute the warm water hits Juliet's back, she moans into my mouth. This is what she needs, and it's my mission to make sure she always gets what she wants.

"Jesus, Juliet. I can't do this anymore," I say against her mouth.

I know this might not be the best time since she's a sex kitten icicle right now, but when will be a good time? After we sign divorce papers?

No.

I have to do this now.

I have to lay it out and tell her what I want. And if it's not reciprocated, then it's not reciprocated.

"You can't do what?" she asks but doesn't pull away.

"I can't pretend this is fake anymore and that I don't have feelings for you."

I push her into the corner of the shower, using it as leverage to feel her body pressed tightly against mine. She moans at the pressure I apply between us, our lips never breaking away from one another.

"Date me," I say. "Date me for the next two years and give me a chance to convince you to stay as my wife."

"You want me to stay as your wife? You don't want a divorce?" she asks softly as if she can barely believe what I'm saying.

"I know this isn't what we agreed to but—"

Before I can get the words out, Juliet pulls my mouth to hers and kisses me harder.

This isn't a kiss where we can't seem to get enough of each other. And it's not a desperate kiss made from lust and need. This is an answer... the answer I've been waiting for.

"Yes, I'll date you. It's been real for me for a while now too," she admits.

Pure relief and happiness fill my lungs as my heart thumps wildly against my chest. She's giving me a shot, and now I have two years to build a life that's too irresistible for her to leave.

"I want you, Ryker. Right now," she says, reaching between us and wrapping her hand around my cock.

It dawns on me that I only had one condom in my wallet and I used it on her at the bar last night.

Fuck.

"I don't have a condom. Damn it, I'm sorry. I forgot to reload my wallet this morning."

"Do we need one?" she asks.

The question takes me off guard because condoms have always been a requirement. I've never entertained the idea of not using one, and I've never had a woman suggest we go without... until now.

It's not as if I've never thought about how good it would be to go without one. But going bare with Juliet is a temptation I don't think I can turn down.

"That's your call. All of this is your call," I tell her because it's her body and I have no idea if she's on birth control.

I had a full physical after Amelia and I broke up, so I know I'm clean.

The build-up of need for this woman is at a boiling point and I think she feels it too.

"I'm on the pill. And I don't want to stop here," she says, pumping my shaft with her hand. "Make love to me."

"I have been making love to you. Since the first time," I tell her because it's the truth.

Her eyes glimmer back at me.

For once, I said something right.

She adjusts her position a little higher, lining up my tip with her entrance, and then presses down over me.

We both groan at the feeling of me almost filling her in one solid thrust. The feeling of no condom—the slippery heat of her—the trust she's giving me... it all takes me to the edge, teetering on losing control and taking her as hard as I can to fulfill the carnal need to solidify this bond.

It only takes a couple more thrusts until I'm buried to the hilt inside of her.

Juliet whimpers into my shoulder to muffle her noises from the unsuspecting... or maybe suspecting, family on the other side of the house.

If we were in my home, I'd demand to hear her cries and every moan she makes for me. But I've probably already scarred her for life from the looks we got walking out of the men's bathroom last night. Though I walked out proud as fuck to have Juliet's hand in mine.

"Ryker, more," she begs, her fingernails clawing into my shoulder blades.

I can feel her legs beginning to shake around me.

She's close.

I reach between us and circle her clit with my thumb.

"Oh..." she whimpers.

I know I have her now but I don't know if I can hold back.

Being bare inside of her gives me more friction and sensation than I've ever had. Everything feels so much more vivid.

"Harder... please," she says.

I do as she asks.

"I'm your husband, Juliet. I'm yours now," I tell her.

I feel her nod against my shoulder as she keeps her grip on me.

"This cock is yours and I'll give it to you whenever you want... however you want it."

I increase my thrusts until finally, I hear her moan loudly and grip the back of my neck. My name comes out of her mouth as a plea and her body pulsates around me, milking me so tight that I can't hold it any longer and I come right after her, unloading deep without a condom. The experience is unmatched—like nothing I've ever felt before.

Everything with Juliet is like something I've never felt before. And I plan to hold on to this feeling for as long as she lets me.

I give us both a minute to recover from what we just did, and then I lower her feet to the porcelain bathtub and back up so that she can wash off first.

I pick up the body soap at the end of the shower and hand it to her.

"That was... amazing," she says, and then trails off.

"Yeah," I say back, doubting that there's even vocabulary to properly explain the feeling I just had.

I pull her hair off her shoulders and watch as her long raven locks cascade down her bare back—one of my favorite images.

I lean down and set a soft kiss on her shoulder as she washes her body.

"Do you think anyone heard us?" she asks.

"I hope so," I tease.

"Ryker, be serious for one second," she says, turning around to switch positions with me.

I squeeze some body soap into my hand and start to wash myself too, though I'd rather keep her scent on me all day.

"I am being serious. You sound good when you come."

I know that comment is going to embarrass her more but poking at her is my new favorite pastime.

"Ryker!" she squeals. "Fine, I'm getting out if you can't be serious."

I turn around quickly and grab her arm before she exits the shower.

"Whoa, hold on," I tell her, pulling her back behind the shower curtain.

I take a step closer to her and slide my hand behind her neck, pulling her lips to mine to kiss her.

"Are we really doing this?" I ask, because it almost seems too good to be true.

"Yes," she says, grinning up at me. "We're really doing this."

I release her and she gets out, drying off with a towel while I finish washing off. Then, she and I both get dressed and head back out to the kitchen. It must have started snowing while we were in the shower because large snowflakes cover the sky and my entire family is out in the backyard dancing in it.

There's no chance anyone heard us in the shower, not that I would have cared.

Since Juliet and I leave first thing in the morning, we spend the rest of the day at my mom's playing board games, coloring with the kids, and watching old home videos of our childhood.

It seems like it always gets harder and harder to leave this place and these people but I still have a commitment to the Hawkeyes and Juliet and I have a lot to work out.

Will she agree to move away from her business and family in exchange for a life with me in Vancouver?

I guess I should have asked that question before I handed her my heart and my future because I won't be asking for it back.

CHAPTER TWENTY-FIVE

Juliet

It's been four days since we got home from Vancouver and things with Ryker are even better than I imagined.

The new bed he ordered got delivered and set up before we got home and he convinced me to move all of my wardrobe into his walk-in closet. It's even bigger than the one in the second master and, shockingly, still has growing space for more clothes.

Today is the first of three alumni-inspired home games that Shawnie and I will be setting up. After spending the entire day nitpicking every little thing we put up, I think Shawnie and I are really showcasing what we are capable of.

"Whoa... this looks good," a familiar man's voice says as Shawnie and I stand at the Hawkeyes' front door entrance to get the full picture of the lobby.

I look over to find Ryker walking out in his uniform.

The fans are already at the doors to get let in but Shawnie and I still have twenty minutes before early admission starts, in case we need to change anything.

"Do you like it?" I ask.

He walks up and lowers his lips to mine, laying a sweet tender kiss against my lips before looking at the space again.

Large Hawkeyes-colored balloon arches are placed over every single concession stand. Throwback pictures of each of the three alumni members coming in tonight are blown up and hung in different places around the space. All three jerseys are hung up high, and fans can see them framed in glass the minute they walk in.

"You two outdid yourselves. Has Marjorie seen this yet?"

"Not yet, but Autumn, Tessa, and Penelope have been in here and helped blow up balloons earlier today, so they've seen it and love it."

Ryker gives the space one more look and then smiles down at me.

"I'm proud of you. I just came up to check in before the game starts. I have to get back before the doors open. I'll see you after media?" he asks.

"Yeah, I'll see you after."

"Is this what you're wearing tonight?" he asks, giving me a full body scan, taking in my hoody, jeans and platform Keds.

"No, I have jeans, heels and your jersey stuffed in a backpack that I'll change into."

I know he wouldn't have said anything if I told him that, in fact, I would be wearing this tonight.

"You look good in anything but I love seeing the name Haynes anywhere on your body," he says with a devilish grin.

"Then I guess you'll like the panties I'm wearing today," I tease.

He licks his lips and now I wish this game was already over.

"When are you going to make that name permanent?" he asks.

"You want me to change my name?"

We'd never discussed this before. Probably because it's a lot of work to change everything when we were planning to divorce anyway. Then I'd have to go through the hassle of yet another change... but now, the idea of it makes me giddy.

Having Ryker's last name would make this feel so much more official, even though we're technically a married couple that just started dating.

"Only if you feel comfortable with it," he says, rubbing my back. "But we can wait if you don't want to."

Getting rid of Di Costa, the name still attached to my father, and trading it in for a man who's asking for a future with me feels like the exact thing I'd like to do.

"When would you want me to change it?"

"Yesterday," he says simply.

I chuckle at his eagerness.

"Ok, I'll start the paperwork tomorrow, how about that?"

"I like that a lot, Juliet Haynes."

He bends down and sets a kiss on the top of my head.

"I have to go before they open the doors. I'll see you later," he says over his shoulder as he turns, taking long strides away from me back toward the locker rooms.

Juliet Haynes.

I can barely wait to fill out the paperwork.

Ryker

After a long grueling game, we pulled out a win, but my body is going to feel this one tomorrow.

My plans to convince Juliet to take a long shower with me tonight is on the top of my list.

When I walk out of media in my suit with my duffle bag over my shoulder, I see Autumn and Tessa, but not Juliet.

"Hey," I say to both of them.

"Good game, Haynes," Tessa says.

"Thanks. Any chance you know where my wife is?" I ask.

"I think she's still breaking down a few things with Shawnie," Autumn offers.

Right, that makes sense. Juliet said that the janitors for tonight would take down her balloon arches, but she probably wants to take the pictures down carefully and stow those away somewhere.

"I'll go find her... thanks," I tell them. I'm about ready to head to the stadium until I hear my name.

"Ryker Haynes?"

I look down the hall, the opposite way that I was headed, to see a guy in slacks and a blazer standing further away from everyone.

I head in his direction, doubling back past Autumn and Tessa and the opening to the media room where Powers is being interviewed. Autumn and Tessa seem completely immersed listening to Lake's answers.

"Yeah, that's me. Are you part of media? I just finished so if you have other questions you'll have to—"

"No, Mr. Haynes, I'm with immigration."

Immigration? No one told me we'd need another interview this early on but whatever. Juliet is still in the building and we can pound this out right now and send him on his way.

"If you need another interview, my wife is at the entrance of the stadium. I can get her."

"That won't be necessary, Mr. Haynes. I only need to talk to you."

Only me?

"Ok... what can I do for you?"

"Mr. Haynes, my name is Henry Morris and I'm the supervising officer over an immigration employee by the name of Frank Bishop. Does that name ring a bell?"

Shit... the look on this guy's face says that this isn't a house call visit.

"Yes, I met with Frank for my K-1 visa interview. Why?"

"It's come to my attention that you applied for the K-1 visa with the intention of fraudulently marrying someone to stay in this country. Is that correct?"

I can feel the tops of my ears heat and my stomach drop. How the hell am I supposed to answer that question?

"Wait, hold on a second, where are you getting this information?"

"It has also come to my attention, after a fair amount of digging, that Mr. Bishop has money on the Hawkeyes winning the Stanley Cup. Is that true?" he asks.

"Where are you coming up with this information? My wife and I are in love. You can't prove that we did anything fraudulent," I say, looking quickly over my shoulder to make sure that Autumn and Tessa don't hear this conversation, but they're still glued to Lake's interview.

Henry pulls out his phone and hits a button, then turns the phone toward me.

It's the video that Amelia asked the water boy to record of me proposing.

Fucking hell...

He hits replay and I hear my voice over the speaker.

"So what I was going to say is that we've been together for a while now and ... and with my visa about to expire, I think it makes sense that we get married."

"Where did you get that?" I ask.

"Just a concerned citizen who doesn't like it when someone tries to take advantage of our laws."

A concerned citizen, my ass.

You mean a jealous spoiled brat who didn't get the televised proposal and the big diamond ring she was angling for? The same one who ended up empty-handed after Mateo Easton dumped her?

"That doesn't prove that Juliet and I are defrauding our fiancé visa. We fell in love—I proposed—we got married. People do it every day."

He doesn't have anything. He can only accuse me of proposing to Amelia for the K-1 visa, but there's no recorded evidence of Juliet and I making any deal.

"Mr. Haynes, we can do this one of two ways. The first option is that we take this to court, play the video message to the jury, along with this same concerned citizen testifying against you and Juliet's relationship, and prove that Frank Bishop fast-tracked your application for his gambling addiction," he says, slipping his phone back into the pocket of his button-up shirt. "If you're found guilty, you will get deported and I'll have your eligibility to reapply for a visa revoked for up to ten years. Juliet will be looking at up to five years of prison time, felony charges, and a possible fine of two hundred and fifty thousand dollars."

I swallow hard at the outlook for Juliet if we lost that court battle. The shame of not only putting Juliet in this predicament but also for being the one who gave my ex-girlfriend the ammunition to cause this kind of damage weighs heavy on my conscience.

I can't let Juliet take the fall for this.

I need to fix this. And ideally without Juliet knowing the details about Amelia's evidence against us and the fact that I took a deal from a guy with a gambling addiction. All of which is my fault and is sealing our fate.

"And option two?" I ask.

"Because Frank is under my jurisdiction, and my boss will demand a department-wide audit of all the employees who work under me if this abuse of power gets out, I want this to go away as quietly as possible. If my ass wasn't on the line, I wouldn't be offering this to you... do you understand? This is a sweetheart deal."

I wish the guy would shut the fuck up and just tell me what the hell I have to do to get Juliet out of this mess.

At this point, I'll do anything he asks. I won't let my wife spend a day in prison for this.

"What do I have to do?" I ask, pinching my hand on my hips and glancing over my shoulder one more time. The girls have left the hall.

"I'll give you until tomorrow by ten am to pack up and leave the country... quietly. You don't tell a single soul why you're leaving. No one can know about what happened, just in case it gets out."

"And if I agree to this, you'll leave Juliet alone?"

"If you do this, Juliet will not be charged, and I'll allow you to reapply for the yearly visas you've been applying for to play sports here after two years."

"The Hawkeyes will drop my contract before then," I argue.

"That's not my problem, Mr. Haynes."

"I need to at least tell my GM that I'm getting deported. I have a four-year contract I have to get out of. I need a good reason."

"Fine, your GM but that's it, Mr. Haynes. And leave the fiancé visa out of this. Do we have a deal?" he asks.

He's not giving me time to think about this but I don't have a choice. Juliet can't get in trouble for this and protecting her is more important than the Hawkeyes or my contract. A contract that I'll violate for failing to meet my terms.

All this shit because someone didn't mail in a goddamn check.

"Yes, we have a deal. I'll be gone by ten am. You have my word."

"Good. Enjoy your win tonight," he says, before turning and leaving toward the illuminated exit sign.

Two years... I'm going to be deported for two years.

My phone vibrates with a text.

> **Wife:** It's taking us a little longer to break down. Head out with the guys for a beer, I'll see you at home.

> **Ryker:** My body knee is killing me. I'm going to head home instead. I'll see you there when you get done.

The only thing I care about now... will Juliet come with me?

CHAPTER
TWENTY-SIX

Ryker

I've been texting her for the last couple of hours to make sure she's ok but it turns out that breaking down a project of that magnitude takes a lot of time.

But every minute that passes, and she isn't home, is a minute I won't get back and the anticipation of her answer to my question makes it hard to think about anything else

"I'm home." Juliet's voice comes through the door as I sit on the bed with an ice pack on my shoulder and knee.

I'm about to jump up and race to her but I can already hear her down the hall coming my way.

"Hey," I say, the second she walks through the door.

"Hi," she says in one exhausted breath, dropping her purse inside the door before heading for the walk-in closet. "I'm so tired. That took forever."

"I'm sorry to hear that. What happened?" I ask.

"We had issues getting the picture frames that we hung up to come down but the alumni guys wanted to take them home with them. So we had to call one of the stadium mechanics to come help with the rigging to get it to work. We had to wait an hour for him, and then the janitorial team wanted to know how we wanted them to take the balloon arches down. These are just first-day issues. Shawnie and I will have it better organized for tomorrow's game, don't worry," she says, her voice muffled from where she stands in the closet.

I won't have to worry... I won't be here.

The gravity of that hits finally, now that Juliet is making future plans and I have no idea if I'll get to stay in those plans after tonight.

She walks out in her shorts and the Hawkeyes shirt I gave her. I want to pull her into me and beg her to come to Canada but I have to go about this the right way.

I can't bring myself to tell her how close my actions brought her to seeing the inside of a courtroom... and maybe a prison cell. My job as her husband is to protect her and I couldn't have protected her if the Immigration office had decided to press charges instead. I would have taken her prison time if they would let me, but that's not how it works.

The truth is, I got flat-out lucky.

As much as I want to be honest with her and tell her what's going on, I can't stare back into those violet-blue eyes and see her disappointment in me. If I did come clean with her, will she follow me to Canada because she feels the same obligation and duty to me as she does to her brother? The same kind of obligation and duty that led her to marry a complete stranger to give her brother a better opportunity. Will she give up her business? Will she give up her weekly visits with her brother, just to make me happy?

She might… and I can't live with that.

As much as I don't want to ask her to choose, I also selfishly want her with me. So I'll let her decide and then I'll live with the outcome that led me here.

"I feel like I could sleep for days, but I have to get up bright and early to meet Shawnie. We agreed to a last minute setup for tomorrow. Marjorie wants to do a special alumni brunch for all the old players that are in town."

"That's nice of Marjorie," I say.

Though all I can think is how Juliet should be leaving with me by ten in the morning to head for Vancouver. Though, I know that even if she agrees to move, she can't do it tomorrow… she'll have to come later to fulfill her commitment and set someone up to take over her business.

"I know we were going to celebrate your win but I have to get up so early to get to the restaurant that Marjorie wants all the food from that I need to get to sleep. Could we do a raincheck for tomorrow?" she asks.

I know there won't be a raincheck tomorrow. Not in this penthouse and in this bed, at least.

She pushes the sheets down on her side of the bed, clicks off the bedside table light, and lays down.

I turn toward her, hooking an arm around her middle and pulling her against me.

"Mmmm," she hums blissfully. "You feel so good. Like home."

Hearing her say that brings me hope.

Because I am her home and she's mine.

I could live anywhere if I got to keep her.

"Juliet?" I say softly.

Her eyes are already closed and she seems to be fading to sleep quickly. I don't have much time to ask my question.

"Hmm?" she mumbles.

"What do you think about moving to Canada?"

She takes a deep yawn.

"Meeting your family was great but my brother and my mom—I can't just leave them. And my business... it's going crazy. I can't leave now. Let's revisit this after you retire, ok?"

She thinks retirement for me is in four years, but it's actually in about twelve hours.

Her answer isn't far from what I expected. This was the answer I thought I'd get, but I was hoping for a different conclusion.

I can't tell her the truth about immigration now because I know it will change her answer. She does so much for everyone else and if she's going to be with me, it needs to be because she wants it for herself. I asked her if she would move and she listed her priorities—moving to Canada with me isn't on it.

"Hey, Juliet?" I say, shaking her gently to wake her but she barely moves this time.

She's falling asleep fast.

"... just know that no matter what happens after tomorrow, everything I do from here on out is because I love you."

Now, there's only one answer for what I have to do tomorrow. I have to set her and her family to live as comfortably as I can, and then I have to end all communication before I step over the border.

Seeing her name come across my phone will make me turn back around.

Seeing her text messages asking where I am and why I left will have me confessing how badly I fucked up and gave Amelia evidence that she's using against us.

What's so fucked up about the whole thing? I'm going to do the same thing that her dad did to her. I'm going to repeat the same reasoning for her trust issues that kept her from trusting me in the beginning.

Unfortunately, I only have one option to protect her.

If I love her... I have to leave her.

CHAPTER
TWENTY-SEVEN

Juliet

When I get up this morning, Ryker's no longer in bed, but it's not unusual for him to go for a run or lift weights with one of the guys early in the morning.

I get ready for the brunch today as quickly as I can, throwing on a sweater dress and bootie heels, tying my hair back in a bun and quickly doing my makeup.

I look at the time and I see that I'm going to be late if I don't hurry up.

> Shawnie: Are you getting food?

> Juliet: Yes, on my way there now.

I make a mad dash out of the bedroom and head for the door. I probably won't have time to grab my coffee before I have to be back at the Hawkeyes stadium with brunch.

A colorful display catches my eye as I near the kitchen and I'm surprised to find a bouquet of flowers and my iced coffee waiting for me.

Ryker must have done this.

Little butterflies flap wildly in my belly at the thought that he would do this for me before he left this morning.

I grab my coffee and head for the door.

Ryker

Penelope isn't at her desk when I walk into Sam's office so I knock on his door.

"Come in," I hear him say.

I turn the knob, taking a deep breath, and push through the door.

"Do you have a minute?" I ask.

Sam looks to be reading an email but pulls his eyes off his computer screen and smiles up at me.

"Sure thing. I always have time. What's up?"

My stomach is twisting to the news I have to share as I walk closer to his desk. How do I even begin to tell the GM of the Hawkeyes about what I've been up to and the consequences of those actions?

Just plain spitting it out is my best option. Sam will respond better to me delivering direct information instead of beating around the bush.

"I need to let you know that I'm being deported from the US, effective this morning. I have to leave in a couple of hours and I won't be allowed to obtain a visa to play hockey for another two years."

Sam's eyes go wide, and his mouth falls open. "You're what?!" he says, standing out of his chair, his hand flattening against his desk as he leans forward toward me. "But you have a K-1 visa. Did something happen between you and Juliet?" he asks, his voice elevating with alarm.

"No, it's not that. It's more like... my original visa had an administrative issue due to my sports agent's assistant not sending in the check with my application. My visa wasn't going to get approved in time. I ran into Juliet by chance and asked her to marry me in order for me to get my green card."

I thought it would be hard to tell him, and I wasn't supposed to tell him it all, but once I started, it all came rushing out.

"You paid Juliet to marry you for a fiancé visa... have you lost your mind? You could get deported indefinitely and she could do prison time for that."

I knew he was going to be pissed about the decision I made.

"Not to mention that this could look really bad on the Hawkeyes if this comes out. Did you consider that?"

"No sir, I didn't. It was the only option for me to stay in the States and help out the team," I say.

"We could have put you on leave for a few weeks or a month, for Christ's sake, until the application went through. You've jeopardized yourself, Juliet, and this hockey franchise."

Shit, I know he's right and letting him down is the last thing I want to do. This team has been good to me and I never considered the team giving me a few weeks in Canada until my visa got approved. Players can't just miss games. Especially not the starting lineup. But I should have come to him first and worked something out.

And Juliet... I could have helped her out without marrying her and going through the immigration office. I could have simply started dating her and that would have been enough for Marjorie to have given her the job.

At the time I thought I was doing the right thing by not putting this on anyone in the Hawkeyes franchise and fixing this myself. I was wrong.

"Sam, I don't know what to say. I screwed up and I have no recourse—they'll take this to trial. And the Hawkeyes and Juliet need to stay out of a legal battle over this. I don't have any other option. I have to leave this morning."

Sam blows out a breath and leans back, resting his hands on his hips.

"Losing our center and captain right before the playoffs..."

"I know. But this team is solid without me and they're going to bring home the cup. I have full confidence. And as for a center... Slade Matthews on the farm team is due a shot. I can't believe no NHL team has tried to snag him away yet."

Sam doesn't seem pleased with my recommendation, but he doesn't have a lot to go on right now and he knows I'm right.

He'll have to fill my position fast, and he'll have to do it with a player they already have in reserves.

I wish it were me playing for the championship, but it won't be and I still want to see my team win.

"You're right. I'll look into him." He comes around the desk and shakes my hand. "Thank you for your years on this team. I'll talk with Phil and with legal and see how we can get you out of your contract as easily as possible without backlash."

He's offering more than he has to and I appreciate it.

"Thanks, Sam. Can you do me a favor and leave the K-1 visa issue on a need-to-know basis? The immigration office doesn't want this getting out and I don't want anyone around here looking at Juliet differently."

I don't think Marjorie would revoke the contract with Juliet now. Besides, what she pulled off yesterday was better than anyone has done in the years I've played here. Letting her go would be a mistake. Besides, Marjorie isn't the kind of person to go back on her word.

"Juliet's not going with you?" he asks, his eyebrows stitching together in confusion.

"No. She's staying where she belongs."

He lets out a disappointed sigh. "That's too bad. You two looked good together. I thought you two were going to make it."

Yeah... me too.

"It wasn't meant to be."

He gives a slow nod but looks away in thought.

"Ok, so, if I can't tell Phil and Legal about the asshole who's deporting you, what do you want me to tell everyone?"

"I'll call all the guys myself and let them know that my visa got denied due to mixed-up paperwork and I'm getting deported. Can we leave it at that?"

"Fair enough, I understand." He nods. "And just for your information, I've heard whispers that the Vancouver Vikings might be looking for a new head coach. Your retirement plans might be panning out after all."

I hadn't heard that yet but there's no consolation prize to losing Juliet, and letting down my team is a knife to the chest. Not even the opportunity to honor my dad could make up for leaving everyone else to pick up the pieces in my wake.

But taking a job like that will give me something to do so that my days aren't spent sitting around my house thinking about Juliet. I don't know how I'll get in my car and leave this city with Juliet still inside it but I have to keep her safe and this is the only way I can do that.

"I'll reach out to the GM. He's a friend of the family's. Thanks for the heads up," I say.

I nod and then turn back toward the door.

"Haynes," he says, and then walks quickly around his desk. "If you ever feel like coaching a team in the US when you can apply for a visa again, keep the Hawkeyes in mind, will you? We're always looking to add talent to the coaching side of things and Bex would be happy to have you."

The fact that Sam is keeping the door open to the Hawkeyes for me means everything.

I have one last stop before I head home and pack a few things.

"Good morning, sir. How can I help you today?" the woman at the front desk of Jerrin's new facility asks.

"Hi, yeah... I wanted to come in and make an advance payment for a resident that you have here. Can I do that?" I ask.

"Certainly sir. What is the resident's name?" she asks, breaking eye contact with me to quickly click the keys of her keyboard.

"The name is Jerrin Di Costa."

She flashes a smile up to me. "Oh, we love Jerrin here. He has really settled in well and he comes down once a day and plays the most beautiful music on that baby grand for us here in reception."

I'm glad he seems to be doing well and I hope they've mentioned all this to Juliet. After all the dust settles, I hope that she still feels, if nothing else, that what happened over the last few weeks was worth her brother getting into this facility.

"And how much would you like to apply to his account today?" she asks.

If I could, I'd just ask her to set up auto pay on my unlimited spend black card and pay the monthly payment indefinitely, but I have no idea how Juliet is going to take me leaving without telling her the real reason and I can't risk her being upset enough to cancel the account set up.

Instead, I'll pay a lump sum and make sure that my credit card company refuses any refunds... just in case she tries.

I know how she feels about her father for abandoning her. I can't imagine she'll see me any differently.

"I want to pay ahead for the next two years," I tell her.

"Oh…" she says, shooting her eyes back up to mine from her computer screen. "Are you sure you wouldn't rather pay per month? It's about ten thousand a month—"

Before she can finish her sentence, I slide my black card over the desk.

"That's not a problem. Two years will be fine for now. Thank you," I tell her with a reassuring nod.

"Ok, then."

She starts typing and then slides my card through the reader.

Who knows what will happen two years from now when I'll be eligible to apply for a work visa again. My spot on the Hawkeyes will be filled by then and I don't want to play for another team. The only reason I'd come back is for Juliet. But asking her to wait for me is unreasonable. I deserve to lose her for what I put her through. She deserves better than that.

As the receptionist is finishing charging my card and applying it to Jerrin's account, a blob of black silky hair catches in my peripheral. I look up quickly to see who is walking in this direction, a tingle of panic setting in that Juliet is here and is going to catch what I'm doing… but it's not Juliet… it's Theresa, Juliet's mom.

She's dressed in full scrubs and seems to be too preoccupied with her thoughts to notice that I'm standing at reception.

I turn to face her and her eyes flicker to me. It takes her a second to register that it's me but once she does, she slows and I'm surprised at the small smile she gives me. I half expected her to pretend she didn't see me and keep moving.

"Ryker… this is a surprise. What are you doing here?" she asks.

Shit, I didn't think about what it might mean if Theresa sees me here and then later tells Juliet that she saw me minutes before I skipped town. What will Juliet think?

"I just came down to donate. My accountant is always hounding me about making them during the tax season. It's a write-off," I say, hoping she buys it.

Not that it's untrue. I am making a donation... I'm making Juliet's life as easy as I can since I won't be here anymore to do that day-to-day.

"That's very thoughtful of you. And I never got a chance to thank you for what you've done to help my daughter and my son. I know I've been wary of my daughter dating a professional athlete, but you have done so much and you make her very happy."

Her words hit me. I have just started to crack Theresa's guard against me and within a matter of hours, she's going to think that I did to her daughter what her ex-husband did to her. I'll never gain her trust again after this, but it may not matter anyway at this point.

"She means everything to me, and I would do anything to take care of her and protect her," I say, hoping my words ring through her ears when her daughter calls her in tears later today.

Fuck, the thought of causing Juliet tears makes me physically ill.

The door opens to one of the small offices near the reception desk and a woman walks out.

"Theresa, what a pleasant surprise to see you," the woman in a nice pantsuit says, walking toward us.

"It's good to see you too," Theresa says.

She gets close enough that I can see her name tag.

Linda Ottis, Human Resources.

"I'm glad I caught you before you left. I got your application for the Occupational Therapist Assistant position and I discussed it with the head of staff. Unfortunately, that position requires that you either finished your schooling or that you're enrolled in the course at the time of being accepted for this job."

Theresa nods back in understanding but her eyes lower to the ground for a moment in disappointment.

"I see, well thank you for looking into it for me. It was worth a try," Theresa says.

"I believe classes start at the institute next week. If you can get enrolled, I can throw your name in the ring for the position," the woman in the suit says.

Linda is bright-eyed with excitement at the news she has to share. I don't know much about Theresa's work except that she doesn't make enough money to help Juliet with the monthly payments for this place. I don't know how much an Occupation Therapist makes but it must be more than she makes now. This seems like a great opportunity for Theresa to work near Jerrin.

"I can't afford that at the moment," she says, swatting her hand in the air to act as though she doesn't feel awkward saying she doesn't have the money. "Maybe I'll be able to apply the next time you have an opening."

"Sure, right... of course. We would love to have a CNA with your years of experience working as a therapist here. Please consider trying again once you get enrolled—you're a shoo-in," the woman says, giving Theresa a warm smile.

"Yeah, I'll do that," Theresa says, but something tells me she won't try again. If she doesn't have the money now, I don't see how she'll have the money later. "I'd better get out of here. My shift starts in forty-five minutes."

Theresa waves to the woman I was talking with in reception and then thanks Linda, giving me a small wave before she heads back out of the building.

As soon as the automatic doors open and she walks out into the parking lot, Linda starts heading back to doing whatever she came out of her office to do.

"Linda," I call out.

She stops and glances over at me.

"Yes, can I help you?" she asks with a professional smile.

"I think so. Can you tell me the name of the institute that teaches the Occupational Therapy Assistant courses?"

"It's a program within the WU. You can contact them to get registered."

I nod. That should be easy enough for my agent to handle. Though I've thought that before and now I'm getting deported. This is his chance to redeem himself and take care of things on this side of the continent for me.

"Thanks for your help. Theresa will be enrolled by the end of the week."

"Oh... ok..." she says, probably wondering who the hell I am and how I know Theresa well enough to make that call for her.

I look back over at the receptionist who pushes my card back over the counter.

"You might hear from my agent, James Potter, now and again to add more funds to the account. Thank you for your help today."

She smiles and nods. "No problem. I'm sure Juliet and Theresa will be very pleased with the credit on the account."

Linda looks at the receptionist and then me, one eyebrow lifted as she tries to determine who I am.

"Have a good day," I say to both of them and then head toward the exit.

I pull out my phone and dial James's number.

"Haynes, please tell me that you're calling with good news. I've been calling all my contacts trying to find a lawyer that can help us fight this."

I called James first thing this morning while I was getting Juliet's coffee down the street and professed my anger over my circumstances. At the end of the day though, I made the choice to go through with this scheme and I'm the one that told Amelia what I did while her phone was rolling.

As much as I'd like to blame this all on James, the decision to go through with the fiancé visa and propose the idea to Juliet was mine and mine alone. Though I can still hang the missing check over his head for a lifetime... and I plan on it.

"It's over James, let it go. But you owe me and I'm cashing it in now."

"Anything. What is it?"

"The Vikings need a new head coach I want you to negotiate my contract—don't fuck this up for me," I tell him.

"I won't. I swear," he says.

"And I need you to look after Juliet. Anything she needs. You have access to the funds you need from me to make it happen. Don't question anything she asks for... that's not your job. Whatever she needs or wants, you'll make good on it."

James has the ability to sign off on my behalf for certain things and has access to funds that I've always kept in a joint escrow account.

He makes sure my leases are paid for, checks get mailed to charities I donate to, and pays other administration fees and fines handed down from the hockey associations that I'm a member of as part of the NHL.

"I need you to transfer the Penthouse lease into Juliet Di Costa's name and ensure the payment is made every month."

I may not be around to take care of her, but I have enough money to make sure she lives comfortably.

"For how long?"

"Indefinitely. Or for as long as she'll agree to stay."

"Got it," he says, I can hear the scratching of the pencil against a pad of paper.

He's writing this down and taking it seriously.

"Anything else?" he asks.

"Yeah. Get Juliet's mom, Theresa, into the Occupational Therapy Assistant course at WU and make sure that she has everything she needs."

"I've got this all down and I will get this all done today, you have my word."

"And James...?"

"Yes?"

"Do this shit all yourself."

"You got it, Haynes. I'll call The Commons first and get the ball rolling on the lease change."

"Thanks."

CHAPTER
TWENTY-EIGHT

Juliet

After a long, successful brunch, I'm exhausted but on cloud nine.

Marjorie wouldn't stop singing our praises for how quickly we set up and how great everything looked with barely twenty-four hours' notice. Not to mention that we stayed under the budget she gave us. That part isn't her expectation but more of a personal challenge that Shawnie and I like to shoot for.

It's great to feel like I'm not just the wife of a player who got handed the job, but someone competent enough to handle the tasks that Marjorie wants done.

"I knew you were the right choice from the moment you walked out of our office," Marjorie says.

"That means more than you can know," I tell her. "I sort of figured I got the job because I'm Ryker's wife."

"Absolutely not, my dear. You were already my top candidate but when I saw Ryker propose on the ice, I didn't think there was any reason to make you wait to hear back," she says. "We love hiring from within if we have someone competent to do the job. We just got lucky that you were one and the same."

My heart warms at her words.

All this time I thought I was only barely on the cusp of making it to the top five candidates who applied for the position. I thought I was the outlier—the event firm that came to the table with the least to offer. And now to hear that we were her first pick... I can't describe the feeling of accomplishment that I set myself apart and that she could see our worth in that meeting.

I look over at Shawnie who's grabbing the last box of rental items she picked up this morning for the brunch event.

She smiles wide at me, overhearing the conversation.

"That means the world to us. We really appreciate the opportunity you've given Elite," I say, including Shawnie since I couldn't do this without her.

As happy as I am to celebrate this win with Shawnie, there's one person I can't wait to share the news with.

Ryker.

I grab the last couple of items off the table and Shawnie and I walk out of the Hawkeyes building.

We load up our vehicles and then we say goodbye.

I pull my phone out of my purse the second I can and see the time is three pm. Since I left home at seven am, I haven't seen Ryker since last night and I can't wait for that raincheck.

Sitting in the driver seat while Shawnie takes off out of the parking lot, I hit redial on my phone and call Ryker.

"We're sorry, you have reached a number that has been disconnected or is no longer in service. If you feel you have reached this recording in error, please check the number and try your call again."

What?

That can't be.

I pull the phone from my ear and go through my contacts instead of recent calls and select Ryker's name again.

But I get the same error.

Something must be wrong with the cell towers because this makes no sense unless he forgot to pay his cell phone bill. That seems like a silly oversight, but I suppose it happens.

I put my car in drive and head home. I'm not sure if he'll be there but his car isn't in the Hawkeyes parking lot, so I know he isn't here working out with the guys.

Pulling into the parking garage of The Commons, his parking spot is empty. I know his car wasn't at the stadium and it's not here either.

Ryker has meetings all over town regularly but now I wish I had asked him what he was planning to do today. Maybe he already knows about his cell phone issues and is down at his cell phone provider getting it resolved.

I get out of my car and head upstairs. All I can do now is wait for him to return home.

Walking into the apartment, I call out his name just in case he parked on the street today.

"Ryker?"

But there's no answer.

I head for the kitchen to get a glass of water when I see a note on the island that wasn't there this morning, placed under the vase of roses.

I see my name in the top corner.

Yep, he must know his phone isn't working and left me a note.

Relief hits me.

For some reason I was starting to get a little concerned since he hadn't tried to call or text all day, which is unusual for him. But I guess that's what childhood trauma does to you. The first lack of communication leads to you believing that they left you.

I take a cleansing inhale and then pick up the note.

Juliet-

I don't know where to begin this letter, so I'll just start by saying that I'm sorry. The last thing I ever planned to do was hurt you.

My stomach turns instantly, and the taste of bile rises to my throat. I grab the letter and instinctively head straight for the bedroom.

I storm through the door, pushing it hard enough that it bounces off the back of the wall and power walk to the closet.

My heart beats wildly against my rib cage. The same rib cage that's designed to protect my heart from the outside world. But no caged heart is safe from what I know I'm about to find.

I crash through the walk-in closet and the second I look to his side where all of his clothes should be hanging, I start to hyperventilate—a wail cracking from my throat—a sound that I don't even recognize. Streams of tears start flooding down my face. I couldn't hold these ones back even if I tried.

I fell for it.

I fell for his promises.

I let my guard down when my mother told me not to and my instinct told me to run.

My tear-filled, blurry eyes fall back to the letter, a slightly more crinkled version of the one I took off the island a moment ago, now shaking like a leaf in my hand. Teardrops begin to smear some of the ink, but not enough to shelter me from his words.

The Vancouver Vikings have offered me a head coaching position and I've accepted it. The Hawkeyes are going to let me out of my contract, and this is my chance to make up for missing time with my dad. I'm going to finish his legacy and bring the Vikings home a Stanley Cup.

I wish the best for you, but I know you'll do just fine without me. I had the lease on the penthouse changed into your name and James Potter and Associates will ensure that the lease and all the upkeep on the place will be paid every month. You can live here for as long as you want, and I hope that you do. I'll list his phone number below. Call him for anything you need… anything, Juliet.

I never meant to leave like this, like your dad. This is why I want to contribute financially to make sure that you and your family are taken care of.

I know it doesn't matter now, and this won't make much sense to you, considering what I'm doing but if I could have done things differently, I wouldn't have asked you to marry me for a green card. I would have asked you for a first date that night out on the parking lot. I would have worked to earn my chance to propose to you, instead of buying it.

I'm sorry I put you through a fake marriage.

I'm sorry for everything.

He left... he actually left.

I crumble to the ground and stare at the empty white built-in cabinets where his things used to be.

There's only one person to call. The one person who will understand.

"Mom..." I say, trying to keep my voice from shaking when she answers. "He's gone."

"Are you sure? I just saw him at the center. I got a call that he's paying for my OTA program. That doesn't make sense."

The shock in her voice gets to me. For all the warnings she told me in the beginning of all this... she can't believe he left either.

"I'm sure," I say, a sob breaking through my throat.

Her voice and tone changes quickly at the sound of my tears.

"I'll tell my supervisor I have an emergency. I'll be there in ten minutes, Juju Bean. Don't move. Stay right where you are. I'm coming, baby."

Chapter Twenty-Nine

Two Months Later

Juliet

"Is that the last of it?" my mom's new boyfriend Felix asks, carrying out the last suitcase from the penthouse.

He's a single father who has a son at the same center as Jerrin. He's a nice guy who owns a string of rock-climbing gyms around Washington and does well for himself. And the best part... he treats my mom like she walks on water. It's time she found love again, and I've never seen her happier.

"Yep, that's the last of it," I say, taking a last look at the place.

He nods and heads out the door with my brother right behind him, carrying my laptop bag. The Occupational Therapist who works with Jerrin daily has made so much amazing progress with him. Jerrin's even come to a couple of home games with me which he wouldn't have been able to do before because of his anxiety around large crowds and noise. It's still a work in progress but I can already see him taking the tools they're giving him and applying them in real world situations.

"Are you sure you want to do this?" Tessa asks.

"It's time. He's not coming back, and I shouldn't have held on this long," I say, handing my penthouse key to her.

She said she'll coordinate with James to get the key to him when he comes by to take over the penthouse.

Since she lives with Lake in the penthouse across the hall, she's been coming over with wine and movies or dinner ever since Ryker left.

We've become close, and not having her right next door will be a bummer but I'm at the Hawkeyes stadium at least twice a month. And Shawnie and I get regular invites to coffee dates at Serendipity's Coffee Shop with the girls.

Besides, I can't live here anymore with the memories of the life I *almost* had. It's too painful.

I see him everywhere between these four walls and the muscle memory of his kiss is still so vivid.

His cell phone never started working again, though I called a dozen times or more over the space of a week, until finally it was too pitiful to continue trying.

My landlord already rented out my old place but with the money I have since I don't have to pay for Jerrin's lease, I rented a two-bedroom in the same building with double the square footage. I also hired an assistant to help Shawnie and I, and gave Shawnie a big fat raise, which she deserves with how much she's taken on.

I wanted to ask the center to send the funds back but my mom convinced me not to.

"He put you through enough, Juliet. Take this advantage and get ahead with your business. Who cares if it makes him sleep better at night? It helps us sleep better too, doesn't it?"

As if I know what sleeping at night feels like anymore. But I won't tell her about the sleepless nights where I reach out for him hoping this all is just a nightmare. It's bad enough that I haven't taken off his ring. Every time I try to, I replay him begging me to never take it off in the bathroom of his childhood home in Vancouver... and I stupidly promised that I wouldn't.

I guess I'm the only one that keeps my word.

So, I did what she suggested and left the money on Jerrin's account. However, I still don't understand what his motivation is for paying the lease on my brother's apartment, for my mother's classes for her OTA program, or for paying the penthouse lease for me to stay in. But whatever it is, I hope he's done.

I pull out my phone and call James's office for what will be the last time.

"James Potter and associates," his assistant answers.

"James Potter please, this is Juliet Di Costa."

"Of course, Ms. Di Costa, one moment."

I hear the hold music as she transfers me.

"Juliet." I hear James's booming voice. "Have you changed your mind about the penthouse? Why don't you just hold onto the key, just in case? Maybe you could use it as an office space for your growing business," he says, trying to sway me before I even get a word in edgewise.

I don't know what James's reasoning for wanting me to stay is. I would assume he's in communication with Ryker but he's never said as much, and I'm too prideful to ask. Either way I won't be persuaded, whether it's James asking me to stay or if it's Ryker using James as his puppet. Though I don't know why Ryker would care either.

If he cared, he would have at least had the decency to break it off with me in person instead of leaving a note.

What Ryker wants is irrelevant to me. He didn't care what I wanted.

"I've already moved into my new apartment and I'm looking for an office space that I don't have to ride up eight flights to get to. You can tell Ryker that if he would like to discuss this further, he can call me himself. That is, if he finally has a phone number that hasn't been disconnected," I say, and then hang up.

I don't feel good about hanging up on James like that but all he's going to do is keep saying things to make me stay, like he has for the last couple of months. I don't need any more connection to Ryker.

It's bad enough that we're still legally married.

I've been waiting for the divorce papers from his lawyers to arrive, but they haven't.

I hold my breath every time someone knocks on the door, expecting it to be a courier with the papers, but it never is. I can't live like this.

I would send him the divorce papers myself, but every time I'm about to call a divorce lawyer to book an appointment, the diamond on my hand catches my eye and I'm reminded that even though things were fake when I said "until death", I meant those words... even then.

And I wish so badly that I didn't.

But I still mean them now.

CHAPTER THIRTY

Juliet

It's the first morning in my new apartment. I haven't unpacked a single thing since we moved everything yesterday and all my luggage is still in the back of my SUV.

Since I don't have any appointments today, my day is free. I thought I would set up my brand-new office with the furniture I ordered online that got here a couple days ago. If setting up my first home office in my brand-new apartment doesn't cheer me up, then I don't know what will.

But first... coffee.

I head for my kitchen and to the house warming coffee maker that my mom bought me for my new apartment, and load a single pod into it.

It hisses and moans as the coffee maker comes to life, pouring liquid gold into my cup.

I pour it over a cup of ice and give it a minute to melt.

My phone starts ringing next to my cup.

It's not a number programmed into my phone but under the phone number, the area code is weird. I look below the number to see that it tells me the number is an international phone number from Canada.

My heart literally skips a beat. In less than a second, I debate both answering and screening the call to make Ryker sweat it out. Maybe he should wonder where I am and why I'm not answering, but I can't do it. I don't have enough self-restraint when it comes to him, and I still have so many questions that I want answers to.

Like, why did you leave a note instead of telling me in person?

Why didn't you ask me to go with you?

Do you ever think about me?

And my least favorite but the one that keeps me up at night... are you seeing anyone?

I click on the green 'accept' button and lift the phone to my ear. "Hello?"

"Hi, Juliet?"

It's a woman's voice.

I couldn't be any more confused.

But maybe she's Ryker's divorce lawyer?

"Uh, yes. Who's this?"

"It's Harper, Ryker's sister."

Relief hits me and soothes my racing heart just a little. It's not a divorce lawyer asking for my new address.

"Hi Harper. How are you?"

And where is your brother?

Why did he leave me?

"I'm good. I'm in Seattle right now and I know this is really last minute, but I have an event that my boss just told me he wants 'the works' for. I'm kind of in a pinch. Any chance you would have availability to pull off an event for me?"

Part of me wants to say yes because this could be great exposure with the kind of clientele that attends art galleries but the other part of me doesn't know if I can see her and not break down in tears.

I'm not a crier by nature but when it comes to Ryker, nothing has ever made sense.

"I'm not really sure if—"

"We'll pay anything. My boss knows this is an expedite situation, but our firm doesn't just work with art galleries. We host large art conferences and big parties. If you can make this happen, I can guarantee that my boss will turn to you for more work."

"I'll have to discuss this with my business partner," I say, using Shawnie as my delayed tactic.

I need some time to decide if I can do this or not. Can I handle being attached to Ryker's sister when I just cut off all other ties to him? Technically this woman is still my sister-in-law.

"Ok, could you talk with her and then meet me for coffee? You can give me your answer then."

"What if it's no?" I ask her.

"Then at least I get to see you while I'm here and I'll keep looking for another party planning agency to help me with the event."

I know I can't turn this down. It's too big of an opportunity. And if Shawnie finds out I didn't take on a huge new client with massive elbow rubbing and referral potential because I couldn't put my big girl panties on and meet with my ex's sister... she'll kill me. There's also no way I'm telling Shawnie that I'm about to meet up with Harper. She'd hunt us down at the coffee shop and hit Harper with every question under the sun about Ryker and why he left, including if he got dropped on his head as a child.

Shawnie is so mad at Ryker that I hope he never shows up anywhere she and I are both at. His balls wouldn't be safe.

"Ok," I agree, trying to think of a coffee shop that none of the girls visit. Serendipity's Coffee Shop is off the list. It's a regular hot spot for all of my friends.

I think of a place on the opposite side of town and then give her the name.

She agrees and I end the call, reminding myself that this will be worth it because of the business growth. After all, I lied to James—I do want a penthouse office with incredible views of the city on the eighth floor.

I just don't want Ryker's.

I walk into a quaint little coffee shop an hour later. The smell of coffee and toasted bagels hit me right away, settling my anxiety with my favorite smells in the world.

It's a cute little corner shop in a brick building with floor-to-ceiling windows on two of the four walls. It's bright and airy but small with only six tables.

It's a little busy when I walk in. The second I pass through the door, I see a hand shoot up and wave at me.

A smiling Harper in an off-the-runway green military-styled jacket with copper buttons, designer jeans and wedge platform heels stands out of her seat to make sure I see her. It's weird to see her like this since in Canada, she was dressed in hockey gear during the charity event and then jeans and rainboots for a sledding race. However, the woman is an art curator so it shouldn't surprise me that she knows how to dress in higher fashion when she needs to.

I make my way to the table as she steps away from it, opening her arms and giving me a hug. Just as Everett said, they're a hugging family.

I wrap my arm around her too and hug back.

"It's good to see you," she says.

"You too," I say, though I wonder if she can feel the racing of my heart that started the moment I saw her.

I have no idea if she'll bring up Ryker and drop details about his life in Canada. I'm not even sure if I hope she does, or if I hope she keeps this completely professional without any mention of the family at all.

"Thank you for meeting me. I know that your business is extremely busy so I can't tell you how happy I am that you're at least considering helping us."

"We're certainly willing to try to help you as best as we can. We brought on some extra help recently so we're able to accommodate more work."

"That's great news. I know this is a big ask, but I also know that this could be huge for you as well. We have many clients that host large charity events, corporations that throw big parties, and one of our clients is the event planner who puts on the Super Bowl every year. I will make sure that you never miss an introduction to any of these high-profile clients who could potentially send you big ticket item projects."

I knew that this would be an important meeting to agree to. I'm glad I didn't let my nerves get the best of me and chicken out. I won't let Ryker spoil anything else in my life.

"Where do I sign up?" I ask.

She laughs.

"Good. I'm glad to hear that. The art showing is in ten days and this is a huge up-and-coming artist so we want a huge splash. There's no budget for this. It just needs to be done right."

I pull out my tablet and start writing down notes.

"Do you have thoughts on inspiration for this show?"

She smiles. She likes this question.

"The artist has a very Parisian inspiration so let's go with that. Not an obvious Paris theme but the color pallet, the food, that kind of thing."

"Perfect. No problem. Shawnie, my assistant, loves the whole Parisian aesthetic, so I'll put her as the lead on this one," I say, jotting down more notes.

There's a small silence that sets in as I'm writing. I look up to see if she got distracted but she just stares back at me as if she is studying me.

"Is something wrong?" I ask.

"Your ring."

Shit.

My hands turn clammy instantly and I feel like I can hear my heartbeat in my ears. I've been caught by my soon-to-be ex-husband's sister.

I forgot to stick it in my pocket before I walked in. Not taking it off is hard wired now into my brain and I hate it that I can't seem to bring myself to take it off.

I lift my hand and straighten out my fingers, locking my sights down on the diamond that represents so many broken promises.

"Right, well... we're not technically divorced yet so I guess..."

I have no idea what to say next. What do you say to an almost total stranger who's also your in-law and the woman who has probably seen Ryker since he came home... without his wife.

But there's a part of me that's mad at her a little too. She sat in that kitchen and lectured me about how I was the one who could hurt her brother. The fact that she thought I held enough of his heart to crush him is almost laughable now.

But I gave him more of me after she told me he was in love with me. I believed she knew him well enough to know his heart. It turns out that none of us know Ryker at all.

"I need to tell you something," she says, biting down on her lip as if what she has to say isn't something she should say at all. "And I've been debating whether or not I should get involved..."

I try to swallow down the clog in my throat at how serious she looks as her eyes narrow on me and she leans in a little.

"Ryker might kill me if I tell you this, but I think you deserve to know..."

Oh God, please don't tell me he's seeing someone else. I don't think my heart can take it.

I just sit there, waiting to be run over by a semi-truck and flattened like a pancake.

"Ok..." I barely squeak out, not completely sure if I want to hear what she has to say.

"He didn't leave because of the Vikings like he told you. He got deported."

"What?!" I say, my voice louder than intended.

Most of the people in the coffee shop all rubber neck toward us. Harper gives them all a reassuring smile but I can't take my eyes off her.

"He has a K-1 visa... he can't be deported," I tell her, trying to keep my voice down this time.

"That's the thing... he doesn't anymore."

"I'm not following. Why would he say that in the letter he wrote me?"

I need more information and I need it right now.

"Because Amelia sent incriminating footage to the supervisor of the immigration officer who pushed you two through. Then he found out the same officer has money on the Hawkeyes winning the Stanley Cup which is why he fast tracked your application."

"Amelia did that?"

I can't even believe someone would do something so horrible. But then I remember that night she was in the penthouse and how she warned him he'd regret it.

"That's correct, and if karma hadn't hit her hard last month by way of cancel culture, I would hunt her down and make sure the only jobs she can book is for hand modeling. Her face wouldn't be palatable for public consumption."

"Cancel culture?" I ask.

Not that I follow Amelia but I have no idea what Harper is talking about.

"You didn't hear? She faked volunteering at a soup kitchen a week after Ryker left town, and when she got called out for it, she said that the needy and homeless don't deserve her time because they don't pay for it," Harper says and then takes a sip of her coffee. "Evidently, that didn't resonate well with her audience, and she lost all million plus of her followers. Her social media account is dead and no one's booking her for modeling jobs anymore."

Whoa, that happened fast.

"That kind of thing happens?" I ask though I'm not heartbroken for her at all after what she did.

"Oh yeah. And it couldn't have happened to a better person."

My eyes drop to the table as I try to get ahold of all the information she's telling me.

"Still, why didn't Ryker tell me about the immigration officer and Amelia's footage?"

"From what I could pull out of him, the immigration supervisor showed up the night of the first alumni game and gave him an ultimatum."

"What kind of ultimatum?" I ask, my eyebrows stitching together as I stare back at her.

"He had to leave in the morning and couldn't tell anyone that he was getting deported because of the fiancé visa."

"Why?

"Ryker wouldn't tell me. But he did say that the supervisor said that if he didn't comply, he'd press criminal charges and you were looking at prison time."

My stomach drops at her explanation.

I know she's right... criminal charges against me would be steeper than deportation for Ryker but why didn't he tell me this? And why didn't he offer me the option to go with him?

Something is still missing.

"It still doesn't explain why he left without giving me the option to go with him."

She nods like this is a missing link for her too.

"I'm not sure. I couldn't get that out of him either. But did he ever tell you why Amelia turned him down, and why he's never had a serious relationship stick since high school?"

I rack my brain for what he told me when he mentioned their break up. Something in my gut tells me I screwed up... somewhere... somehow.

"He told me she turned him down because she didn't want to live in Canada."

"Yep. She refused to move if their fiancée visa got denied and he got deported anyway."

"But what does she have to do with me?"

"Have you two ever had the conversation about moving to Canada?" she asks, her eyebrow lifting, hoping that my answer is the missing puzzle piece she's been trying to find.

Then the sleepy, barely coherent conversation we had the last night he was in Seattle hits me.

"Oh God, I think I might be sick," I say, my gut twisting in my belly.

My arm grips around my stomach as I actually feel physically unwell.

"I told him I couldn't leave my brother and my mom. They needed me at the time. I told him that we could talk about it again after he retired."

But if he had told me he was getting deported, I would have found a way to make it all work. Vancouver is less than an hour's flight and only a three-hour drive plus border control. I could have found a way to do it all... I think.

He didn't even ask.

"I'm going out on a limb here and saying that he didn't want to make you choose between your family and him. So he took himself out of the equation. Whether he did that so he wouldn't get rejected yet again, or because he knew your family needed you more... I don't know. But I know he still loves you."

"How do you know he still loves me?" I ask, hoping she has a really good solid reason because I believed her last time.

"He hasn't taken his ring off since he got home."

My whole body seems to spark back to life and the twisting in my gut turns to butterflies. How is that possible?

"What do I do now?" I ask her, because I truly need someone to direct me. My brain is short circuiting with all this new information that I can't seem to process fast enough.

"If it were me..." She looks at me and I nod, asking her to continue. "I'd get in my car straight from here, knock on his door and demand answers."

CHAPTER
THIRTY-ONE

Ryker

Practice today was good. I like the way the Vikings are starting to look with the few tweaks that me and the assistant coaches are making with the team.

It's dark out when I leave my office and head for my truck. I spend as much time here as I can because I don't like being at home. It doesn't offer me the distraction of the Vikings stadium to occupy my thoughts. And if my thoughts aren't running through plays and tactics to try to win our next game, they end up on a highlight reel of Juliet and every moment we spent together.

I pull into the garage of my house and head inside, debating whether to make something to eat or just head to bed.

It's after nine o'clock, so I could go either way at this point since I've come home to an empty house. At least on away games, I get to stay in a hotel where I don't have memories of taking off her ex-boyfriend's shirt and exchanging it with mine, or lying next to her while she slept.

I can't even walk into the bar I took her to that night because my mind races to her being in a bar in Seattle at the same time without her wedding ring on. The thought of her going home with anyone besides me boils my blood and has me thinking about calling her and begging her not to see anyone else. But that's the biggest dickhead move I could make, and at this point, I don't think she'd take my call, anyway.

Not since I abandoned her and canceled my phone service. I couldn't risk her calling my phone because I wouldn't have been able to not answer. And if I answered, eventually I would have broken down and asked her to move to Canada for me. But asking her to move would be the most selfish thing I could do, because I believe she would have if I asked. She would have done it for me... not for her.

She told me the night before I left what mattered to her, and I'd never let her give that up just to be with me.

I make the decision to opt for bed. I'm still training with the team like I did as a player for the Hawkeyes so I should refuel with carbohydrates and protein, but I ate a late lunch and I'm too damn tired to care tonight.

I head for the staircase when I hear a knock on my door. It's late for anyone to be here and the usual late-night guest, Harper, who's been coming around and hounding me with questions, is in Seattle... where I should be.

I hear the knock again.

"I'm coming. Hold on," I say, walking toward the door.

If this is one of my brothers coming over for a late-night beer, I'm kicking their asses out or they can play darts in the media room in the back of the house but I'm going to bed.

"I'm not interested in company tonight," I say as I unlatch the door and swing it open.

And see the last thing I'm expecting.

My wife.

"Oh uh, ok..." Juliet says with a frown, and then turns to leave.

"Whoa. Hold on." I practically jump out of my house and grip gently around her arm to turn her back to me.

Fuck, she looks beautiful, but it wouldn't matter if she had spent the day rolling in pig shit, I'd still want her all over me.

The flood of emotions I feel right now couldn't be sorted out if I tried.

I'm relieved to see her at my front door but terrified she's here with divorce papers or to give me my ring back because she met someone else.

James told me she moved out of the penthouse today even though I asked him to tell her to keep the key and turn the place into her office. She still left. It was the last string that attached me to her and she severed it.

She turns around to face me, but she doesn't look as happy to see me as I am to see her. She's still sporting a frown and those violet eyes don't hold the sparkle they used to have for me.

I deserve it.

"What are you doing here?" I ask, though I'm worried I won't like the answer.

"I saw your sister today."

Harper didn't say she was going to see Juliet while she was in Seattle. However, I don't know if she would have. She's been pissed at me ever since I came home without Juliet.

"You did?"

"Yeah. She told me everything. Or... everything she knows."

Goddamn it, I should have kept my mouth shut and not told her a damn thing.

"What did she tell you?" I ask, because I'm not giving anything more away than what my sister did.

I don't even remember everything I told her. She got me wasted one night when I first got back and started asking questions. Not that getting me plastered was hard, I tried drinking Juliet away the first few nights I got here, but it didn't work. I still thought about her drunk or sober and hangovers past thirty-five are a different animal, so I quit and threw myself into work instead.

"That you had a visit from an immigration officer that you didn't tell me about."

"Juliet, I wanted to, trust me I did. But part of his condition was that I don't tell anyone why I left, only that I was getting deported."

"But that's not what you told me. You told me you were offered a job with the Vikings and that you couldn't pass it up. And then you canceled your phone service so I couldn't get ahold of you," she says, with fire in her eyes and her eyebrows knit together.

She's right to be pissed.

I handle everything poorly with her, but Juliet married a stranger to pay for her brother to be in a better center. She's selfless and I couldn't let her give up everything she cares about just because I want her.

"You told me that night that you wouldn't consider Canada because you need to think of your family's needs and your business first, and I understood. It fucking hurt not to be on the list, but I understood, and I wasn't going to make you choose."

Her eyebrows furrow even deeper as she stares at me through her dark eyelashes.

"Make me choose? I was half asleep when you asked me that and I thought we had four years to decide, not twelve hours. And as far as not listing you as a priority, I didn't think I needed to. I thought that was obvious. I thought you and I were falling..."

She stops short and lets out a defeated sigh, but I can guess the ending.

"In love?" I ask.

She covers her face and shakes her head, and that's when I see it.

Her ring.

She's wearing it and that might be the first indicator that she's not here just to curse me out. This isn't over for her... just like it's not over for me.

"You're wearing your ring," I say.

She pulls her hands off her face and stares back at me, looking almost tortured over my observation.

"I never took it off," she admits.

"Why not?"

"Because you made me promise not to and because they never retracted our marriage license. We're still married."

I hold up my hand and show her the ring that I haven't taken off since she slid it on my finger in that courthouse when we said our vows.

"Neither have I."

She studies the ring on my hand for a moment.

"And why not?" she asks.

"Because I'm still in love with you."

Her eyes tick up from my hand to reach my eyes.

I look behind her to find her SUV parked along the curb.

"You drove here? Why?"

"Because my car was already packed with all of my luggage from the penthouse and it would have been too expensive to fly all my things here."

"All of your things?" I ask, my eyes shifting back to her.

"Shawnie and I talked the entire three-hour drive. I'm giving her half the company and she's going to run things while I start a new branch in Vancouver."

A feeling of hope, something I haven't felt since the day Juliet showed up at the Hawkeyes stadium on Valentine's Day, comes over me.

"You're staying? With me? What about your mom and your brother?"

Though selfishly, I don't care right now. I just want her to tell me she's staying with me.

"Well, someone put my mom through schooling and made sure that she now makes a good living, and she gets to spend five days a week with my brother. Jerrin has never done better than he is right now. He's thriving with the support he's getting," she says, a smile stretching across her face as she talks about them. "I'll still have to go back and forth from here to Seattle every other week to help with Elite, but for now Shawnie and our new assistant can take on the bulk of it. And I'll get to see my brother when I'm in town."

She worked it all out so she doesn't have to give up anything and now I wonder what would have happened if I had told her from the beginning. Could we have avoided the last two months of misery?

"You're staying? Even after I left the way I did?"

It's hard for me to imagine that she could forgive me that easily.

"You underestimated what I would do to be with you. But I know you gave up everything to protect me from a criminal investigation. And you set up my family so that they can take care of themselves. All I've ever wanted is for them to feel secure and happy, and now they do. You've given that to us."

I take a step closer, letting myself hope for the first time in two months.

"I need an answer, Juliet. Are you staying with me?"

"Yes. I'm staying with you," she says.

I lunge at her, picking her up into my arms and planting my lips against hers.

Her warmth—her smell, the way her body melds to mine like she was made for me.

There's nothing in this world that is better than this.

No starting line position with an NHL team.

No championship wins.

Juliet is the only thing I won't give up again. She's the only thing worth fighting for.

I pull back from our kiss. It's not an easy thing to do but I have a couple more questions.

"We'll have to start the fiancé visa here to make you a Canadian citizen. Are you ok with that?" I ask.

"I live where you live, so yes."

"Will you marry me?"

"We're already married," she says with a smile.

"In Vancouver. Will you marry me here and plan the wedding I should have given you to begin with?"

"Yes, I will."

Now I have all the answers I need.

I turn around and head for the door.

"Where are you taking me? I need my clothes," she says with a giggle.

"To our bed. We have two months to make up for and you won't be wearing anything for a while."

I walk through the door frame with Juliet's lips back on mine.

I kick the door closed, reach back and lock it, and then I start toward the stairs.

"How long are you planning to carry me to bed?" she teases.

"Until death."

EPILOGUE

Three years later

Ryker

Being in Wisconsin for the championship game with the Vancouver Vikings is surreal. I had plans to push this team to a championship win to honor my father, but I never expected us to be here this soon.

With my wife, my mom, my siblings, Jerrin, Theresa, and Felix, as well as our six-month-old daughter sitting on my mom's lap, the only thing that would make this day any better is if my father was here to witness it all. I know somehow, he's watching. I hope he's proud of not just the success of the Vikings' season, but also of the husband and father I've become.

I watch as the last few seconds wind down on the timer and we're tied. We'll go into overtime if we don't make this goal. Our center passes the puck to our left wing, who makes it past one opposing player and quickly cuts through the ice. He's barely down the rink, with the opposition right on his ass. He's coming up to the goal and looking to make the shot, but the opposition comes out of nowhere, ramming him into the sideboards—an instant after he shoots the puck back to the center. Center takes possession, skating around the net and taking his shot at the last second, sinking the puck into the goal.

Score!

We won!

We won the Stanley Cup! All the Vikings players rush out onto the ice.

But my attention shifts up straight to Juliet who's jumping up and down out of her seat, clapping her hands and pointing at me.

I can see her mouth to me. "You did it! You did it!"

It was all worth it.

Everything that happened to get Juliet and me to this place.

The fake marriage—the deportation—losing each other only to realize that we're each other's priority. It was all worth it.

And now I've done what I needed to do to honor my father.

This feels like a chapter I can close now with my dad. I'll still never get those missed years back, but coaching his team for the last three years made me feel a closeness to him I haven't felt since he passed. It's brought me healing that I didn't think I could achieve.

"Coach Haynes, you have a visitor," one of the security guards says.

Assuming it's Juliet, I step out of the locker room to see her and whoever she's brought down with her. But the second I walk out past the door, I see Sam Roberts.

"Sam," I say, my eyes widening at the sight of him in Wisconsin when his team isn't playing.

"That was a great game, Haynes," he says, walking over and shaking my hand. "You made good on what you set out to do. Your family must be very proud of you."

Hearing him say that means a lot. I've looked up to Sam for so many years.

"Thank you but I'll admit I'm a little surprised to see you here."

"I came to watch you win the Stanley Cup, and to offer you a coaching position for the Hawkeyes. Coach Bex is talking about retirement, but he doesn't want to leave until he finds a replacement he trusts to take over for him."

Sam's offering me a coaching position?

It's tempting, I can't deny that. And now that I can apply for a work visa in the US and Juliet and I still have the penthouse, which Juliet uses when she's working in Seattle, it would be an easy transition.

"That's an appealing offer, Sam. It's something I really need to think about, and Juliet has to be in on this decision."

I made a big decision once without my wife and it ended in us almost not finding our way back to each other. I won't make that kind of call again without her input.

"Of course. I understand. Take your time and enjoy your win. You earned this one. The position will be there if you decide to take it. You're Coach Bex's first pick," he says.

I see Juliet headed down the hallway with baby Enes on her hip and my mom in tow.

"Sam?" Juliet calls out.

"I was just leaving," he says, smiling down at Enes and rubbing her back. "You two have a beautiful family and I'm happy it all worked out for you. I was rooting for you since day one."

"I know you were," Juliet says.

Sam turns back to me. "Just remember, I'm only a phone call away."

"I'll think about it," I say, reaching out for Enes and taking her into my arms.

Then Sam nods and heads back down the hallway.

"Sam came to watch the game?" Juliet asks with wide eyes.

She's surprised too.

Enes plays with my lanyard while I bend down and kiss my wife's forehead.

"He offered me a coaching position for the Hawkeyes," I tell her and my mom.

"You're kidding?" my mom asks with a wide grin. "Things come back around full circle, don't they?"

"Are you going to take it?" Juliet asks.

"I don't know. You and I really have to discuss it. But right now, I want to focus on the Vikings and our win tonight."

"Of course, this is a big night for you. We'll wait and discuss it when you're ready," Juliet says.

"It's all exciting news and I'm proud of you, honey," my mom says, rubbing my arm.

"We'd better get back to the family. I just wanted to see you for a minute," Juliet says.

"I'm glad you did," I tell her, bending down and pressing a kiss to her lips. "I'll see you guys in a bit."

Juliet takes Enes back and then the three of them head back down the hallway while my head spins with everything that just happened tonight.

Right before I open the door to the locker room, I hear the echo of my mom's voice.

"The Haynes' family are going back to Seattle."

The END

Want to keep reading? Continue the series with Book 5, Penelope's Story DIRTY SCORE!

To be in the KNOW about all the NEWS, subscribe to Kenna King's newsletter so you don't miss a thing click HEREor visit www.kennaking.com

Thank you for reading and supporting my writing habit ;). If you missed any of the other books in the series, you can find the series in Author Central or on my website!

Feel free to reach out via email (kenna@kennaking.com) or Instagram (@kennakingbooks)! I love hearing from you.

Thank you for reading Rough Score!

To read the next book, Dirty Score, you can find it on Amazon or on my website.

Keep up with Kenna by following here: